RESIST

STINGRAYS HOCKEY

BOOK 2

MARI CARR

Cover Photography: WANDER AGUIAR PHOTOGRAPHY LLC

Cover Design: Qamber Designs & Media

Editor: Kelli Collins

Final Line Editor: Nan Mabbitt

Created with Vellum

To the fun bunch…Mike, Lisa, Sandra, Nan, and Garrett. I love our monthly "meetings" more than I can say!

RESIST

This one-night stand is going into overtime.

The Stingrays call goalie Coulton Moore their gentle giant. The tall, imposing man is the team's rock, their steadying influence on and off the ice. However, that mild disposition disappears completely when the beautiful bartender he's been lusting after from across a crowded bar is attacked. Then, it's all bets off as he steps in to defend her, protect her, and claim her as his.

Ainsley doesn't have time for any more men in her life. Between serving a rowdy bunch of guys in her family's dive bar, caring for her ailing father, and dealing with her brother and his ever-growing pile of gambling debt, her cup overfloweth when it comes to the male population.

When her brother's enemies track her down, looking for retribution, a sexy, dominant stranger steps forward to save her. At first, it's simple enough to accept his help and his kisses and his tantalizing touches because, after a lifetime of crap, she figures she's due a night of mind-blowing passion with Coulton, the hottest man she's ever met.

The problem begins when morning comes and he informs her

what they shared was never going to be just a one-night stand. Nope. Coulton, the stubborn, determined, possessive man is settling for nothing less than her.

And forever.

TRIGGER WARNING

Resist contains explicit sex, depictions of violence, and attempted sexual assault.

CHAPTER ONE

"JESUS. I ain't straight, but damn if that man doesn't make me think I could learn to like dick."

Ainsley Hall finished pouring a beer, pushing the tap back then glancing toward the tavern door, curious who could have captured the attention of sixty-two-year-old retired Marine and hardcore lesbian Maren.

Because Maren didn't do guys.

Period.

Then Ainsley saw…him.

"Hello, Thor," she murmured under her breath. "Jesus Christ."

"Right?" Maren replied with a deep, raspy laugh that said the waitress should at least *try* to curb her two-pack-a-day habit.

Ainsley let her gaze slide down the guy—it took a while because he was so tall—then back up again, grateful for the unexpected eye candy.

"He must be lost," Ainsley said, when the man hovered in the doorway of Mick's Tavern.

She followed the direction of his gaze, even though she knew exactly what he was seeing. Ainsley had grown up in this place, her dad the owner and namesake. Some people would probably think it was cool having a dad who owned a bar, and if her dad had owned one of those upscale, ritzy waterfront bars on the Inner Harbor, she would have agreed. But Mick Hall owned this piece of shit in the middle of Cherry Hill, one of Baltimore's less-than-desirable neighborhoods.

Mick's Tavern was the stereotypical dive, with too-dim lighting, windows covered with thin curtains that used to be white but were now yellowed with age and dust, sticky linoleum flooring that was torn in too many places, booths and chairs upholstered in cheap plastic—many of which were cracked with the stuffing coming out.

The place didn't just need a facelift to be habitable. It needed to be completely gutted and rebuilt.

Not that the regulars gave a shit what the place looked like. Mainly because they matched the décor.

Grizzled old men occupied the tables and stools in front of the bar, dressed in dirty jeans, faded flannel shirts, and scuffed boots.

A few patrons were looking the same direction she was, studying Thor, who was still standing by the door. New faces at Mick's Tavern were rare. Guys who looked like this one, in his crisp, new jeans, name-brand sneakers—though she didn't have a clue which brand, because she'd never been able to afford anything with a name—and button-down shirts never darkened the door, so it stood to reason he captured a bit of attention.

Ainsley crossed her arms when his perusal of the tavern ended with her. She raised one eyebrow, giving him her best "well?" expression, because she expected him to turn tail and get the hell out fast. Or maybe he'd ask for directions to anywhere that wasn't this dump because there was no way he was sticking around.

She was surprised when he held her gaze for longer than was polite, and then—what the hell?—smiled at her. And not a fake smile or a smirk but a real one. One that looked…friendly. The fact that a smile took her aback was definitely a sign that she was not hanging with the best crowd.

Or any crowd really, unless she counted Maren and this room of miserable misfits, none of whom flashed their pearly whites—okay, stained teeth—much.

"Do you know him?" Maren asked.

Ainsley shook her head. "I don't think so. Pretty sure I would remember if I did."

"True. You don't forget a guy like that."

"Maybe he's already drunk? Or lost a bet?" Ainsley continued trying to come up with logical reasons why a guy as sexy as this one would walk into Mick's Tavern and smile at her.

Before Maren could add her own theories, Thor approached the bar and sat down on a stool at the end.

Ainsley walked over to him. "Uh…can I get you something? Directions or…"

The man—who was even more gorgeous up close—nodded his head toward the taps. "I'd like a Natty Boh, please."

Please?

Jesus. She really needed to get out of the bar more often if this man's smile and manners were throwing her for this big a loop.

"Sure thing." Ainsley grabbed a mug from the shelf behind her and poured the beer, surreptitiously stealing looks at the man.

He was at least six-five, and practically that wide, with broad, muscular shoulders and thick arms. He looked like he could bench a couple hundred pounds without breaking a sweat. She appreciated that he wasn't one of those guys who felt like they had to wear their shirts a size too small to accentuate their beefcake statures. Thor did the opposite, because while his clothing fit, it was a tiny bit loose. Not that it was hiding anything. He was built like Mt. Everest, and she sure as shit wouldn't mind scaling him to reach the top.

Because having a body like his should be blessing enough,

but the man also possessed a seriously hot face. He had dark hair and eyes, a chiseled jaw, and he sported a beard.

Sure…most of the old guys in this place had beards. However, theirs were unruly and long and made them look like a bunch of rejects from a ZZ Top audition. But not Thor. Nope. His beard was neatly trimmed, short, and the perfect frame for his perfect face.

Ainsley shook herself for staring like an idiot, then walked over to deliver his beer. "Here you go. Wanna start a tab?"

The man nodded and tossed her a credit card. She ran it, sneaking a peek at the name.

Coulton Moore.

She snickered when she realized his last name rhymed with Thor.

Appropriate.

She handed him the card back, then glanced at the sketch pad behind her on the counter. On slow evenings like this one, she passed the time by drawing. It was either that or play games on her phone, because she had zero interest in watching whatever sport was in season and playing on the ancient TV hanging behind the bar.

She started to pick up the pad when Maren returned from making a trip around the tavern, gathering dirty glasses and plates. She gave Ainsley a pointed look, then not so subtly tilted her head toward Thor…er…Coulton.

Ainsley narrowed her eyes and shook her head, because in what world would a guy who looked like him pay even the slightest bit of attention to a girl like her? She didn't need to know a goddamn thing about Coulton to know she wasn't his type. *GQ* Greek gods didn't typically go for scrawny women with too many tattoos and piercings, jet-black hair tinted magenta at the ends, and a fashion sense that ran strictly along the grunge line.

Tonight, she was rocking black jeans that were ripped to hell—torn naturally through years of wear—and a faded Steve

Miller Band T-shirt she'd lifted from Dad's dresser this morning because she was behind on laundry. It was also due to a lack of clean clothes that she was going commando right now.

Ainsley was Courtney Love.

Coulton was Captain America.

Maren, her beloved waitress and only friend because she had zero social life, had been riding Ainsley's ass lately about dating, something she hadn't done much of in the past year or two.

"Much" was probably the wrong word. Because Ainsley didn't date at all.

She'd washed her hands of the entire male population because, in her experience, they were shitheads and not worth her time. Of course, she knew they weren't *all* shitheads, but Ainsley had learned the hard way that the only ones she seemed to attract sure as hell were.

She'd only had three long-term relationships in the past, and that included her high school boyfriend Tiger. Tiger was the actual name on his birth certificate, which probably should have been Ainsley's first red flag because it turned out the asshole was always on the prowl. Tiger—unbeknownst to her—slept with at least a dozen other girls while they were dating, several of whom had been good friends.

From there, she moved on to Jagger, a struggling musician who struggled to hold down any real job for long. She'd dated Jagger for three years, and for about half of it, they'd been happy. Happy enough that she agreed to get an apartment with him because she was desperate to move away from Mick and her brother Eli.

Unfortunately, after they became roommates, Jagger's true colors were revealed. He had a drinking problem, and damn…he was a mean drunk. Ainsley didn't consider herself weak or a pushover, but she was also tied to a stupid lease. Which sucked, because Jagger was a stage-five emotional abuser, textbook example. When drunk, he found countless ways to tear her down, only to apologize and beg for forgiveness the next morning.

It was the explosive end of her relationship with Jagger that led to the third—and last—guy she'd ever slept with.

Montgomery Miles.

Again…the name should have been an indicator of trouble ahead, because Montgomery was a prep-school, country club, up-and-coming prosecuting attorney. Completely different from every guy she'd never known. She'd thought all those Richie Rich things were incredibly impressive when they were dating. It was only after the blinders were ripped off that she realized his background served to make him the snooty-ass, condescending jerk he really was.

So yeah…

Three strikes and she was out.

Done.

Maren held Ainsley's gaze, lifting her eyebrows in that stubborn *do as I say* way of hers.

"Talk to him," Maren mouthed.

Ainsley shook her head again, so Maren—the bitch—casually picked up Ainsley's drawing pencils, slid them in her back pocket, and walked through the swinging door that led to the bar's small kitchen to wash dishes, smirking over her shoulder as she did so.

Ainsley didn't care. She still had her phone, so the last laugh would be hers. All she had to do was pull it out and play games to kill time, but she made the mistake of looking at Coulton instead.

She expected to find his gaze glued to the TV, so she was shocked to realize he was looking at her. Shit. Had he just watched that whole exchange?

Ainsley expected him to smirk, but instead, he just smiled at her again.

"Nice tats," he said, opening the door to a conversation.

Before she could think better of her actions, she stepped toward him and—God help her—started making small talk.

"Uh…thanks. You have any?"

He shook his head. "No, but I've always wanted to get one. Just hard to decide what you want to ink on your skin forever, y'know?"

She nodded. "Yeah."

"I guess all of yours have meanings?"

They did, but Ainsley's reasons for choosing her tattoos were personal. "Sure do. So, what brings you in?" she asked, in an attempt to change the subject. She was still certain he'd made a wrong turn.

Coulton took a swig of his beer. "Got a friend who lives nearby. I've driven by the tavern quite a few times the past year. Thought I'd check it out."

Ainsley frowned, because as uninviting as the inside of Mick's Tavern was, the outside was worse. "A friend, huh? So you don't live in Cherry Hill?"

Coulton shook his head. "Nope."

"Lucky you," she muttered.

He gave her a curious look.

"You have to know it's not a great neighborhood," she added.

"*You* live in Cherry Hill?"

Ainsley nodded. "My whole life."

"I'm Coulton, by the way," he said, introducing himself.

"Ainsley Hall," she replied, just before her phone started ringing.

She pulled her cell out of her back pocket and grimaced when she saw the caller ID. She wanted to ignore the call but couldn't, on the off chance there was an emergency.

"Excuse me," she said to Coulton, turning her back to him. "What's wrong?" she asked, as she answered the phone.

Her father, the only chain smoker she'd ever known who could give Maren a run for her money, had been diagnosed with emphysema and COPD a couple years back. He'd continued to run the tavern for about a year afterward before it got to be too much for him. Nowadays, he just sat in his ratty recliner in the apartment they shared with her useless brother, hooked up to oxygen, watching crime drama on TV all day and waiting to die. Given the gray pallor of his skin lately, she was starting to worry he wouldn't have much longer to wait.

"You pick up my prescription?" Mick asked…or rather, barked.

"Yeah," she replied, wondering how in the hell he thought she could forget, given the way he'd badgered her about it all damn morning.

"Good. Just took my last pill."

"Okay," she replied.

"Stop on your way home and grab me some nicotine patches. I'm out," he demanded.

Ainsley closed her eyes, her temper flaring. Why hadn't he asked for those this morning when he was nagging her about the stupid pills? Now, she'd have to go four blocks in the opposite direction to hit the all-night convenience store before walking home after closing.

The Hall family wasn't known for their patience, and as she was a Hall and her father's daughter, she failed to find any. "Why didn't you ask this morning, Mick?" she asked, voice raised.

Mick, taking exception to her tone, lost his temper bigger. He always did. "Because I didn't fucking know I was out, you stupid cow!" When she was younger, Mick's loud, intimidating bellow used to scare her, but nowadays, while his words were still hateful, he couldn't say them with the same volume and tone. Due to a lack of air, the best he could manage was a wheezy grumble.

"You can't wait until tomorrow?"

"Are you fucking kidding me, Ainsley? I ask for one goddamn thing and you act like it's some big damn deal."

She rolled her eyes. He asked for one goddamn thing a

minute, but pointing that out would only prolong this fight and she didn't have the energy. For the last year, she'd been running this tavern with only Maren's help, which meant she was here from open to close, six days a week, for three hundred and twelve days a year. Mick didn't believe in closing for the holidays because the regulars at the tavern preferred to do their celebrating over pints rather than with their families. Considering the patrons, she suspected their families didn't mind their absence around the Christmas trees or Thanksgiving tables. Of course, she wasn't one to judge because she preferred working on those days rather than spending them with her family too.

"Fine," she huffed. "Anything else, oh lord and master?"

"Yeah. Lose the fucking attitude. It's no wonder you're not married. What man's going to saddle himself to your smart-ass mouth?"

Before she could respond to that lovely comment, Mick hung up on her.

She wrapped her hands around her phone and throttled it, imagining it was her dad's neck. Then she shoved the phone in her pocket and sighed heavily. It wasn't like she expected him to say thanks or show her any appreciation.

That wasn't Mick's way. He was a spare the rod, spoil the child kind of guy. Spankings—and the well-placed backhand when she became a teenager—were pretty much part of the daily routine during her childhood. Maybe that wouldn't have been such a bad thing if her mom had stuck around to offer something resembling affection. However, Mom had cut and run when Ainsley was six, Eli eight.

Mick had raised them on his own, though she used the word *raised* sparingly. Mick's life as a single parent had been exactly the same as when he'd been married. The only difference was he'd started dragging two kids along with him to work.

As such, she'd grown up in this tavern, sitting at a booth with her brother doing homework or coloring, watching whatever sport was on TV, eating the cheap microwave food her dad sold to the drunks for dinner. Her bedtime was split into two halves, the first happening on a lumpy couch in the back storeroom that doubled as her dad's office. Once he closed the tavern for the night, he'd wake up her and Eli, the three of them would walk home at midnight, and she'd spend the rest of the night in her bed.

Child services would have had a field day with her father, but no one who drank at Mick's gave a shit about the two little kids sitting in the corner, listening to their dirty jokes, watching their drunken brawls, and sucking in all their secondhand smoke.

Ainsley had never taken a puff of a cigarette in her life, but she figured she could look forward to the same ailments Mick now suffered from, given all the secondhand smoke she'd breathed in as a little girl.

She rubbed her eyes. God, she was tired. And it was still three hours until closing time.

"Boyfriend?" Coulton asked, making it clear he'd been listening.

She shook her head. "My father."

"You call him Mick?"

"Yeah. The word dad doesn't apply to him. Indicates a relationship that's not really there."

"So you're not close?"

She shook her head. "I don't know what the fuck we are. This is his place."

"Oh, of course. Mick. Should have put that together," Coulton said, giving her a self-deprecating grin. "Is it his night off or something?"

"No. Mick hasn't been able to run the tavern the past year, so I do."

"Hey, Ainsley," Petey called out. "You fucking working or what? I'm empty. Get your scrawny ass over here."

And that was a perfect example of why Coulton's "please" had sounded so strange.

"You just took the last swig, asswipe, so I'm pretty sure you're not dying of thirst," she retorted.

She'd gotten her Miss Manners lessons at Mick's, so she probably shouldn't throw a stone when it came to other people's rudeness. Glass houses and all that crap. Trudging in Petey's direction, she decided she was done making small talk with the hot guy. Nothing was going to come of it, so why bother?

She refilled drinks for a few of the guys, purposely remaining on the opposite end of the bar, away from Coulton. He made it easy to stay away by nursing his beer. As long as it was half full, she didn't need to go ask if he wanted another.

Ainsley listened with half an ear as Petey and Brant bitched about some supervisor at the factory where they both worked. Apparently, their new boss was a third their age and fresh out of college with some fancy degree in manufacturing or management or something else equally useless. Petey was pissed because the young guy was trying to make a lot of changes that wouldn't work.

"Same fucking thing every year. Some new asshole comes in, tries to fix what's not broken, then moves on, leaving us to deal with the next twat and his big ideas," Petey griped. "Got a right mind to fucking quit."

Ainsley rolled her eyes in unison with Brant, because Petey threatened to quit his job—the same one he'd worked for nearly forty years—every day.

She started to say as much when the tavern door opened.

Shit.

Just when she thought the day couldn't get any worse.

She walked toward the cash register, which was unfortunately on Coulton's end of the bar, as her brother Eli strolled in and made a beeline for it.

"Hey, Painsley," he said with a smirk. He'd been using that same stupid nickname since she was a kid, thinking it such a clever play on words.

"You come in to work?" she asked, even though it was a

waste of breath. She and Eli were supposed to be running the tavern together, but she could count on one hand—with fingers left over—how many times her brother had chipped in since Mick's illness left him homebound. For the first couple of months after taking over, she'd made a schedule, foolishly thinking Eli would abide by it. More the fool her.

Eli crossed his arms, looking around at the dozen or so people scattered around the bar. "Seriously? You and Maren can't handle this?"

"What do you want, Eli?" Ainsley had officially hit the limit on what she could take from her dad and brother today.

"Came to get an advance on my pay," he said, moving into her personal space, trying to force her away from the register.

"You have to work to get paid," she pointed out, not budging. The only way this son of a bitch would get to the cash register was over her cold, dead body.

"Stop fucking around," Eli grumbled.

"What is it about my face that gives you the idea I'm fucking around?" she asked, scowling, crossing her own arms.

"Move," he said, with that slight tinge of desperation she recognized all too well. "I need some cash."

She groaned. "Tell me you aren't gambling again."

Eli's eyes darted to the side, a sure sign he was about to lie. "I—"

"You said you were done with that," Ainsley continued, without letting him spout a bunch of crap. She wasn't in the mood to hear his bullshit. "Mick told you last time he wouldn't bail you out again. You start this shit up and he's gonna kick you out of the apartment for—"

"It's a sure thing," Eli insisted.

Ainsley scoffed dramatically. "Oh, well, if it's a sure thing," she said sarcastically. "Why not take *all* the money from the cash register? Hell, let me grab my purse. I think I have a few bucks in there. Maybe we can dig behind the cushions in the booths, see if we can drum up some extra change to kick in."

"You don't always have to be such a fucking bitch," Eli retorted.

She shot him a nasty grin. "I don't have to, but it's just so much fun."

"Goddammit. Get out of the way, Ainsley." Eli bumped into her, intent on physically shoving her away from the register.

From the corner of her eye, she saw Coulton start to rise, but she responded faster. She and Eli had been brawlers since childhood, so she knew right where to hit.

Reaching beneath the counter, she pulled out her baseball bat, shaking it in Eli's face.

"Back the fuck up," she said through gritted teeth. "This isn't an ATM."

Eli scowled but took two steps away. He was familiar with her bat and well aware that she had no problem swinging it. "You're forgetting that half this bar is mine."

"*None* of this is yours. It's Mick's."

Eli gave her a shitty grin. "Yeah, but we're going to inherit it when the miserable old bastard kicks off, which if we're lucky should be any day now. He's not looking so good."

Ainsley hated how much Eli looked forward to their father dying, but she understood where it was coming from. While her relationship with their dad was strained as shit, Eli and Mick's bond was shattered. They'd butted heads since the day Eli learned to talk, neither of them bothering to hide their outright hatred for each other. While she and Eli had both gotten plenty of beatings when they were kids, Mick seemed to take a perverse sense of pride in *really* hurting Eli, who was scrawny like her and nowhere near as tough as he liked to think he was.

Ainsley could only assume Mick viewed his beatings as a way of toughening up his son. She and Eli could probably keep a team of therapists busy for months, analyzing the impact their fucked-up childhood had on them.

Regardless, she wasn't in the mood to play this game with Eli. "Yeah, well, for now, the tavern is still Mick's, so try to take money from here again and I'll break your hand." Ainsley held the bat in front of her, her threat genuine.

The tavern barely made enough to cover the rent on their shitty apartment, feed them, and cover their father's medical bills. They didn't have enough to squander on Eli's "sure things," which were never sure.

"You're a fucking cunt, you know that?" Eli shouted.

This time, Ainsley didn't have a chance to respond before Coulton interfered. Not that she would have responded. Cunt was her brother's second-favorite nickname for her after Painsley. Due to his constant use of the word, it didn't have the power to wound her anymore.

Coulton, however, clearly didn't feel the same way. One second, her brother was giving her a dirty look, trying to crowd her, the next, he was shoved against the back wall of the tavern, his feet dangling a couple inches off the ground.

"You need to watch your mouth," Coulton said.

Eli, the idiot, didn't seem to gather just how outmatched he was when he spit back, "She's my fucking sister. I can call her whatever I want."

Coulton shoved him against the wall again, harder, and Eli grunted in pain.

"No. You can't," Coulton said.

Ainsley hadn't been wrong about her first impression of him. The guy really was Thor. Which was wreaking havoc on her libido, because as he held her brother aloft, his muscular arms rippled and his brawny shoulders flexed…and her girlie parts woke right the hell up.

She caught a glimpse of Maren, standing on the other side of Coulton and Eli, the waitress's lips curled in a too-satisfied grin. Maren hated Eli, so Ainsley was surprised the waitress was merely smiling. Maren loved to see a few fists fly, so she was showing great restraint in not urging Coulton to pummel Eli.

Glancing around the tavern, she realized everyone was watching the scuffle unfold. Ainsley considered letting it play out a little longer, because the old guys led very small lives and she figured they deserved a bit of entertainment.

However, Coulton's grip on Eli was a strong one, and her brother was red-faced and struggling to breathe.

Ainsley put her hand on Coulton's forearm. She couldn't resist giving it a squeeze. Jesus Christ. She was going to have to rethink her superhero. Coulton might actually be Superman, because the man was made of steel.

"We're cool," she said to Coulton. "My brother was just leaving." She stared Eli down until he gave her a quick nod, silently agreeing to get out.

Coulton held her gaze long enough that she started to question whether he was going to do as she said.

"Seriously," she added. "This is just another Sunday night around here. No biggie."

Finally, after thirty more seconds, Coulton loosened his grip and released her brother.

Eli tried to straighten the wrinkles from his shirt, scowling at Coulton, then at her.

When it looked like her brother was going to say something else stupid, she shook her head in warning. She'd called the giant off this time. She wasn't sure she'd be able to again.

One, because Coulton looked seriously pissed.

And two, because she didn't want to. Like Maren, she thought a few punches to the head might be the only way to knock some sense into her idiot brother. Not that it had ever worked in the past. God knew Mick had given it the old college try.

Eli scowled, then sidestepped Coulton and stormed out of the tavern without another word.

"You shouldn't let him talk to you like that," Coulton said.

Ainsley shrugged. "I've been called worse." She intended for her words to lighten the mood, but they sent things in a different direction.

"By who?" Coulton asked.

She laughed, despite his deadly serious tone. "You want a list?" she joked.

For a second, it looked like he was going to ask her to start giving him names, but Coulton finally calmed down, his shoulders loosening as he gave her—goddamn, his teeth were white and perfectly straight—another one of those gorgeous smiles.

"All better?"

He nodded. "Yeah."

"Thank you," she said softly, trying to recall the last time anyone had stood up for her.

Now it was Coulton's turn to shrug as if he was embarrassed by her gratitude, the fierceness she'd seen in his face as he'd held her brother, melting away completely. "No problem."

She tilted her head and smiled before she could catch herself. "Nice biceps, by the way."

Jesus, Ainsley. Stop flirting.

"Nice bat."

Ainsley laughed. But before she could say anything else flirty, the room erupted into a flurry of noise and movement as Coulton reclaimed his stool.

Maren slapped Coulton on the back and told him she was buying him a beer. Petey and Brant shifted along the counter so they could sit next to him, asking if he'd ever done any boxing. Another group at a nearby table ordered a pitcher, despite already closing their tab, just in case there was any more excitement, they explained.

The atmosphere in the bar shifted from depressed and silent to something akin to a party. People started talking to each other rather than staring at the TV or their phones, and for the first time in months, someone asked to borrow the darts, asking Coulton if he wanted to play.

Ainsley was shocked when he said yes.

Maren shifted next to her, the two of them leaning against the counter, watching a small crowd of men stand in front of the dartboard, trash-talking and laughing.

"What the hell happened?" Ainsley mused.

Maren chuckled. "Something."

Ainsley gave her a confused look.

"When is the last time something—anything—happened in this place?" Maren asked.

Ainsley had to give it to Maren. She made a valid point. "Still not sure why he's here," she muttered.

Maren shoulder-bumped Ainsley. "Who gives a shit why? I swear to God, I'm pissed I didn't think to pull my phone out and take a picture of that giant slamming your waste-of-flesh brother against the wall. Nat is getting so lucky tonight."

Ainsley snorted. Nat was Maren's longtime girlfriend. "I'm sure Nat will be thrilled to know it was a sexy guy who got you all hot and bothered."

Maren shrugged. "She doesn't care where I get inspired as long as she's the recipient of my creative juices."

Ainsley crinkled her nose. "Ew. No, no, no. No talking about your juices because…gross."

Maren barked out a loud, raspy laugh. "Prude."

"Slut."

Maren continued laughing, one that dissolved into a wet cough, as she went to see if anyone needed another round.

Ainsley remained where she was, watching Coulton throwing darts with Petey and Brant. When he first walked in, she thought he looked out of place, but his easy camaraderie with guys who were at least twice his age had her rethinking that.

Of course, with his back turned, she also had the opportunity to enjoy the new view. Of his tight ass. Maren made a valid point about Coulton's ability to inspire.

Ainsley hadn't felt a sexual attraction to anyone in so long, she thought that part of her had died.

It was now very painfully clear it had not.

Her eyes quickly darted away when Coulton looked over his shoulder and caught her staring at his ass. Her cheeks heated—Jesus, was she blushing?—when he gave her a quick wink.

Ainsley snorted then turned around, pretending to wipe the counter behind her. Unfortunately, a huge mirror hung on that wall, so when she chanced a glance, she saw he was still looking at her and grinning like the cat who ate the canary.

She narrowed her eyes, the two of them staring at each other through the reflection, then she forced herself to look away and escape to the kitchen to regroup, because she wasn't the type of girl who ogled. Or flirted. Or blushed.

Grabbing a tray of clean glasses, she took a steadying breath, determined to put the pretty man out of her mind and focus on the job at hand.

Something easier said than done when she returned to find Coulton back at the bar.

"Finished playing darts?"

He nodded. "I was putting more holes in your wall than the board."

She lifted one shoulder. "It's not like the holes would make this dive look any worse."

Coulton grinned, then started a conversation about his preferred drinking game—beer pong—as she restocked the glasses. He was surprisingly easy to talk to, probably because they weren't talking about anything personal, the two of them chatting about favorite cocktails, bands, and movies. When he asked about the sketch pad, she played off her art, called it doodling, even though her drawings were so much more than that to her.

The sad part was, the entire time they talked, Ainsley found herself wondering what the hell was wrong with the guy because there was no way anyone could be this nice.

Trust issues much, Ains?

After an hour or so, Coulton stood. "Got an early morning. Guess I should head out," he said.

She was tempted to ask what he was getting up early for, but instead, she just nodded, sorry to see him go because she very seriously doubted he'd return.

"I'll cash out your tab," she said.

Handing him the bill, he signed it, then stuffed three twenties in the tip jar.

"Thanks," she said, trying for an air of casual indifference and failing. That was a hell of a tip. She was lucky to get a few lousy bucks from the rest of these guys, and that was after they'd spent hours here guzzling beer after beer.

"See you later, Ainsley," he said.

She frowned, trying to decide if he meant those words or if that was just his way of saying goodbye.

"Um, sure," she said. "See ya."

Coulton gave her another one of those easy smiles, then turned and left.

See you later.

God, she really hoped she did.

CHAPTER TWO

COULTON LEANED HIS HEAD FORWARD, relishing the hot water on sore back muscles. Following this afternoon's game, he'd spent an hour doing his postgame workout and stretches to warm down, before hitting the showers.

The Stingrays won, but Coulton wasn't sure how much credit he could take for that W. He'd let in three goals, struggling to find his rhythm and to get his head in the game—literally.

Fortunately, his teammates had been on fire, Tank and Blake both sinking two goals apiece, while the rookie, Lucas, gave them the fifth to put them up by two when the last buzzer sounded.

Coulton bent his neck side to side a couple times, working out the kinks, while silently kicking his own ass for letting any goals get by him at all.

Typically, he didn't have a problem shutting down the outside world when he was out on the ice. In the arena, the only thing that ever mattered was him keeping the puck out of the net, and that was his single focus.

Today, other things crept in, distracting him.

Actually, just one thing.

A beautiful woman with tatted arms, a nose ring, thick dark

hair, and piercing blue eyes, who cussed like a sailor and wielded a baseball bat like Babe Ruth.

It had been a week since his impromptu visit to Mick's Tavern. Seven days, during which his fascination for the badass bartender seemed to have crossed the line from attraction to obsession. The team had been on the road four days this week, so he hadn't had the opportunity to drop by the tavern again.

That was probably a good thing, because he wasn't even sure if he should go. He'd enjoyed talking to Ainsley, and while she had been friendly on the surface, the woman had sent out some pretty hardcore *don't get too close* vibes. He felt like he should respect those, but instead, his curiosity was piqued.

Coulton turned off the water and reached for his towel, trying for the millionth time to put Ainsley out of his mind because this was getting ridiculous.

"Hey, Moore. Get your head out of your ass," Tank said, rinsing shampoo out of his hair. "I've been saying your name for a full minute. What the hell are you thinking about?"

"Nothing," Coulton lied. He and Tank were good friends, so he could tell his teammate about the bartender who'd been consuming his thoughts lately. In fact, it might be nice to have someone to talk to about her.

The reason he didn't was because he knew exactly what Tank would say. He would tell Coulton to go back to the bar, take Ainsley home, and fuck her out of his system.

Because that was always Tank's answer when it came to female concerns. Apparently in his world, one tumble between the sheets was all he needed with a woman before he was good to move on to the next.

Coulton wasn't wired that way. He was the king of long relationships. Like *looooooong* ones. So long, he'd reached the ripe old age of thirty-two and had only seriously dated two women. Sure, there'd been the occasional hookups because…he had needs. But those one- or two- or few-night stands were few and far between.

Jocelyn had been his high school girlfriend, and when he said high school, he meant all of it, the whole shebang, ninth to twelfth grade. After graduation, it ended because he bounced around the junior league for a while, moving from city to city until he was signed to play professionally with Vancouver.

He met Evelyn, his last girlfriend, while living in Canada, and he'd dated her for five years. If he hadn't been traded to the Stingrays, Coulton didn't doubt they'd still be together. Instead, the relationship ended fairly soon after his move to the other side of the continent.

Since moving to Baltimore two years earlier, Coulton had gone out on at least a dozen dates, but none of those had advanced to a second…or even to the bedroom. Which meant he'd been living like a goddamn monk for twenty-four months, his acts of intimacy limited to shower time spent with Rosey Palmer and her five sisters. His masturbation game was strong.

So perhaps his keen interest in Ainsley was purely physical. There was no denying the instant sexual attraction he'd felt for her. Maybe his body was doing the thinking and he'd be right to adopt Tank's philosophy this time around.

"You've got something on your mind," Tank pressed. "I can tell."

Coulton shrugged, because the truth was he didn't have time for one of Tank's lectures on how it was bad for a man's health to go so long without sex. When he'd admitted to his teammate a few months ago about his painfully long dry spell, Tank's eyes had nearly bugged out of his head, and he'd said—with unshakable conviction—that if Coulton didn't start having sex soon, his dick was going to wither and fall off due to lack of use.

One time on the receiving end of that conversation had been enough.

Sure, Tank was a lot to take, but during Coulton's time in Baltimore, the man had become a good friend—along with his teammates Blake, Victor, and Preston. So good, it wasn't unusual for them to spend as much time together off the ice as they did on it, gathering at each other's apartments for movie or game nights or blowing off steam over a pitcher of Natty Boh at Pat's Pub.

"I swear I'm okay," Coulton said, offering his friend a smaller piece of what was bothering him. "Just pissed that I let those three goals in."

Tank slapped him on the shoulder as the two of them walked out of the showers, towels wrapped around their waists. "As always, Eeyore, you're focusing on the negative. You also had at least a dozen wicked saves. So give yourself a break."

Coulton appreciated Tank's pep talk. "Thanks, bro."

"I'm heading to Pat's Pub with Preston and Lucas. Wanna join us?" Tank asked.

Coulton shook his head. "Can't. Gotta get Slade home."

Coulton had brought his Little Brother, Slade, to the afternoon game, tucking the kid in the team box with McKenna Bailey. McKenna worked in the Stingrays' administrative offices as the team's director of social media marketing. She was young and new to the position, but Coulton really liked her vision for the team and the way she was branding the Stingrays players.

She was moving the media coverage away from them looking like a bunch of stereotypical cocky jocks and portraying he and his teammates as a tight-knit group, a family. Rather than focusing exclusively on their time on the ice, she'd begun humanizing them by sharing personal small peeks into their real lives, giving fans fun posts that included favorite recipes, current reads, and other interesting facts.

When McKenna learned Coulton participated in the Big Brothers Big Sisters program, she asked if she could meet Slade and take some pictures for promotional purposes. Coulton had been resistant to the idea, because he was protective of his time spent with Slade, and he hadn't joined the program as a way to show off. To him, that time was sacred and private.

However, when he ran McKenna's request by Slade and his aunt Barbara, they were both excited by the premise and anxious to participate. Slade's aunt was a huge advocate of the Big Brothers Big Sisters program, and she was hopeful McKenna's promotion would encourage others to volunteer their time.

Slade, however, was less enticed by the altruistic component, drawn in by the opportunity to be in the limelight. Not that Coulton couldn't fault him for that. The kid was part of a large family, so Coulton suspected it was sometimes hard to feel seen in the crowd. Plus, Slade had a huge personality and loved to be the center of attention, always talking the loudest, laughing the longest. Which wasn't a problem for Coulton, because the kid was funny as shit.

It had been McKenna's idea to bring Slade to a Stingrays game, and because Barbara worked long hours and couldn't afford to take time off, McKenna said she'd be happy to hang out with Slade while Coulton was on the ice.

Following the game, she'd brought Slade down to meet some of the players in the weight room, while they did their postgame workouts. The kid had gotten a slew of autographs from his teammates, and McKenna had taken a ton of pictures.

"It was good to finally meet the infamous Slade," Tank joked. "Nice kid."

Coulton grinned, aware he tended to talk about Slade a lot, but that was just because he was so fond of the boy and proud of how much he'd grown in the past year, since they'd been paired together.

Barbara had signed up Slade for the Big Brothers Big Sisters program because he'd started getting into trouble at school, running with a rough crowd and failing tests. Coulton had encouraged the boy to get into sports, hoping Slade would join a junior hockey league. No such luck. Instead, he'd signed up to participate in little league baseball.

Because…of course, he did.

Coulton had put on a happy face as he'd sat through countless baseball games last summer, but it was tough. There wasn't enough action in the damn sport in Coulton's opinion, but that didn't bother Slade, who was a natural shortstop and a hell of a hitter.

So far this school year, the kid had all A's, probably because Coulton wasn't above buying good grades. They'd come up with a payment plan—one they kept on the down-low—with Slade earning twenty bucks for every A on his report card, ten for every B, and a five for C's. Coulton had learned early on that money was a huge motivator for Slade, which made sense, considering the kid had spent too many of his early years with a drug-addicted mother who often forgot to feed him.

For Slade, having some money in his pocket gave him peace of mind, even now, when he lived in a safe home with plenty of food.

The locker room was quiet, since the rest of the team had already taken off, either to head home or to Pat's Pub to celebrate their win.

"You sure you don't want to join us?" Tank offered again. "It's not going to take long to drop the kid off. Gonna be plenty of puck bunnies there. Maybe you can invite one back to your place and take one of Blake's famous victory laps."

Coulton rolled his eyes, all too familiar with his teammate's horizontal victory laps, not that Blake was taking any of those lately. Regardless, Coulton had zero interest in picking up one of the countless women who swarmed whenever he and his teammates went out together.

"No, thanks. I'm looking forward to having a quiet night at home." Or at least, he was telling himself that was the plan.

Chances were good that once he'd dropped Slade off at home, he'd swing by Mick's Tavern again. He had to see if his infatuation was still there, justified and real.

Who knew? Maybe he'd see Ainsley again and the spark would be gone.

Though he wasn't sure if he was rooting for that outcome or not.

Even now, he couldn't figure out what had prompted him to

walk into that tavern in the first place. God knew there was nothing appealing about the decrepit building that made it look inviting.

But for some reason, it had captured his attention countless times over the past year.

Last week, he'd made a spur-of-the-moment decision to check the place out because the idea of going home to an empty, quiet apartment held no appeal. The tavern reminded him of a dive bar his dad would occasionally go to with his friends after work called Moxie's, and feeling slightly homesick for Detroit, he'd decided to check it out.

He hadn't made it two steps inside Mick's Tavern before he'd taken a long look around and decided to retreat because, damn…the place really was a dump. It was as if someone had decided to open a legit dive bar, then decided to go the extra mile on making it even worse.

If despair was a place, it would be Mick's Tavern.

Or at least, that was what he thought until he'd spotted *her* standing behind the counter.

Ainsley had captured his interest and held it in a way he'd never experienced. Because she was the complete opposite of what Coulton considered "his type."

His previous girlfriends were soft-spoken, book smart, sweet, girl-next-door types who were more like McKenna. They'd been understated beauties who didn't seek to draw attention to themselves with a lot of makeup and revealing clothing, like so many of the puck bunnies did. In addition, he'd always been drawn to tall, willowy blondes, as evidenced by the fact Jocelyn, Evelyn, and at least fifty percent of those failed first dinner dates matched that description.

Ainsley did not fit that bill. Not even close.

Not with her countless tats, piercings—he'd counted ten alone in her left ear—and dark hair that just barely brushed her shoulders, tipped with a bright purple dye at the ends. She'd been wearing an old band T-shirt tied with a knot on one side and low-slung jeans that gave him a healthy peek of her midriff. She was in a class completely her own…and he'd been captivated from the first glance.

So the fact that Mick's Tavern was a shithole and its bartender wasn't his type didn't matter at all, because the second his gaze landed on Ainsley, it held. It didn't help that she'd been staring him down, looking at him like she'd expected him to get the hell out of Dodge. She'd given him a self-confident, in-your-face smirk that was equal parts challenge and badass.

And damn if he hadn't picked up the gauntlet she'd tossed at his feet as he walked over to the bar and ordered a beer.

He'd sprung a boner when she'd pulled that baseball bat out from under the counter and threatened to pummel her brother. There'd been nothing soft-spoken or demure about the way she'd cussed Eli up one side and down the other. It had been the mother of all turn-ons.

"Text if you change your mind about coming out with us," Tank said.

"Will do," Coulton said, giving Tank a wave over his shoulder as he stepped out of the locker room.

There would be no text.

And there would be no more pretending he wasn't going to Mick's.

Subconsciously he'd known that all along, because he'd purposely brought an extra change of clothes with him. There was no way he could wear the black dress pants, button-down shirt, tie, and blazer he'd worn to the arena, in Mick's. It was an expectation of the Stingrays organization that the players dress up on game days.

He could just imagine if he walked into Mick's in his dress clothes. Instead, he'd opted for dark jeans, a T-shirt, and gray hoodie, so he wouldn't stick out like a sore thumb, even though he suspected he still would. Even his casual clothes were new and clean and didn't look like he'd worn them through a couple of wars, like the attire sported by most of the patrons at Mick's.

"Hey, Coulton!" Slade bounced over to him the second he stepped out of the locker room with some serious Tigger-level energy, which told Coulton the kid had taken advantage of the large candy selection in the team box.

"Did you have a good time?" Coulton asked Slade, taking note that McKenna looked a hell of a lot less peppy. He'd warned her Slade could be a handful, but she had insisted she was cool with watching the game with him, determined to go the extra mile to jazz up her social media posts.

"I had the best day ever!" Slade shouted dramatically. "I got nine autographs, ate four candy bars, two bags of chips, and drank three Mountain Dews. And it was all free!"

Coulton exchanged a glance with McKenna, who grimaced. "Free is apparently a very big deal," she said. "He was determined to take advantage of the offer."

Coulton chuckled, unsurprised by Slade's delight. Money was tight at his aunt's house, as she was a single mom, raising not only her nephew, Slade, and his sister, but five kids of her own. Her oldest son, Jerome, still lived in the apartment and was contributing toward the bills and groceries, but because they both worked minimum-wage jobs, the money didn't stretch far.

Given the bulges in Slade's jacket, Coulton guessed the boy had taken some of those free treats for the road.

"I appreciate you keeping an eye on him." Coulton placed his hand on Slade's shoulder in an attempt to calm him down, because the kid was hopping around like he had snakes in his pants. "We've been trying to get Slade to a game for ages, but we never found a way to make it work with his aunt or cousin's schedules."

"We had a lot of fun," McKenna said. "And we got some awesome shots to use on our socials. Slade is a natural in front of the camera."

Slade grinned over his shoulder at Coulton, delighted by her compliment. "A *naaatural*," the kid repeated, drawing the word out for effect. Coulton laughed.

"Thanks again, McKenna," Coulton said, giving Slade a pointed look that he understood.

"Yeah, thank you, Mac," the boy added. Apparently, he'd given McKenna a nickname. "I had a lot of fun. And I can come to another game if you need more pictures."

McKenna laughed. "I'll let you know."

"You ready to head out?" Coulton asked the boy.

Slade groaned. "Do we have to go home? I'm not tired."

Coulton ruffled the boy's hair. "*You* might not be, but I just played hockey for sixty minutes, then tacked on a postgame workout. I'm looking forward to chilling." He figured it wasn't lying if he did his chilling over a cold one at Mick's Tavern.

"Okay," Slade said sadly, shoulders slouching.

"Besides, tomorrow is a school day, and your aunt said you still had some homework to do."

Slade grimaced. "Yeah, but that's not fun."

Coulton swung his arm over Slade's shoulders as they walked out of the arena. "I think you've had plenty of fun today." Then he poked one of Slade's pockets, the crinkle proving his suspicions. "You going to share those treats with your cousins?"

"Do I have to?"

Coulton chuckled. "Might be a nice thing to do, since they didn't get to come." Coulton was bound and determined to get Slade's whole family to a game, but given how many hours Barbara and Jerome worked, it was tough.

"Okay," Slade groused, in a tone that said he wasn't happy about sharing his booty.

They climbed into Coulton's truck, the conversation on the trip from the arena to Cherry Hill one-sided as Slade replayed every single second of the day for him. Coulton had hoped the effects of the sugar would start to wear off by the time they reached Slade's apartment building, but no such luck. The boy was still wired for sound.

"You coming up?" Slade asked, as they climbed out of the truck and trudged up the stairs to the family's apartment.

"Yeah, but I'm not coming in. Just going to knock on the door and then run like hell, because your aunt isn't going to be happy with either of us when she hears how much junk food you ate."

Slade cracked up. "Run like hell," he repeated.

Coulton shot him a look for cussing—not that it would do any good. Slade's colorful vocabulary was something they'd talked about a lot in the first couple of months they were together. Mainly because the then ten-year-old was dropping the F-bomb into every sentence like a damn comma.

"We're home," Slade announced as he walked inside.

Jerome was standing near the door, sliding on a jacket. "Hey, little man. How was the game?"

"Great! We won," Slade proclaimed in such a way it sounded as if he'd been on the ice with the team. He took a few minutes to catch Jerome and his other cousins up on the day's events. Then he reached into his pockets and withdrew a candy store's worth of sweets.

Jesus, Coulton thought. He might have to slip into the team box at some point this week to replenish.

He grinned as Slade and his cousins divvied up the goods, acting like Halloween had come early this year.

"Mom is getting a quick shower," Jerome said. "I was just about to head out to hang with some buddies."

"I'll walk down with you." Coulton said goodbye to Slade, then he and Jerome trudged down the three flights of stairs, stepping outside into the chilly fall evening. The sun was setting low over the horizon.

"Gonna play video games at my friend Malcolm's place," Jerome said. "If you wanna come."

Coulton smiled at the offer. He'd become quite close to Slade's family over the past year. "Afraid I can't tonight. Got plans."

"Oh yeah? Please tell me these plans include some hot chick, because dude…you realize you're wasting your superpower?" Jerome, like Tank, believed Coulton should be using his professional athlete status to get laid every night.

"I was going to stop by Mick's Tavern for a beer."

Jerome frowned. "Is there another Mick's? Because I know you don't mean the shithole down the street," he said, pointing in the right direction.

"That's the one."

"Don't you have any rich-guy bars on your side of town?"

"Mick's is fine. I stopped in there last week."

"Were you wasted?" Jerome asked. "Did you lose a bet?"

Coulton chuckled. "No. It reminded me of a place where my dad used to drink in Detroit, so I thought I'd check it out."

"Okay. That explains the first time, but, bruh…"

"It wasn't that bad."

Jerome lifted one eyebrow in genuine disbelief. Coulton didn't blame him, because the place *was* that bad. It was the company, however, that wasn't.

"It's your funeral, man. Hey, do me a favor and tell Ainsley I said hey," Jerome added.

"You know Ainsley?"

"Yeah. We went to school together. Me and her and a bunch of our gang skipped our last-period class a shit ton during our senior year to get high."

Coulton laughed, instantly adding that tidbit to the list of ways Ainsley didn't fit what he considered his type. His past girlfriends would never get stoned. Hell, Evelyn barely even drank, unless he counted the occasional glass of what he'd referred to as her "bubble-gum pink wine" with dinner. Even now, just the thought of her ordering the super-sweet Moscato made his teeth hurt. "What class did you have last period?"

"Algebra with Mr. Dickinson. And believe me, the first part of that name was right."

"You and Ainsley don't hang out anymore?"

Jerome shook his head. "Nah. Not since we graduated. I

know her dad is sick, so she runs the bar. I see her around the neighborhood every now and then, and we catch up real quick, but that's it."

"Gotcha." Coulton wasn't sure what to add to that without making it obvious to Jerome that he was interested in Ainsley.

"Well, see you 'round, Coulton."

Jerome lifted his fist and Coulton bumped it, the two of them saying goodbye.

Coulton climbed into his truck. If he was in his neighborhood, he'd just walk to the tavern because it wasn't more than five or six blocks away, but in Cherry Hill, he felt better having his vehicle close by, where he could keep an eye on it. Considering Slade always looked genuinely surprised each time he picked him up and they returned to the street to find his truck still there, it told him he was right to be concerned.

Parking near the tavern, he crossed the street and walked in.

Just in time to see Ainsley thrust her finger in some mammoth guy's face.

"I told you, I'm not serving you, Tuffy, so stop fucking asking for a beer. Goddammit, I'm sick of this shit!"

Coulton took a step closer, concerned about Ainsley's safety, especially when the man scowled and leaned toward her.

"Jush wanna beer. Not whishkey," Tuffy struggled to say.

"Jesus Christ," Ainsley barked, taking a step back. "Do us all a favor and invest in a toothbrush, you gross bastard."

Several of the guys sitting at the bar chuckled, but none of them seemed overly concerned about the safety of their bartender. In fact, their lack of interest in the whole drama made Coulton wonder how often this same scene played out.

Ainsley answered that for him with her next comment. "Every Sunday, you drink that cheap-ass rotgut whiskey at Lefty's until he stops serving you, then think you can come here and keep going. I'm not serving your drunk ass."

The man—Tuffy—wavered, struggling to stand still, his gaze darting in such a way that Coulton suspected he was seeing at least three fingers pointed his direction instead of the one, and he couldn't figure out which was the real deal.

"I ain't that drunk, 'Sley" Tuffy slurred, missing the first half of Ainsley's name completely. "Leffy's jush an ash-hole."

Ainsley narrowed her eyes. "You're right, he is, but that's not my problem. You got two choices. Go sit your ass down in that corner booth and start drinking coffee, or I'm calling your wife to come pick you up."

Tuffy threw his hands up. "Jesush, 'Sley. You don't gotta be a bitcsh. I'll go sit down. Jush don't call Ann."

Coulton watched, somewhat amazed, as the big gruff man looked genuinely threatened by Ainsley, who was half the man's height and weight. He shuffled to the booth without continuing the argument.

With Tuffy taken care of, Ainsley glanced in his direction, her eyes widening in surprise as he approached the bar and claimed the same stool as last week.

She stared for a second, looking at him a bit like Tuffy had been studying her, like she was trying to decide if he was real. "Back again?" Her tone held the same level of disbelief as Jerome's, when he'd said he was going back to Mick's for a second time.

"Yep," Coulton said, smiling.

"Why?"

He chuckled. "You're good company."

Ainsley frowned at what he'd thought was a charming reply. Then she scoffed. "You must not know many people. You want a beer?"

Coulton nodded. "Natty Boh."

She poured him a pint from the tap, then slid it in front of him.

He handed over his card. "I'm gonna hang out awhile, so I'll start a tab."

"Um...okay," she said, as she rang up his card.

"You working alone?" he asked, when he didn't see the same

waitress who'd been here last week. The tavern wasn't exactly busy, but there were more people than had been here during his initial foray into Mick's, over half the tables claimed.

"Yeah. It's Maren's birthday. Her girlfriend, Nat, surprised her with a trip to D.C. for the weekend."

"Nice. She the only other employee?" Coulton recalled Jerome mentioning he didn't see Ainsley much, now that her dad was sick.

"My brother is supposed to work here too, but as you saw last week, he's a total piece of shit."

Coulton couldn't fault that observation. He wasn't a violent person, but when her brother had insulted her, he'd seen red. His teammates would have flipped out if they'd seen him shoving Ainsley's brother against the wall, the action completely out of character. Somewhere along the line, he'd gotten the nickname Gentle Giant on the team, and it circulated enough that McKenna had used it in some of her posts about him.

The door to the tavern opened, casting a ray of light across the floor, despite the setting sun. Because of the dingy interior of the place, it was easy to tell when someone new was coming in, the brief burst of light from the open door almost blinding.

Ainsley glanced over his shoulder. "Hey, Petey. Where the hell have you been?"

Coulton recognized the man as the one who'd pulled him over to play darts last Sunday.

Petey stepped next to him, also surprised to see him again. "Hey, Colt," the older man said, slapping him on the shoulder.

Somehow, Petey had misheard Coulton, thinking he'd said Colt when he introduced himself, and he hadn't bothered to correct the man.

"Wife dragged me to my mother-in-law's for a fucking Sunday dinner," Petey said in response to Ainsley's question. "Tells me I don't spend enough time with her mother. Told her that's because I hate the bitch, which started a big fucking fight and next thing I know, I'm sitting with Atilla the Hun, pretending to like her cooking. I swear to God, it took me too many bites to figure out what the hell I was even eating." Petey glanced back at Coulton. "It was ham, by the way, but it tasted like fucking leather."

Coulton chuckled, amused by the man's story. He hadn't lied to Ainsley when he'd said he enjoyed the company at Mick's. While the old guys in the place were grizzled and grumpy, they were entertaining storytellers.

"Anyway." Petey shuffled down the bar to a stool Coulton assumed was the guy's usual. "Get me a beer."

Ainsley had the pint in front of Petey before he settled onto the stool.

"Turn the channel," the older man demanded gruffly, pointing to the ancient TV. "See if you can find highlights from the hockey game. Atilla got rid of her cable, so I had to sit there and listen to her and my wife talk about a bunch of boring bullshit. Who the fuck gets rid of cable?"

So far, no one in the tavern had recognized Coulton, which wasn't that surprising. As goalie, his face was completely covered by his helmet, so he was better able to go places incognito than his other teammates. He'd wondered last week if Ainsley recognized his name when she ran his credit card, but if she did, she didn't give any indication.

Ainsley flicked through the channels until she found the highlights. Coulton didn't bother watching them because he'd had a front-row seat to the game, and he was still pissed about letting those pucks get by him.

He watched Ainsley to see her reaction to the game, but she didn't spare the TV a second glance, grabbing her sketch pad from the counter and picking up her pencil, chewing on the end as she studied whatever drawing she was looking at.

Coulton's curiosity was piqued—by her disinterest in the game *and* her artwork. "Not watching the highlights?"

Ainsley shook her head.

Then Petey cussed at the TV. Or more specifically, *him*. "Jesus

Christ. Moore needs to get his head out of his ass. How the fuck did that puck get in the net?"

Coulton grimaced, wondering the same goddamn thing. Then he looked at Ainsley and remembered *exactly* how it had flown by him. He'd been thinking about her.

"Not a hockey fan?" Coulton asked.

"Fuck no. Though to be fair, I hate all sports equally. Sat through enough of them when I was a kid because it's all these losers around here watch."

Petey rolled his eyes at her comment, clearly unaffected by her insult. Coulton wondered how long the older guy and Ainsley had known each other. There was a familiarity that seemed to indicate it had been a long time.

"That's a shame," Coulton said. "Because I was going to invite you to a hockey game."

Ainsley stared at him for a couple seconds, blinking like she was trying to translate what he'd said. He had never met a woman like her. She was a ballbuster, overflowing with confidence when it came to running this tavern. She seemed to literally hold the rough patrons in the palm of her hand.

Yet, when it came to his flirting, she was completely flustered.

"Pass," she finally said. "Hard pass. Not interested in going to a hockey game."

So much for using his superpower with Ainsley, he thought, grinning.

Ainsley gave him a curious look. "That's funny?"

"Not really," he said with a shrug. He didn't mention his career because he liked being able to sit unrecognized in this bar. "What are you drawing?"

She responded to that question exactly how he expected. She closed the pad and shoved it out of sight under the counter. "Nothing."

"Can I see?" he asked.

She shook her head. "It's all crap."

He doubted that, but he also knew she wasn't going to waver on giving him a peek, so he let it drop.

Despite her unease, she leaned on the counter to continue talking to him. "Visiting your Cherry Hill friend again?" she asked.

Coulton nodded. "Yeah. By the way, Jerome says hi."

"Jerome Walker is your friend?"

"His cousin, Slade, is my Little Brother," Coulton explained.

"Oh sure. I can totally see the family resemblance," she joked.

Coulton cracked up, because he was clearly white and Slade Black. "We're partnered up through Big Brothers Big Sisters."

"You volunteer to be Slade's Big Brother?"

"Yeah," he replied.

"That's seriously cool."

"Cool enough that you'll let me take you out to dinner? No hockey game," he quickly added.

"You mean like on a date?"

Coulton laughed again. "Dinner *is* one of the things people do when they go on a date. You don't hate food too, do you?"

Something shifted in Ainsley's expression, something that wiped away the easy smile that had just been there. The problem was, Coulton couldn't understand what he was seeing because she turned to stone, leaving him to wonder if she was mad, sad, scared, or annoyed. It could have been any or all of those things. What the hell had he said wrong?

"Not interested in dating, either." She turned away from him, wiping the counter behind her—even though it didn't need to be cleaned—and not bothering to offer him any reason why.

He sat there for a few minutes, trying to figure out how to recover. Ainsley was a puzzle, one he was obsessed with solving.

As she continued to clean the counter, carefully avoiding his gaze through the mirror, he studied her more closely. Her hair hung loose, the ends just brushing her shoulders. She wore a black tank top, so with her back turned, he was able to get a good look at most of the tattoo on her right shoulder.

"Is that an empty birdcage?" he mused aloud, hoping that by changing the subject, she'd relax and chat with him some more.

Ainsley twisted back around slowly. "Yeah."

"No bird?"

She shook her head. "Nope. It flew away."

Well, there was definitely a story behind that tattoo, but now, as always, Ainsley shut him down before offering anything more.

Rather than turn from him, she tilted her head, looking at him like she was trying to figure him out too. "You gonna keep coming here?"

Coulton nodded. "Yep."

"Why?"

He considered lying, because he didn't want to push her away, but there was a larger part of him that wanted to tell her the truth, simply to see how she would respond. "Because you haven't agreed to go out on a date with me yet."

Petey snorted, making it obvious he was eavesdropping on their conversation. "Good luck getting this one out," he said to Coulton, as he tilted his chin toward Ainsley. "She hasn't dated since—"

"Since I got saddled with running this dump," Ainsley interjected too quickly and too loudly. "This dump *you* come to every goddamn day."

That was not what Petey was going to say, but the old guy had clearly gotten the point, and he didn't seem any more anxious to piss off the bartender than Tuffy had. So, instead, Petey huffed and turned his attention back to the TV.

Oh yeah, Coulton thought. This woman had lots of stories.

And he wanted to hear every single one.

CHAPTER THREE

AINSLEY LEANED OVER THE COUNTER, her chin resting on her palm, simply to prop her head up. She was tired as shit and bored out of her fucking mind.

The tavern had been dead most of the night. So dead, she'd considered closing early.

The only problem with doing that was, it meant going home, and she'd rather stay here with the one lonely soul sitting in the corner, nursing a beer, than spend any more time than necessary with Mick.

He was usually in bed by the time she closed for the night, so she could have the living room to herself, watching whatever she wanted on TV, chilling for a few hours before heading to her own bedroom to sleep until eleven. She was a nocturnal creature. Always had been. Her ex, Jagger, used to swear she was part vampire.

Her work and sleep schedule suited Ainsley just fine, because it limited her unpleasant interactions with Mick to a couple hours every morning. Which was two hours too long for her.

She rubbed her eyes wearily, her gaze drifting to the door despite her best efforts to stop looking.

Coulton had shown up two Sundays in a row, so when he

didn't come this past Sunday, she'd been more disappointed than she wanted to admit to herself. The tavern was closed on Mondays, so she had spent all yesterday running errands and telling herself she didn't give a shit that he hadn't shown.

He'd asked her out, she'd turned him down, and he'd moved on.

Good riddance.

She didn't have the time or desire to date. Because men were douchebags.

Usually repeating that mantra worked for her, but she was having a hard time shoe-horning Coulton into the same category as guys like Jagger, Tiger, and Montgomery. Or her dad or Eli, she mentally added.

She rolled her eyes when she thought about her brother. He'd been absent lately, something that never boded well because he only disappeared when he was losing money at the track, stoned out of his mind, or hiding from someone stupid enough to loan him money.

Which meant when he returned—and he always returned—he was strung out, smelly, and mean.

Too many times in her life, she had wished he would stop coming back, and then she'd feel guilty for thinking that. She prided herself on trying to be a good person overall, but whenever she thought about Eli, her karma took a serious hit.

She glanced at the door again, and then at the time on her phone. Two hours to closing.

Fuck this shit.

She walked over to the lone patron. "I'm closing up early tonight."

The guy, Rat, was a regular, though she didn't know much more about him than his name fit his appearance. His nose long and pointy, his mustache limited to a few whiskers, his eyes small, beady, and shifty, and he was always three days overdue for a shower, his greasy hair clinging to his equally greasy forehead. He tended to drink alone, and he only had one expression—resting bitch face.

She half expected him to argue, because it was two hours earlier than the usual time, but then his eyes darted around the tavern and he merely shrugged, reaching into his pocket and tossing a few bucks on the table rather than handing them to her. Even though she was standing right next to him.

She sighed, picking up the cash—which covered his bill, with none left over for a tip—and grabbed his glass. She turned, intent on following Rat to the door to twist the lock, but as dictated by Murphy's Law, two men walked in just as the other guy left.

"We're closing early," she said, meeting them before they could make it more than a few steps inside. Now that she had her nose pointed toward home, there was no going back. All she had to do was endure a couple of shitty remarks from her dad on the way in, then retreat to her bedroom. She was tired enough that even her lumpy mattress felt inviting.

"We're not here to drink," said one of the guys, the bigger of the two.

"Well, that's good. Because you're not drinking." Ainsley had spent so much of her life in this tavern that she'd pretty much stopped looking at the guys who came in. Because, with the exception of Thor, they were all a dime a dozen.

However, these two didn't exactly fit the bill of a Mick's Tavern drinker any more than Coulton did. Most of her guys were older, no strangers to long work hours, poor diets, and hard manual labor.

These guys—Mario and Luigi, she dubbed them—were worse than that, with their wifebeaters, low-slung, loose jeans, thick gold chains, and enough product in their dark hair that a hurricane wouldn't mess it up. They were also younger, closer to her age, though she didn't recognize them from school, which either meant they'd moved into the area, or they'd dropped out early in their educational careers.

Regardless of where they'd started, they were currently standard, run-of-the-mill thugs as far as Cherry Hill was concerned.

Ainsley started to skirt by them, anxious to get behind the bar to grab her bat. She didn't like the way Mario was salivating like she was a juicy steak. But Luigi, the smaller of the two guys, stuck his hand out, grasping her upper arm.

She scowled and shrugged it off. "Excuse you," she snapped. Ainsley had learned a long time ago that the worst thing a person could do was show fear.

"Looking for Eli," Mario said to her tits.

Ainsley rolled her eyes as she lifted her arms, gesturing around the empty tavern. "He's not here."

"No shit," Luigi said hotly, not appreciating her sarcasm. "That guy is slipperier than snot."

"Not my problem." She didn't need what was happening here spelled out. These idiots had clearly loaned Eli money and now they were here hoping to collect. Fuck that.

Mario rubbed his pockmarked chin. "That's where you're wrong. Eli owes us money. Thousand bucks. Said we could collect it here."

Ainsley laughed. "Don't think so."

Luigi scowled. "Wasn't fucking asking." He pointed toward the cash register. "So get your ass back there and get our money."

Ainsley didn't have anywhere near a thousand dollars in her cash register, and given the way Mario was eyeballing her, she got the sense he was hoping she'd come up shy.

Which left her with precious few options. None of them good.

She sized them up again, fairly certain they weren't carrying guns. No bulges beneath their clothing and nowhere to stash them in their pants.

Ainsley pretended to play along, because her bat was under the register and fighting her way out of here was the only option she could stomach if they decided the few measly bucks she had weren't enough.

Begging for mercy most likely wouldn't change the outcome.

She crossed the bar and started to walk behind the counter, but Luigi grabbed her again.

"No funny business," he warned her, flashing a switchblade.

Okay, cool. So no gun. Not that a knife was much better. Luigi slipped the knife back in his pocket. Clearly, he and Mario were confident in their abilities to knock her around without weapons until she gave them what they wanted.

Ainsley shook her arm loose again. "Go to hell," she muttered, as she stepped in front of the register. With one hand, she opened the drawer, while the other drifted lower.

She'd just managed to wrap her hand around her bat when Luigi stepped next to her, looking into the register.

"That's it?" he asked, grabbing the handful of twenties she had and stuffing them in his pocket. "Fuck, man. That's not even two hundred bucks. Where's the rest?"

She smirked. "Look around, asshole." She gestured to the empty tavern once more, distracting him while she got a better grip on her bat. She was trying to figure out her game plan because, unfortunately, the space behind the bar was too tight. She wouldn't have enough room to rear back and swing properly.

"Guess you're gonna have to pay up another way," Mario said, licking his lips.

Yep. That was what she thought.

It was now or never. All she had going for her was the element of surprise, but given she didn't have enough money to pay Eli's debt, it wasn't like she had any other options.

She quickly took a couple of steps back as she raised the bat. Without time to aim, she swung too low, catching Luigi on the meaty part of his upper arm. Nowhere near hard enough to hurt him but plenty hard enough to piss him off.

He reached out and wrapped his hand around the thick end

of her bat, planning to wrestle it away from her. Ainsley had zero intention of letting go, so she tugged back as she kicked upward, managing to nail the asshole right in the nuts.

Luigi dropped to his knees, cursing a blue streak. "Motherfucking cunt!" he said, gasping. "Gonna pay for that."

While he tried to pull his balls out of his stomach, Ainsley twisted, swinging her bat once more as Mario tried to rush her from behind, circling around the bar and climbing over the counter to hem her in. This time, she aimed higher, cracking the bat against the side of the man's head. He howled in pain.

She hadn't hurt either of them enough, so time was not on her side. She tried to leap over the counter, and almost made it, but at the last minute, Mario grabbed her ankle, throwing her off-kilter. She hung over the bar, head pointed toward the floor. She was forced to drop the bat in her attempt to grab the edge of the counter as he tightened his grip, pulling her toward him. She couldn't let him drag her back behind the bar because she'd be trapped—without her weapon.

Ainsley kicked wildly with her free leg, landing a couple times as Mario grunted in pain. Glancing over her shoulder, she aimed the next kick, clipping him in the jaw. His grip loosened, and unfortunately, without him holding her, gravity took over and she flew forward, crashing into a couple of stools before landing hard on floor on the opposite side of the counter.

Her right arm took the brunt of the fall, the pain enough that her vision went gray and bile rose in her throat. It took her a few seconds to recover enough to move again.

Those seconds were too many. She tried to rise but failed as Mario leapt over the bar, landing next to her. He reached down and grabbed a handful of her hair, pulling her to her knees, her scalp burning.

"You're going to pay for that, you stupid bitch." Mario released her hair, but only so he could back that threat up with a hard kick to her stomach.

Ainsley doubled over, coughing hard, certain she was going

to throw up. Even as she fought to breathe, her eyes flew over the floor. If she could just find her bat…

After this, she was buying a gun. They'd never gotten one for the tavern because in his heyday, Mick had been a big, mean son of a bitch, who never needed more than his fists to keep the drunks in line. Ainsley hated guns, but she felt her stance on that changing with each passing moment.

Luigi rounded the bar, his hand still cupping his crotch, his expression pure fury as he lifted his arm and backhanded her, the side of her face scorching as if she'd pressed it to fire.

"We were just gonna take the money," Mario lied, grabbing her hair once more, tugging her toward him and out of reach of her bat. "But now, we're gonna collect interest."

He grabbed a handful of her T-shirt, ripping it in his attempt to pull it over her head.

Ainsley hurt all over, but none of that pain stopped her from fighting with everything she had. She kicked and punched, gouged, and pinched, managing to get free, though she didn't expect that to last long.

"Jesus Christ." Luigi, who was still covering his balls lest she nail him again, yelled at Mario. "Fucking grab her already!"

Mario was just reaching for her when the tavern door open. "Get the fuck out!" he screamed, without looking at whoever had walked in. "Bar's closed."

The door shut with a slam, and Ainsley sent up a prayer that whoever had cut and run would at least call the cops. Though even if they did, they would arrive too late.

Mario had just managed to grab one of her arms, his hold tighter than a vise, when she heard Luigi yelp.

One minute, Luigi was standing in front of her, the next, he was laying on the ground halfway across the tavern in the middle of the splintered remains of a table.

Ainsley blinked rapidly, blinded by tears of pain and trying to figure out what the hell happened, when Mario pushed her forward roughly, using her as some sort of human shield. She bounced off a rock-hard wall of muscle, but the hands that touched her now didn't hurt. They were gentle.

"Call the police, Ainsley."

She looked up—and nearly sobbed when she saw Coulton standing there. His gaze, however, was locked on Mario, who was standing behind her.

Coulton carefully set her to the side, and then he moved forward with the force of a wrecking ball. He picked up Mario, swinging him like a rag doll as he tossed him next to Luigi, who was either unconscious or playing dead.

Mario slowly clamored to one knee, attempting to rise, but Coulton didn't give him the chance, kicking the man in the gut the same way Mario had done to her.

Ha! Fucking karma, asshole.

That was when Luigi moved, grabbing Coulton's ankle in an effort to pull him off his feet. He almost succeeded as Coulton stumbled back a few steps.

Both men used that to their advantage, quickly rising and lifting their fists.

"You're gonna fucking die," Luigi threatened, reaching into his pocket for the knife.

Assholes like these two enjoyed beating on women, as if crushing someone who was physically smaller and weaker somehow made them big, tough men, but when it came to fighting Coulton, they were prepared to gang up and cheat, using their weapons against an unarmed man.

"Fucking cowards." Ainsley reached down, grasping her bat and screaming like a banshee as she charged. She heard a crack after she swung, and Luigi's howl of pain as his hand dropped the knife, his arm hanging uselessly at a strange angle.

"My fucking arm!" he cried out.

Coulton had moved at the same time, throwing a punch at Mario that took the man down in one. Petey had asked Coulton if he'd done any boxing. If he hadn't, he was missing his calling.

Mario shook his head, trying to clear his vision, twisting over to his hands and knees, rapidly crawling toward the door.

Luigi beat him there, shoving his partner out of the way with his foot, in his haste to get away. Ainsley chased him, her bat raised above her head.

Mario scrambled to his feet, racing out just a step behind Luigi, who was cradling his broken arm and cussing loudly. "Crazy fucking cunt!"

Ainsley had every intention of chasing the motherfuckers down the street, but a strong arm banded around her waist, holding her back.

"Down, wildcat," Coulton said, reaching to take the bat from her.

She struggled briefly, adrenaline coursing through her veins, until Coulton placed his lips next to her ear. "Shhh. It's over now," he said softly. "It's over."

It took at least a dozen times of him repeating those same words, "It's over," for it to finally sink in.

She stilled in his arms, soaking in the strength and warmth of his embrace for as long as she dared.

When was the last time anyone had held her like this?

Wrong question.

Had anyone *ever* held her like this?

Sadly, the answer to that question came easily.

No.

Ainsley had lived an entire lifetime painfully short on hugs. Which explained why it was so difficult for her to push Coulton's arm down and step away.

She turned around, ready to thank him. He'd saved her from… She couldn't let herself think the word, so she swallowed it down, not letting her thoughts drift beyond the fact that he'd saved her.

He'd been gentle as he held her, but when she faced him, his expression immediately morphed to one of anger.

Ainsley took a step back, until he said, "You need to go to the hospital. You're hurt."

She took mental stock, trying to pinpoint the painful places. Her scalp was tender, her lip was throbbing, and her arm hurt like hell. Those were the sharpest pains. Everything else had receded to a dull, throbbing ache.

"I'm okay. It's not that bad."

"Not bad!" Coulton said hotly. "You're bleeding."

She reached up and winced when she felt her split lip. "Fucking asshole. What is it with guys? Why do you all think it's okay to backhand a woman?"

"All?" Coulton froze. "Have you been hit before?"

She rolled her eyes. "What part of 'I've lived in Cherry Hill my whole life' did you miss?"

He leaned toward her. "Who hit you?" he asked darkly.

She tilted her head, trying to come to grips with what she was seeing. The man looked seriously ready to go on the warpath. On the two occasions he'd sat at the bar, they had talked, and he'd been super chill.

Well, apart from his showdown with Eli, but Eli tended to bring out the worst in everyone. It was her brother's one true talent.

Coulton's desire to take on anyone who tried to hurt her was one of the things that had captured her attention, despite her efforts to put the pretty man out of her head. It was hard, because no one—and she meant *no one*—had ever tried to protect her before.

"I've been mugged a time or three," she responded. "And my dad is no fucking prince."

Suddenly, it felt as if the temperature in the tavern had dropped a good fifty degrees.

"Your dad backhanded you?"

She shrugged. "Plenty of times. Not sure if you've noticed or not, but I'm kind of a smart-ass."

Coulton drew in a slow breath through his nose, his eyes

dark with an anger that should have scared her…but instead made her horny as fucking hell.

Quite the feat considering she'd almost just been…

Nope. Not thinking that.

"I'm taking you to the hospital," he repeated.

She shook her head. "No. You're not. I've got some bumps and bruises and that's it. All they'll do at the hospital is give me a three-hundred-dollar Tylenol and a seventy-dollar ice pack. No thanks. I've got that shit at home."

Coulton didn't like her answer. "If I take you home, will someone take care of you?" he asked, his voice so low, she had to lean closer to hear. God, at this rate, she'd be pressed against him again.

She laughed, then winced again because her lip hurt like a bitch. "Oh yeah, Coulton. Mick will kiss all my boo-boos, make me hot chocolate with marshmallows, and then tuck me into bed."

Ainsley's second language was English.

Sarcasm, her first.

"What's really going to happen when you get home?"

Ainsley closed her eyes, too weary to continue this conversation. "Mick will want to know if the assholes got the money, and he'll be pissed at me when I tell him they did," she said, also angry that they'd gotten away with the cash. They really needed the money. Mick had stupidly decided to do a cash-out refinance on the tavern when the medical bills got to be too much, the short-term solution leaving them even deeper under water, thanks to the high interest rate.

"They came in to rob you?"

She narrowed her eyes, her anger toward Eli resurfacing. "Not really. They were trying to get me to pay off my brother's debts, and fun fact…there wasn't enough money in the register."

"Your brother gonna be home?"

Ainsley got a sick pleasure out of the murderous way

Coulton asked that. Like he was hoping to keep the night's brawling going.

"Probably not, considering he sent those guys to *me* to pay his debt. He'll lay low. Either at a friend's house, or maybe he'll find some woman stupid enough to sleep with him. Won't see him anytime soon because he's a coward."

"He sent those men here," he said, no question in his voice. She got the sense he was repeating those words simply to make them sink in.

"I was getting things under control," she lied, uncertain if she was trying to convince him or console herself.

Coulton pierced her with a look that told her she most definitely wasn't getting *anything* under control.

She lowered her head, looking at the floor. "What was happening…" She paused, her brain skipping over how closely she'd come to being sexually assaulted. "It was *going* to happen, Coulton. I didn't have enough money to pay them."

"Jesus," he muttered. "They were going to—"

"But they didn't," she cut him off, unable to hear that word.

He reached for his cell.

"What are you doing?"

"Calling the cops," he replied.

She put her hand over his, pushing his phone down. "No. They don't come here. Besides, the guys got some money. I doubt they'll come back after the ass-whooping we just handed them."

She wished she could believe that was true, but the fact was, they were still shy about eight hundred dollars and now had an ax to grind.

"Ainsley. You were assaulted and robbed. You need to file a report."

She shook her head. "You don't understand how things work around here."

Coulton had gotten stiller and quieter with each of her responses. Then his gaze drifted lower, not in the creepy way most guys looked at her. Instead, she got the feeling he was checking her over to make sure she was okay.

She followed his gaze, cussing when she realized her shirt was torn and hanging open, her tatty black bra showing. "Goddammit. They ripped my favorite shirt."

"Get your stuff," Coulton said darkly.

She glanced up at him. "What?"

"Your stuff. Get it," he replied, enunciating every word like she was four cards short of a deck.

She wanted to take offense, but she also wanted to go home, lick her wounds, and crawl into bed for the next thirty years or so.

So she did something she never did. Followed an order.

Walking to the register, she took out the crappy few one-dollar bills the assholes left behind. She'd pulled a ten-hour shift and had all of seven dollars and twelve cents to show for it.

She shoved the bills into a bank bag and locked it into the safe behind her. Only she and Mick had the combination, something that made Eli see red every time she opened it to lock their money away from him. Because of the previous muggings she'd mentioned, neither she nor Mick ever carried cash out of here at night, doing their bank deposits in the bright sunshine of morning, when there were a lot more people out and about.

Once the safe was closed, she grabbed her purse, glancing around at the destruction. Several of the barstools had been knocked over in her attempt to scale the counter to escape. A few other tables and chairs were askew from their brawl, and one table—the one Coulton had thrown Luigi into—was damaged beyond repair and headed to the dumpster tomorrow. Her baseball bat lay in the middle of the floor.

She started to bend over to pick up one of the stools.

"What are you doing?"

"I should..." She sighed.

"Leave it," Coulton said. "You should leave it."

He was acting strangely, but not in a bad way. In truth, she was kind of touched by how concerned he was. Especially since they didn't know each other that well.

She nodded, walking to the door. Once they were both outside, she locked the door, then pulled down the metal gate, listening as it snapped into place.

"Well," she said awkwardly as they stood there. "Um, thanks."

Coulton gestured to a truck parked across the street, offering to drive her home.

"I only live a few blocks that way," she said, pointing down the street.

Coulton's scowl returned. "You walk home alone at night in this neighborhood?"

She grinned. "Of course not. My driver will be here with the limo any minute."

Coulton ran a hand through his hair. "I don't want you to go home if there's no one to look after you. You took some hard hits, and your lip is still bleeding. I have a guest room. You can stay with me."

Ainsley laughed. "Yeah. No. That's not happening. I might have taken a couple of knocks to the head, but they didn't knock me senseless. I barely know you."

Coulton considered that for a few moments, then pulled his phone out of his pocket, calling someone before putting it on speaker. "Hi, Jerome, it's Coulton. Sorry for calling so late. I'm here with Ainsley."

"Hey, Coulton, Ainsley. How's it hanging, girl? Haven't seen you in a minute."

"I'm cool," she lied.

"There was an incident at the bar, Jerome, and Ainsley was hurt," Coulton replied.

Ainsley wasn't sure whether she was more confused by this call or pissed that he was sharing her private information. She didn't like for people to know her business.

"She won't go to the hospital, so I've offered to take care of her. Got first-aid stuff back at my place. She's leery," he continued, looking at her. "And rightly so, because we don't know each other that well. But I was hoping you would vouch for me."

"Oh, hell yeah, man. Coulton's a stand-up guy, Ainsley. You can trust him. He's awesome with Slade, changed the kid's life."

Ainsley blinked a couple of times as her eyes teared up. She was blaming exhaustion, refusing to attribute anything else to this unfamiliar emotion. Coulton wanted to take care of her, but he also wanted her to feel safe.

Who the hell *was* this guy? Because genuinely good men were few and far between in her world.

"Thanks, Jerome," she finally managed to say, her voice sounding thicker than usual.

"No problem. I'll stop by Mick's one day and we can catch up."

"I'd like that." Ainsley had always liked Jerome, but they'd drifted apart after graduation, their loose connection based on the fact her high school friends had been friends with his.

"Hope you're okay, Ainsley."

"I'll be fine," she reassured him.

Coulton added his thanks, then hung up the phone. "So you'll come home with me?"

Ainsley glanced down the street, the idea of walking into her shitty apartment that still stunk of stale cigarettes, despite the fact Mick had stopped smoking a year ago, too depressing to consider.

Coulton frowned when she didn't answer right away. "Do you seriously think I'm trying to pick you up? After what you just went through? Those guys were planning to rape you, Ainsley."

She shivered, preferring not to think about that. She'd been losing the fight, but pride wouldn't let her admit it.

Tonight could have been so fucking bad, and she would have been powerless to stop it.

She was used to feeling hopeless, but not helpless.

"I'm offering you my guest room," Coulton added. "Where you will be sleeping alone. Did you eat dinner?"

She shrugged. "Heated up some of those crappy microwavable pizza bites at the bar."

He sighed. "I'll make you something healthy to eat, after I check your injuries. Then you can soak in a hot bath and go to sleep. So are you coming with me or not?"

"Yeah," she said, nodding. "I am."

Coulton smiled like she'd done something nice for *him*, when it was really him offering the kindness. Then he placed his hand on the small of her back and walked her to his truck, where he opened the passenger door for her.

They were quiet on the drive to his place. She hadn't even thought to ask where he lived, so she was shocked when he pulled up in front of an upscale apartment building on the waterfront in Fell's Point. It was a nice area, and a far cry from Cherry Hill.

"You live here?" Ainsley asked, as she stepped out of the truck. She belatedly realized she knew next to nothing about this man she'd come home with.

But she wasn't afraid. Because, even with the lack of specific details, she'd gotten a feeling about Coulton from the first second he'd sat down at the end of the bar. Between her instincts —which admittedly usually sucked—and Jerome's reassurance, she felt safe with him.

Safe?

Jesus. Maybe she'd taken some harder hits tonight than she thought, because her trust issues had fucking trust issues. And *no one* made her feel safe.

"I do. Been here just over two years," he said, entering the security code for the building before opening the door and escorting her to the elevator with that gentle touch on her back that she liked way too much.

He pushed the button for the top floor.

"Where were you before?" she asked.

"Vancouver," Coulton said.

"Oh, cool. I didn't realize you were Canadian."

Coulton chuckled. "I'm not. I'm originally from Detroit. My parents still live there, so I go back to visit a few times a year."

"You're close to them?"

"Hell yeah. Only child of older parents who never thought they'd have kids."

"So what I'm hearing is you were spoiled rotten," she teased.

Coulton laughed but didn't deny it.

Before she could ask what had taken him to Canada and then brought him to Baltimore, they reached his floor. Coulton opened the door to his condo—and her mouth fell open as she took in the large, open space with floor-to-ceiling windows. His place was on the waterfront, and the moon sparkled off the river, the sight so beautiful, Ainsley had to force herself to tear her gaze away. If she were alone, she would spend hours taking in that view.

When she continued her perusal of this place, her eyes landed on a wall that contained a huge shelving unit filled with countless trophies and photographs of Coulton.

In goalie gear.

More specifically, professional hockey gear.

"You play for the Stingrays?"

Coulton nodded. "And Vancouver before that."

"Holy shit. When you said you wanted to take me to a hockey game, and I said…"

He grinned, both of them recalling her comments about hating the sport. "Yeah, my ego took a bit of a hit there. Was kind of hoping taking you to a game might impress you."

Ainsley hadn't underplayed her disdain for sports. When the patrons of the tavern were getting wasted and bitching about whatever team was losing, she tuned it out, completely uninterested.

"I'm the goalie," he added.

She pointed to a collage of photos of him on the ice. "Yeah. I figured that out. Do you even have to move when you're playing, or do you just stand in front of the net? Because I can't imagine much getting by you," she said, gesturing to his large frame.

Amused, Coulton laughed. "I have to put in a little work."

"Jesus, if the guys at the tavern figure out who you are..." Ainsley couldn't even begin to imagine how excited they would be. Professional athletes were the equivalent to the royal family at Mick's.

Coulton shrugged, clearly unconcerned if that should happen. "Petey seems to think my name is Colt."

Ainsley laughed. "He's hard of hearing. Even so, I'm surprised they didn't recognize you. They really like watching the Stingrays play."

"It's easier for me to walk around unrecognized, thanks to my helmet. But it's not a big deal if they find out. I like talking to fans. It's nice connecting with them."

"Yeah, you'll definitely rethink that if it gets out at Mick's. You think they swarmed you after that confrontation with Eli? Finding out you're on the Baltimore team will be next level."

Ainsley continued her perusal of his condo, because the first few minutes here had been enlightening to say the least. Her attention was drawn to a cage on a cabinet across the large living room. She stepped up to it, but it was empty.

Coulton followed her. "Sofia is in there. You just have to dig around a bit."

Ainsley watched as Coulton gently dug through a bunch of white fluff before he closed his hand around something, pulling it out of the cage. When he opened his hand, he revealed the tiniest, cutest little creature she'd ever seen.

"Oh my God. What is that?" she asked, lifting her hand to touch it.

"A dwarf hamster."

The image of gigantic Coulton holding the smallest pet on the face of the earth was too adorable and hilarious. She laughed. "This is your pet?"

Coulton didn't take offense at her reaction. "She's my sweetest baby," he said, cooing to the tiny creature, gently touching the hamster's head. "Want to hold her?"

Ainsley was dying to. She held out her hand and giggled when Sofia wiggled, tickling her. "She's so cute! But I'm struggling to make this pet fit with you. You seem better suited to a big-ass dog."

Coulton chuckled. "I have to confess, getting a dwarf hamster wasn't my decision. My neighbor across the hall, Lee, got Sofia for his daughters for Christmas, but the girls were too young. They kept taking her out of her cage and they were a bit rough. Lee was afraid they'd hurt her or lose her, so he asked if I minded taking her. The girls are four and six, and they have visitation rights. Plus, they feed her when I'm out on the road with the team."

"That's so cool."

Coulton took the hamster from Ainsley and put her back in the cage. "We can finish the tour of my place after I take a look at you."

Ainsley followed Coulton to the kitchen, where he reached into a cabinet under the sink and pulled out a first aid kit. "Not exactly a stranger to patching up injuries," he explained. "My pads protect a lot, but every now and then, I take a hit." He gestured to a stool next to the island. "Sit there."

Ainsley continued to shock herself as she simply did what Coulton said without arguing. It occurred to her that in addition to her trust issues, she also had some serious problems with authority. God, a therapist could use her head as an amusement park.

All those problems fell away when she was with Coulton, though.

He used his finger to gently tip her head back, his gaze traveling over her face. "You've got a bruise on this cheek," he said, stroking it softly. "But I don't think you'll have a black eye." He cleaned her bloody lip with such care, Ainsley had to blink back some more of those cursed tears. Then he dabbed it with some Neosporin. "It's the good stuff. Includes painkiller."

She nodded appreciatively. Her lip was sore, but nothing unbearable.

Then Coulton lifted her arms, scanning them, frowning at the bruises already darkening the skin that her tattoos were doing nothing to hide. "Motherfuckers," he muttered under his breath.

"You did way worse to them," she said with a grin, hoping to lighten his mood.

It didn't work.

"They should be behind bars for hurting you, Ainsley."

She didn't respond to that.

"What else hurts?" he asked.

She pointed to her head. "Mario was a hair-puller. And not in a fun way."

"Mario? You knew those guys?"

She quickly shook her head. "No. I was calling them Mario and Luigi in my head."

That finally got her a hint of a smile. He ran his fingers through her hair. Even with her sitting on the tall stool, he was able to look down. His touch was more massage than investigation, and it felt like heaven. Ainsley had to work not to moan. It felt *that* good.

"Where else?" he asked.

Ainsley lifted her shoulders because the rest of her injuries were no doubt bruises, just like the ones he could see. The only difference was, these bruises were under her clothes.

"Ainsley," he persisted.

"They kicked me in the stomach," she said, gesturing vaguely to her midsection.

Coulton's scowl was dark as he reached for the hem of her shirt. She'd been holding the giant rip at the top together as best she could, but she let it fall open as she gripped his wrists to stop him. The man was seriously strong. He didn't shake her off, but he also didn't relent. "You could have bruised or even broken ribs."

"I don't."

"How do you know that?" he asked.

"Because I've had them before. They would hurt worse than they do."

"Broken ribs?" he asked.

"Eli and I have had some knockdown drag-outs in our day. He shoved me down the stairs in our apartment building once when I was a junior in high school. Bruised ribs and a concussion."

"Your brother did that to you?"

She shrugged, not mentioning that fight with Eli didn't even crack the top ten as far as ways he'd tried to hurt her. Of course, the list had been adjusted tonight, as almost getting her raped by two assholes rocketed to the number one position. "It's no big deal. Got me out of going to school for a whole week. So silver linings and all that shit," she joked lamely.

Coulton held the hem of her shirt, but he'd stopped trying to take it off her. "I want to check that you're okay, but I understand if it makes you uncomfortable. I think we should revisit the hospital idea."

"Nope. And you can admit it. You're just trying to sneak a peek of my tits." Shyness had never really been an issue with her, so she stopped trying to fight him, shrugging off the shirt. It wasn't like it was serving much purpose anyway. Coulton had already gotten an eyeful of her bra and chest in the bar.

She lifted her arms in a "here I am" gesture. Coulton didn't smile, his eyes sliding over her, his brows furrowed. His scowl was back. "That's a hell of a bruise on your arm."

"Yeah. I sort of fell over the bar and landed on it."

"And on your side." His fingers feathered over her midsection.

"That was where Mario kicked me. Felt like the fucker was wearing steel-toe boots."

He gently poked and prodded her arm, his gaze locked on her face, making it necessary for her to shield her reactions. She had a pretty good idea Coulton would drag her ass to the hospital at the slightest wince.

"I'm fine," she insisted.

He continued probing, but after a few more minutes, he seemed satisfied that she wasn't lying to him. Then he shocked her by taking off his own shirt—hello, Mr. Eight Pack—and pulling it over her head.

"Anything else hurt?"

She shook her head, tempted to mutter "my pride," but she held that tidbit in.

Coulton offered his hand, helping her from the stool and leading her down the hallway. Opening a door, he gestured inside. "The guest room."

Ainsley stepped inside, feeling like she'd walked into a parallel universe, because no place in her real life was anywhere near as nice as Coulton's condo. The guest room was painted a soft gray, and a king-size bed dominated one wall, covered with a fluffy duvet and pillows that looked brand-new, pristine, soft. "This is the guest room?"

What the hell must *his* room look like?

"Bathroom is through that door," he said, pointing without following her into the room. She knew that was on purpose, Coulton holding steady to his determination to make her feel safe.

"Why don't you take a nice long soak in the tub while I make us something to eat. There's a new toothbrush in the vanity and a bunch of other toiletries. You should find everything you need."

"Have lots of unexpected overnight guests?" she asked, wishing her question was a joke rather than misplaced jealousy.

"Nope," he replied. "You're the first one."

Ainsley decided that had to be a lie, because there was no way a hot guy—and professional athlete—didn't have a revolving door of women in and out of this place. Of course, if he did, they weren't sleeping in the guest room.

Coulton left her on her own, so she walked to the bathroom, her eyes nearly popping out of her head when she saw the big tub.

She felt like she should skip the bath and take a quick shower instead. After all, soaking in a stranger's tub would be strange, right?

Unable to let that conviction stick, she plugged the tub and started running the water. Because she hadn't had a bath since… maybe ever? At least not since she was a little baby and too young to remember. No one in their right mind would sit their bare ass down in the bathtub in her family's apartment, thanks to the rust stains and mildew that no cleaning product on the market could touch, and the apartment she'd rented with Jagger only had a small shower stall.

Once the tub was nearly full, she stripped off her clothes and slipped in, sinking into the honest-to-God hot water. The standard temperature for her showers at home was tepid.

Alone, she didn't bother to hold in her moan of pure delight as she lay down, only her head remaining above the steaming water. Reaching for the clean washcloth on a shelf beside the tub, she squirted some bath wash on it, running it over her body. Then she held her nose and dunked her head under the water, wetting her hair so that she could use the expensive citrus-scented shampoo. Rinsing out the suds, she repeated the process with the conditioner, then lay still, letting the heat work its magic on her sore body.

She'd never felt this clean or relaxed in her life.

Ainsley remained in the bath, nearly falling asleep, until the cooling water and her empty stomach told her it was time to get out.

Grabbing a towel, she dried off, the soft cotton so nice against her skin. When she returned to the bedroom, she was touched to discover Coulton had placed one of his T-shirts and a pair of boxers on the bed for her to sleep in. She pulled the shirt on, the huge thing falling to her knees, covering up the boxers completely.

She considered tugging on her jeans but couldn't make herself do it. She wanted to enjoy this feeling of being clean for as long as she could.

She showered every day, so it wasn't like she was dirty, but that soak in Coulton's tub had done more than merely scrub the surface. It had gone deeper than that. In ways she couldn't fully understand or explain to herself.

She roamed around the guest room for a moment, trying to get a feel for the guy. She stopped by the dresser, picking up a picture frame. The photo was of Coulton with an attractive blonde, the two mugging for the camera, looking so happy and in love, it almost took Ainsley's breath away. The blonde looked exactly like the type of woman who *should* date a guy like Coulton—pretty, sweet, clean-cut, with perfect teeth, stylish clothes, soft, wavy, natural blonde hair that had probably never seen a bottle of dye.

She'd bet every dime she had the woman didn't have a single tattoo, and her only piercings were the ones in her earlobes filled with those tasteful diamond studs.

Diamonds.

Ainsley scoffed, put the frame down, and decided she'd seen enough.

Walking to the kitchen, she took a second to watch Coulton, whose back was turned. He'd put on a clean shirt too, which was a shame.

Although, even fully dressed, he cut an impressive form.

Jesus, the man's ass in those tight jeans was a work of art.

"There you are," he said, turning and catching her creeping on him. "I was afraid you'd fallen asleep."

"That bath was... I've never taken..." She stopped. She'd

almost admitted it was her first bath, which felt too personal and humiliating to share.

Coulton looked at her for a second, waiting for her to continue. When she didn't, he finished for her. "Never taken a bath?"

She tried to tell herself the reason her cheeks felt hot was the residual effects of the bath. Not embarrassment. "It was amazing," she said, rather than admitting he was right. His expression told her that her confession wasn't necessary.

"Come eat." He placed bowls on the kitchen island, along with bottles of water, and the two of them claimed stools, side by side.

Coulton handed her a bottle of salad dressing. "Didn't put this on because I wasn't sure if you liked balsamic vinaigrette. If you don't, I have ranch, blue cheese, or Caesar in the fridge."

"This is great." Ainsley tried to remember the last time she'd eaten a salad. If she could even classify this as a salad. Hers were typically the premade variety from the grocery store that she could only afford when they were one day from going bad.

Coulton's salad was as big a masterpiece as his ass. He had three different kinds of greens, fresh tomatoes, cucumbers, red onion, hard-boiled eggs, chunks of blue cheese, real bacon bits, and what she swore looked like homemade croutons. He'd topped it with sliced, seasoned chicken breast, and her bowl alone contained enough to feed a family of five.

"This is delicious," she said, forcing herself to make conversation when all she wanted to do was shovel the mouthwatering food into her mouth.

"I promised you healthy."

The two of them ate in silence, and Ainsley appreciated the fact Coulton wasn't one of those people who felt like he had to fill the quiet with meaningless chitchat.

"Thanks for the shirt and boxers," she said after a few more bites. There was no way she was going to be able to eat the entire bowl. She wondered if it would be rude to ask for a doggie bag, because she hated the idea of wasting such delicious, expensive food.

Coulton must have noticed her slowing down. When she tried to hide a yawn, he put his fork down. "Had enough?"

She knew he was asking about the salad, but her nod covered a hell of a lot more. Because she'd had more than enough of so many things.

This day.

This life.

Coulton reached out, and she took his hand without even thinking about it. He walked her back to the guest room, keeping her hand tucked in his the whole way. He stopped at the door.

"Want anything else? Tylenol?"

She shook her head. "I'm okay."

He pointed down the hall to a closed door at the end. "I'll be right there if you need me."

"Thanks, Coulton. For everything. Tonight was…" She stopped.

"It was shitty, horrible, the worst," he finished for her. "And you and I are going to talk about it. But not tonight."

She would be fine with never talking about it, but Coulton didn't seem like the type of person to let things lie. No doubt he resided in that camp that thought talking made shit better.

Ainsley, in the meantime, was a firm believer in burying all the bad stuff deep and never looking back.

But she didn't get a chance to let him know the conversation about tonight was off the table, because her brain short-circuited and every sore part of her body redirected its pain to her pussy when Coulton kissed her bruised cheek.

"All better," he teased with a wink. His lips were soft and warm and touching in the wrong place, because she really—REALLY—wanted him to kiss her for real. In fact, it was on the tip of her tongue to remind him that her lip was hurt too.

She huffed out a soft laugh instead, exhaustion overpowering even her hormones. It really had been a shitty day.

"Good night, Ainsley."

Coulton waited as she walked into the room and closed the door. It didn't occur to her that she hadn't locked the door until she'd climbed under the sheets. That fact drove home just how safe she felt with Coulton.

She didn't even sleep in an unlocked room in her own home, not trusting her brother not to rifle through her stuff to steal, or her dad not to come in and whale on her if he got pissed. Mick had a hell of a temper, and she'd been woken up more times than she could count by him slapping her after discovering some transgression, like she hadn't done the dishes or had forgotten to buy something he'd asked for from the store.

Ainsley shoved those thoughts away because she didn't want them tainting this single perfect moment.

Her stomach was full.

She was clean and warm.

And this was the most comfortable bed she'd ever been in.

She burrowed deeper under the soft covers and drifted into the best sleep of her life.

CHAPTER FOUR

COULTON LIFTED THE GRIDDLE, giving it a quick swish with his wrist to flip the pancake. He kept an ear out for his overnight guest, anxiously waiting for her to join him.

Last night had started out as a waking nightmare. Walking into that tavern and seeing those two men attacking Ainsley had stolen ten years off his life.

She'd been fighting with everything she had—and as much as that impressed him, he'd known she wasn't going to win.

He had tossed and turned most of the night, thinking about what would have happened if he hadn't stopped by Mick's.

Because he'd walked in and…

Fuck.

He should have taken her to the hospital, and he should have called the cops. He wasn't sure why he'd let her talk him out of it.

"I smelled bacon."

He turned at the sound of her voice. Ainsley stood in the doorway of the kitchen, her arms crossed, looking decidedly rumpled and maybe even grumpy. She was dressed in her jeans but still wore his T-shirt. He liked seeing her in his clothing.

What he didn't like was the dark bruise covering nearly her entire right cheek.

"Morning, sunshine," he said as cheerfully as he could muster, despite the murderous thoughts racing through his brain of what he'd do if he ever ran into Mario and Luigi.

She grunted. "Oh God. You're one of those morning people, aren't you?"

He was, but he didn't bother to admit it. Instead, Coulton chuckled as he slid a couple of pancakes onto a plate and set it in the same place she sat last night. Then he carried over the platter of bacon he'd fried. "There's butter and syrup, but if you want something else, let me know."

Ainsley looked at the plate like it was a snake. "You made me breakfast?"

"Of course, I did. You want coffee?"

"Yes, please," she said, looking like a dog begging for a treat.

He grabbed the pot and filled a large mug. "Cream or sugar?"

She shook her head. "Drink it black."

Coulton handed her the mug. "Me too."

"What time is it?" she asked.

Coulton glanced at the clock on the stove. "Eight thirty."

"Jesus Christ. How are you functioning?" Ainsley didn't wait for a response as she slid onto the stool, buttering her pancakes.

Coulton joined her, adding bacon to his own plate. It was nice having her here. He'd never shared breakfast with a woman in this kitchen.

Ainsley hummed her appreciation after the first bite. "Mmm. These are so good."

He smiled. "Glad you like them. I packed up the rest of your salad from last night. It's in the fridge if you want to take it home for lunch. Figure it's better for you than those damn pizza bites."

She gave him that confused look he was becoming familiar with, the one that had him convinced no one had ever done anything thoughtful just for her. He hated it, hated thinking that she'd lived so long without a simple thing like kindness.

"How old are you?" he asked, suddenly curious.

"Twenty-four. What about you?"

"Thirty-two."

Ainsley continued eating. Fast. Too fast.

He placed his hand over hers just as she was about to shove a third piece of pancake into her mouth before chewing and swallowing the first two. "Slow down, wildcat, or you'll choke."

She put down her fork and took a sip of coffee. "I'm just trying to get out of your hair. I'm sure you have stuff you need to do, and I've already overstayed my welcome."

"I don't have anything to do," he said, determined to learn more about Ainsley. "We have a game tonight, so I don't have to be at the arena until later this afternoon. My morning is wide open. And you'll never overstay your welcome."

"Oh. Okay. Cool." She glanced toward the door to the kitchen, though she looked less intent on making an escape.

"You feel okay?"

She nodded. "Yeah. It's not the worst beating I've ever had."

Every time she mentioned being hurt before, Coulton's chest tightened. "Your brother?"

Ainsley shook her head. "Mick. But I don't want to…" She closed her mouth and looked away.

Coulton let the subject drop there. "I'm glad you're okay physically, but I meant emotionally. Last night was scary as fuck."

Ainsley didn't look at him when she said, "I'm fine," in a way that told him she was lying. And while he didn't know her well, he was getting very good at reading her expressions. This one was telling him she was finished talking about the attack.

She proved it when she turned the conversation to him. "Do you like playing hockey?"

"I love it," he replied. "Greatest job on the planet."

"I guess you travel a lot."

Coulton nodded. "We play over forty away games each season, and when you add in exhibitions and playoffs, it's even more."

"Must be cool to see so much of the country. I've never even been out of Maryland."

Just like she'd never had a bath. That confession had thrown him for a loop last night. And it made Coulton want to know what else she'd never had, overwhelmed him with the desire to expose her to all the amazing things in life that she'd missed out on.

Like baths and travel.

Coulton rose to grab the coffeepot, refilling her cup and his. "Truth of the matter is, I see very little of the cities we travel to apart from the hotels and the arenas."

"That's a shame."

"What's a shame is never leaving Maryland," he replied.

She shrugged, which Coulton was quickly learning was a tell for Ainsley. She shrugged whenever she was uncomfortable.

"I have done a fair bit of traveling, though," he continued. "During the off-season, I usually plan a nice vacation, either to do some hiking and fishing in the national parks or tour around Europe."

"Wow. Europe."

"You ever think about traveling? Have a dream vacation spot?"

She shook her head, her eyes glued to her plate. "No time. Or money," she added softly before picking up her fork, speed-eating again. This whole conversation had been a minefield.

Rather than risk her trying to cut and run, he changed the subject again. She couldn't eat if she was talking. "Tell me about your tattoos."

Ainsley tilted her head. "What do you want to know?"

"I'm curious why you chose them? Like that birdcage. What made you get that one?" Coulton had wondered about that tattoo since first spotting it.

Ainsley bit her lower lip, and he was afraid maybe he'd chosen the wrong subject again.

"I got it when I was eighteen. Because of my mom."

Coulton didn't know much about Ainsley's family beyond the fact her dad was sick, her brother had a gambling problem, and they were both assholes. She hadn't mentioned her mom.

"She left when I was six," Ainsley continued, suddenly fascinated by her coffee cup.

"I'm sorry."

She gave him that shrug. "To be honest, I don't remember her very well. My memories of her are more feelings than actual events."

"What do you remember?"

"Just that she was always sad. She cried a lot."

"Is she still alive?" Coulton asked.

"I have no idea. She didn't leave a note or tell us where she was going or anything. Mick was at the bar, working, like always. Mom was usually at the apartment waiting for us, but that day, when Eli and I got home from school, the door was unlocked and she was gone. We didn't know what to do, so we sat there, watching TV until Dad got back late that same night. He was furious when he realized her stuff was gone and she'd left him."

Coulton would have thought Mick's first response would have been panic when he realized his young children had been alone all evening, but he was quickly coming to learn that Ainsley's family didn't do anything normal. Or kind.

He slid another piece of bacon onto her plate. She was thin, and given the way she'd devoured that salad last night, he was beginning to suspect that her slight frame was because she couldn't afford to eat much. "Mick didn't try to find her?"

"No. He just called her a stupid, worthless bitch and said good riddance."

Wow. Just what every six-year-old girl wanted to hear after being deserted by her mother. Coulton hoped he never met Mick

Hall. Then he decided he hoped he did. Because he had some choice words for the asshole.

"I still don't understand the birdcage tattoo," Coulton said, returning to the original question.

"It was just a drawing I'd been working on for a few years, and I thought—"

"You drew it?" he interjected.

She nodded.

His eyes widened, and he blew out a low, impressed whistle, because the tattoo was seriously beautiful. It made him even more curious to see what else she'd drawn in that sketch pad of hers.

"Mom flew away. She escaped. I liked the idea of that. Of being free."

Coulton reached out and grasped her hand. "You feel trapped?"

For the first time, her gaze lifted to his. "Life is a cage, Coulton."

He didn't have a clue how to respond to that, so silence crept in.

Mercifully, Ainsley found a way to break it, because his thoughts were reeling.

"Can I ask you a question?"

He nodded. "Sure. Shoot."

"How come you don't have a girlfriend?"

Coulton chuckled. "What?"

"You're obviously loaded, with a great condo, super-cool job, and you have to know you're not hard to look at. So why are you single?"

"Are you trying to figure out what's wrong with me?" he asked, amused.

She tilted her head, studying him curiously. "Yeah. Kind of. Because there's no way you don't have women beating down your door. Are you gay?"

He narrowed his eyes. "Not gay."

"Are you one of those swaggering athletes with commitment issues and a revolving door of women going in and out of your bedroom?"

Coulton shook his head. "Nope. I'm not a fan of one-night stands. Prefer real relationships."

Ainsley leaned back. "Yeah. None of that computes. So you must have a girlfriend."

"Do you think I would have asked you out if I had a girlfriend?"

She shrugged. "I don't know. Most of the guys I know have a side piece."

"I don't cheat, Ainsley. Don't sleep around."

She obviously didn't believe him.

"I *did* have a girlfriend, Evelyn."

Ainsley glanced toward the hallway in the direction of the guest room. "Is that the pretty blonde with you in the picture on the dresser, in the guest room?"

Coulton nodded. "Shit. I forgot that picture was in there. I don't go in the guest room much and I didn't really know what to do with that picture, so I just shoved it on the dresser in there. So yeah. That's Evelyn. We were together for five years when I played for Vancouver. We did the long-distance thing for a short while, after I was traded to Baltimore."

"But she wanted to stay in Vancouver?"

"She's a nurse practitioner, and she works in a good practice in the city. Plus, her entire family lives in Vancouver. It's where she grew up, so it's home to her and she didn't want to leave."

"When did you break up?"

"A couple years ago, not long after I moved to Baltimore."

"Why?"

Coulton grinned, pleased by her questions. It gave him hope that she was as interested in him as he was in her. "We both realized splitting up was for the best. She was a born-and-bred Canuck, with zero interest in moving to the U.S."

"You could have moved there."

"I could have, but I'm under contract with the Stingrays. And my plan is to play hockey until my body tells me I can't anymore. I'm hoping that doesn't happen for a while."

"Five years is a long time to date someone, only to give up."

"I wouldn't say we gave up. We just changed the parameters of our relationship."

"What's that mean?"

"It means she's still a very good friend, hence me holding on to the picture. We keep in touch, and she'll always be a part of my life."

Ainsley shook her head, as if remaining friends with an ex was a concept she couldn't wrap her head around, so he sought to explain it better. "We dated a long time, but in the end, I wondered how much of us staying together was due to a sense of familiarity and comfort versus true love."

Ainsley snorted. "True love? God, you don't really think that's a thing, do you?"

Coulton frowned. "Of course I do. My parents have been married over forty years, and it's definitely true love. You don't believe in it?"

"Hard to believe in something you've never seen."

Coulton thought about her parents. It was obvious they'd had an unhappy marriage, but what about Ainsley? Hadn't she ever experienced love? "So no long-term relationships in your past?"

"My record is three years, and that was at least twelve months too long."

Coulton waited, hoping Ainsley would expound on her comment, but she simply took a sip of coffee then glanced at her phone, a sure sign she was anxious to end the discussion.

"Well, I guess I should be going."

Coulton wasn't ready to see her leave, because he'd enjoyed this chance to get to know her better, even if she had only shown him bits and pieces.

Then he considered what was waiting for her at home. She

mentioned that Mick would be pissed off about the stolen money, which pissed Coulton off. Her father was obviously as big a douchebag as her brother, and the more he learned about them, the angrier he became.

However, as much as he hated her returning home, the idea of her returning to Cherry Hill while those assholes who'd robbed her were still around sat even heavier on his chest. He didn't share her confidence that they'd leave her alone now that they'd gotten some of their money. Those men struck him as the type who'd hold a grudge, and the lack of payment was probably lower on their list of concerns now. They'd no doubt want payback for the beatdown.

Which meant Ainsley was in danger.

"Why don't you stay here a few days?" he offered.

Ainsley was shaking her head before he finished issuing the invitation. "Can't. Need to go home and check on Mick. Then I have to head over to the tavern to put the furniture back in place before I open."

"You're opening the tavern?" He'd hoped after last night's events she'd take at least a few nights off.

"Of course."

"Take a few days off," he insisted. "You're still healing."

Ainsley dismissed the idea out of hand. "That's not an option."

"What if those guys come back?"

She shrugged as if it wasn't a real concern, something that chafed. Didn't she have an ounce of self-preservation?

"Ainsley. Last night—"

"I don't want to talk about last night. It's water under the bridge."

Coulton scowled. "Like hell it is. You can't bury your head in the sand on this. Those men were going to hurt you. They were going to—"

Ainsley stood up abruptly, the stool squeaking loudly across the floor. "Look, Coulton. I appreciate what you did for me, but that doesn't make you my keeper. You have zero say-so in my life."

"I didn't say I did, but—"

"I'm perfectly capable of taking care of myself."

"I'm not saying you can't," he argued, even though he couldn't shake the image of her last night. She was fighting for her life, and it still wasn't going to be enough. "It's just—"

"I have my bat," she interjected. "And Maren is working today."

He scoffed. A lot of fucking good that bat did for her last night. He started to say just that, but she kept talking.

"Coulton, I don't have the luxury of not working. I need the money the tavern brings in to pay for my dad's medical bills, plus rent and groceries and the mortgage on Mick's, and so on and so on."

"It's not safe."

She plucked at the hem of his shirt, clearly ready to be anywhere but here. "It's where I live."

It was a shitty answer, but an honest one. He viewed Cherry Hill with an outsider's perspective, as someone who'd never lived in a truly dangerous place. Ainsley, however, had spent her life in that neighborhood, so she had adapted to her environment and found ways to survive.

While he might understand that, he didn't like it. At all.

Ainsley drank the last sip of her coffee. "I really do need to go."

"Just close the tavern tonight," he pressed, hating the fact that he had to work and couldn't protect her. "I'll get you a ticket to the game."

She shook her head. "I can't, Coulton."

He rose, fighting desperately for something that might change her mind, his heart thudding in panic.

"Thanks for last night," she said, grabbing her phone, then looking down at herself. "I'll return the shirt."

He shook his head. "Keep it."

"Oh. Um. Okay. Thanks."

She left the kitchen, Coulton following in her wake as she made her way to the front door. He was overwhelmed by the desire to block the exit, because her returning to work bothered him more than he cared to admit.

Ainsley turned at the door, the sun shining brightly through the window, casting too much light on the bruise on her cheek. "Good luck at the game tonight."

He frowned. "What do you think you're doing?"

She glanced behind her at the door. "Leaving?"

Coulton rolled his eyes. "I'm driving you home."

"I can get an Uber."

He shook his head, grabbing his truck keys from the dish by the door. "Come on, Ainsley. Everything doesn't have to be a fight."

She pursed her lips but let it go.

The drive to her place was a quiet one, Coulton barely able to keep his temper at bay, which was a new emotion for him. He rarely got angry, but his blood was practically boiling. Not that he was mad at Ainsley, just at her really fucked-up, shitty situation. It also didn't help that he had a fixer personality, and he couldn't fix this.

His irritation got even worse when they turned down her street and he took in all the run-down buildings. The idea that she lived in one of them churned uncomfortably in his gut.

"This is me," she said.

Of course, she pointed to the worst building on the block. The neglected place looked like it should have been condemned twenty years ago, and the desire to drag her back to his condo grew.

Coulton's anger sparked, not at her but at the situation, as he pulled up to the curb and put the vehicle in park. "Give me your phone." He didn't mean to bark, but Ainsley didn't take offense.

Instead, she took her cell out of her back pocket and handed it to him. He held it to her face to unlock the screen before adding his number into her contacts. Then he sent himself a text so he would have her number.

"Call me if you need…anything," he said, changing his offer to something vague, because what he really wanted was for her to call him if those guys came back. He had to revise that, aware that if she placed that call when he was on the ice, he wouldn't be able to help her until after the game. Which would be way too late.

She gave him a funny look but didn't question what *anything* might entail.

Unable to resist, Coulton leaned over the console and gave her another kiss on the cheek. He'd done the same last night, pretending he was kissing her boo-boo. Today's kiss was meant to be just as platonic, but the moment his lips touched her skin, they lingered.

Ainsley didn't pull away; rather, she leaned into it, her eyes drifting closed.

"I'll come to the tavern after the game," he murmured in her ear.

"You don't have to."

He tilted her head up with a finger under her chin. "I'll be there."

She gave him a gorgeous smile, but it wasn't enough to calm his unease at leaving her here. "See you later then."

He watched as she walked into the building, the entrance unsecured, leaving all the residents at the mercy of whoever might walk in off the street.

Coulton sighed, trying to convince himself he was overreacting. She'd lived in this neighborhood her whole life. She would be fine.

Unfortunately, those reassurances refused to stick, so by the time he arrived at the arena that afternoon for the game, he was a powder keg about to explode.

"Damn. Who pissed in your cornflakes?" Tank asked, when

Coulton roughly shoved his duffel bag into his locker, slamming the door shut.

"No one," he grumbled, tempted to call Ainsley to make sure everything was okay.

His teammates gave him a wide berth when he started cursing and struggling with the clasp on one of his pads. "Fucking shit equipment."

"You okay?" Preston ventured to ask as they started to head out to the ice.

"I'm fine," he replied, even though he was clenching his jaw so tightly, it hurt. The idea of Ainsley defenseless in that tavern was working on him.

He tried to push those thoughts away when he took to the ice, but he failed. Soon, he was viewing his opponents as Mario and Luigi, taking their shots on goal as personal affronts. He caught every puck that flew in his direction, resisting the desire to shove his stick down someone's throat, resenting the fact he was here instead of protecting Ainsley.

When the final buzzer sounded, the Stingrays emerged victorious. Not that Coulton gave a shit. He hadn't let a single goal in, and while his teammates were jubilant, slapping him on the back and congratulating him for a hell of a game, all he could think about was getting to her.

He cut his postgame workout and stretches way too short because he couldn't relax until he knew she was okay.

He didn't say a word to anyone as he left the arena and hightailed it to Mick's Tavern.

Coulton's gaze drank her in as he stepped inside the dimly lit dive. She was pouring a beer from the tap, rolling her eyes as Maren and some young buck arm wrestled over the counter, several men passing dollar bills back and forth as they bet on the outcome. A cheer went up as Maren won, pounding the guy's arm down to the surface with a surprising amount of force.

When Ainsley turned to see him standing there—and flashed him that same shocked expression she wore every time he showed up at Mick's—the pressure that had been crushing his chest all day lifted.

"Coulton!" Petey cried out, using the right name.

"There's our hero," Maren exclaimed excitedly.

"You really did come," Ainsley said.

Given the warm reception he was receiving, it was apparent Ainsley had outed him. Not that he minded. He was thrilled to know she was looking forward to seeing him again.

Coulton approached the counter, exchanging a glance with Ainsley, who gave him a guilty grin. "We watched your game. You were incredible."

"Thought you hated hockey," he said, as she put a pint of Natty Boh in front of him.

"Oh, I do," she said, in a pure smart-ass tone. "Boring-as-shit game."

He didn't have a chance to respond as the regulars descended, surrounding him at the bar, giving him the same back slaps and congratulations he'd received from his teammates, everyone offering to buy him a beer.

Coulton didn't mind the accolades, now that he was with *her*.

Once he'd answered no less than forty million questions and signed a cocktail napkin for nearly every single person in the place, most of the patrons began to return to their regular spots.

"Ainsley said you came along at just the right time last night," Petey said, perched on the stool next to Coulton's.

His gaze traveled to Ainsley, who was serving pitchers to a table of older women. The volume coming from the group told him this wasn't their first round. Or second. Or third.

Ainsley had made a nominal attempt to conceal the bruise on her face with makeup, but it was still visible, as was the cut on her lip. No doubt she'd had to explain her injuries to the patrons.

"Wish I'd been here," Petey muttered. "I'd've taught those fuckers a thing or two."

"You'd have gotten in line behind me," Maren added. "Not

that there would have been anything left for you by the time I was done."

Coulton had been losing his shit all day, and while he was still uneasy with Ainsley working here, he had to admit he felt easier knowing she had Maren and Petey and all the other regulars in her corner.

Not that it had helped her much last night.

"I'm glad I showed up when I did," he said.

"Shame the assholes got the money," Petey added. "I know things are tight for her and Mick, what with him being sick and Eli gambling and snorting away whatever he can steal from them."

"You know Mick well?" Coulton asked.

Petey nodded. "Oh, hell yeah. Been drinking here for going on thirty-five, forty years. Known Ainsley her whole life. Her and her brother used to sit in that booth right over there after school and during the summers, when they were just wee little things."

Petey noticed Coulton's frown.

"Yeah," the old guy continued, addressing what Coulton hadn't said. "I know it probably wasn't the best place for little kids, but Mick's wife split, and he couldn't afford to pay a babysitter."

"So they stayed here? Every day?"

Petey nodded. "Yup. Mick has an old couch in the back storeroom. When it got to be too late, Ainsley and Eli would sleep there until close."

Jesus. What the hell kind of childhood was that?

Coulton wanted to ask more, but Ainsley returned to her spot behind the bar, leaning on the counter behind her.

For two hours, he listened as Petey and Ainsley shared stories about the bar—recounting drunken brawls, some of the more colorful characters who'd passed through, and Mick's "body count," which was how they referred to the times Ainsley's dad bounced someone out on their ass.

Maren hopped in a few times, adding her own stories to the mix.

When closing time rolled around, Coulton's face hurt from laughing at their tall tales, and the stress he'd felt all day had abated.

Petey and Maren left together, leaving him and Ainsley alone. He helped her clean, then walked out with her, watching as she went through the routine of locking the door and pulling down the gate.

"Talk to your brother yet?" Coulton asked, hoping perhaps her brother would man up and do the right thing, paying off his own debts.

Ainsley shook her head. "Haven't seen him. Fucker is laying low so I can't find him. Probably hiding from those guys too."

"Things go alright with your dad this morning?" Mick's response to Ainsley's injuries had been another item on his never-ending list of concerns today.

"He reacted the way I thought. Bitched about losing the money, but he was more pissed at Eli than me, so you know, small mercies."

"Did he even mention the bruises?"

Ainsley gave him that quizzical look. Growing up with a neglectful, abusive dad had clearly skewed her thinking, made it impossible to see how wrong Mick's reaction was. Then she grimaced. "Of course he did. That's why I had to tell him about the robbery. It wasn't like I was going to volunteer that info unless I had to."

"And what did he say about you getting hurt?"

Ainsley gave him her shrug/tell. "He said I was soft. Said he raised a couple of pussies."

He closed his eyes and counted to ten. By then, he'd only just managed to bank his temper. "Come home with me tonight."

Ainsley frowned. "Why?"

Coulton stepped closer, reaching for her waist. If she gave

him even the slightest indication she was uncomfortable or scared, he'd release her.

But she didn't. Instead, she leaned in, her palms resting flat against his chest, not to push him away but to touch him. Then she lifted her face, her eyes heavy-lidded.

She was begging to be kissed.

"Why?" she repeated, when he didn't respond, her voice was suddenly breathless.

Coulton lowered his head, his lips a mere inch from hers. "So I can kiss all those bruises of yours better."

Ainsley grinned. "All of them? There are a lot."

He leaned closer. "Every." He gave her a quick kiss on her cheek. "Single." This time, he placed his lips gently on her cut lip. "One." This kiss lingered, but he didn't increase the pressure, waiting for a sign from her.

When her hands found their way to his hair, her fingers tightening around it as she held him close, he knew he'd broken through the first of the many, many barriers she surrounded herself with.

Coulton pulled away. "Ainsley," he murmured, waiting for her answer.

"Okay," she whispered.

"Okay?"

"I want to go home with you."

Coulton closed the distance, pressing his lips to hers in a kiss that he'd intended to keep gentle, considering her lip was still sore from the attack.

However, Ainsley had other plans, kissing him back with a hunger that matched the hardcore desire coursing through his veins.

They devoured each other for several minutes until a car passed, blaring the horn, someone hooting from the open window.

Coulton pulled away, his gaze locked on her swollen lips.

Had they been like that before the kiss? The twinge of guilt he felt vanished when Ainsley flashed him a sexy smile.

"Ready to go?" she asked.

He nodded as several truths crashed down on his head.

Coulton was determined to be the one man who never caused her a second of pain, the one to introduce her to new experiences.

But even more than that, he wanted to be the man who brought her joy, happiness…

And maybe even true love.

CHAPTER FIVE

AINSLEY STEPPED into Coulton's condo for the second time in two days. When she left this morning, she never expected to return. Mainly because she'd told herself one night of weakness was all she could afford when it came to the sexy goalie.

If she hadn't been so shaken up and terrified after the attack, there was no way she would have agreed to come home with him last night. She knew better than to follow some rich guy home. Not that she'd had a clue just how loaded Coulton was when she got into his truck.

This morning, after he dropped her off, she'd been determined to toe the line, hold steady to her "no" should he ask her out again. She'd walked this path before, so she knew it was a minefield.

As she drifted over to the large windows, taking in the incredible view of the water, she gave herself a mental headshake.

Because…Jesus.

She hadn't even managed to stick to her guns for a full day.

Personally, she blamed the hockey game. She'd never been interested in the sport before, but knowing Coulton was out on the ice had drawn her in, and once she'd started watching him, she could not look away. As she watched him play, her determination to resist him had given way to something much more powerful.

Desire.

Sex had become a solitary affair for her after Montgomery, because he'd really taken her down a peg and destroyed her self-confidence even more than Jagger had, which was saying something.

At least vibrators didn't hurt her, didn't say cruel things, didn't break her heart. And she hadn't felt a single drop of temptation to break her vow of chastity.

Until Coulton walked into the bar.

She wouldn't have thought the guy could get any sexier, but damn if he didn't prove her wrong tonight. Watching him in front of that net, seeing his agility, his strength, his toughness, had lit a fire in her that no vibrator in the world could put out.

"If you're having second thoughts…" he murmured, wrapping his arm around her waist, his chest pressed to her back.

"I'm not," she hastened to reassure him, aware she'd probably given him that impression by standing by the window for so long.

"I'm just saying. I would understand. After last night…" He ran a hand through his hair as if he was the one having regrets. "Maybe we should talk first."

She shook her head. "I don't want to talk about that."

"Ainsley," he started, using that tone that said he wasn't convinced she was okay.

She turned around, hating that the movement meant he was no longer holding her. "Erase it," she said.

His brows furrowed in confusion.

"Give me a good memory to replace that one," she clarified, her gaze holding his. "I need a good memory," she added with a whisper.

What was it about this man that had her dropping her guard? She kept giving him peeks of her weaknesses, and she should hate it, but she couldn't. Because he didn't look at her like she was frail or helpless. He just…

God, right now was the perfect example. He was looking at her like she was strong, like she mattered.

Coulton cupped her cheek, his expression softening. "I'd like to be a good memory for you."

"I want to be here," she reassured him, turning her head slightly to press a kiss to his palm. "With you."

Despite this being a risky decision on her part, she couldn't help but feel like last night in Coulton's amazing home had been similar to one of those vacations he'd talked about. He'd given her just what she needed. An escape from reality, from the horror of the night, from the hell that was her life.

He'd given her a bath, a healthy dinner, a soft bed, breakfast, and one whole night where she didn't have to be on guard. Hell, he'd *already* given her a good memory.

"I feel safe here," she added, feeling stupid the minute the admission crossed her lips.

Coulton nodded, the clouds in his eyes clearing. "You *are* safe here." Stepping closer, he ran his finger gently along the bruise on her cheek. "Does it hurt?"

She shook her head. "No. Between last night's bath and that ridiculously comfortable bed in your guest room, I'm feeling no pain. I can't remember the last time I haven't felt…" She paused.

What the hell was going on with her? Where had this Chatty Cathy come from? Ainsley always played her cards close to her chest. Always. But with Coulton, she'd lost her filter, her thoughts and feelings tumbling out of her.

"Haven't felt what?" he prodded.

"Tired."

She'd slept so well that even Mick's shitty attitude hadn't bothered her this morning. True to character, he'd taken one look at her face, asked how much the thief had gotten, then raged for a full twenty minutes about the stolen two hundred bucks. His insults and ire hadn't touched her because she'd felt refreshed in a way she hadn't experienced in years.

Regardless, she hadn't looked forward to opening the tavern, because there wasn't enough concealer in the world to completely cover the bruise on her cheek and her cut lip. Which meant she couldn't escape rehashing the attack.

Luckily, it hadn't been as bad as she'd anticipated. Maren, Petey, and the other regulars had expressed genuine concern for her well-being. She'd needed their bolstering words and swaggering vows to protect her in the future more than she realized. Like her, most of the patrons of Mick's Tavern had lived in Cherry Hill long enough to know the score. She'd bet every single one of them had been victim to some sort of robbery or assault.

Initially, she hadn't planned to go into much detail, intending to simply say it was a robbery and move on. However, the moment she mentioned it had been Coulton—she'd called him Thor to jazz up the tale—who'd scared the assholes away, she'd been inundated with questions. That was when she realized her childhood spent at Mick's hadn't been *all* negative. Turned out, she could embellish the hell out of her stories too.

Ainsley had even gone so far as to drop Coulton's position on the Stingrays, since he'd assured her he didn't care.

Thanks to her story, tonight had been her best night in years financially. Because word spread fast in Cherry Hill. Quite a few people had shown up, asking if the famous athlete would be there. Never one to look a gift horse in the mouth, Ainsley said he'd mentioned dropping by. So, everyone stayed, drinking pitchers and pints and ordering Mick's shitty microwaved apps. She'd more than made up for the lost two hundred dollars.

However, by the time the hockey game ended, Ainsley had convinced herself she would never see Coulton again, despite his assurances he was returning. There was no way he'd be in a hurry to return to Mick's Tavern…no matter what he said. Guys said shit like that all the time, simply so they could make an easy getaway.

Then, he'd arrived. And invited her to come home with him.

It had been on the tip of her tongue to say no. That would have been the smarter answer, but no one had ever accused her of being too bright.

Apparently, her strengths lay in self-delusion. Because she'd convinced herself that this Ainsley was wiser and stronger, and her eyes were wide open. She promised herself she wouldn't fall victim to whatever Coulton's game was, since she wouldn't stick around to play for long.

Feeling overly confident in her abilities to remain aloof, she decided to be selfish. To steal another night in Coulton's condo. To treat herself to one night in his bed, because she didn't doubt for a second that he would know his way around a woman's body.

As long as she kept her expectations low—as in, nonexistent—in regard to Coulton, she would grab one night of incredible sex and use it to feed her masturbation fantasies for the next fifty years or so.

Firming her resolve, she studied his face. She could become addicted to the way he looked at her, the way he truly seemed to like what he saw.

That stupid resolve began to falter, so she turned around once more, trying to fortify her walls. "Some view," she said lamely.

Coulton remained behind her, but he didn't wrap her back in his embrace. Instead, his eyes met hers in their reflections in the window. "It is," he agreed, looking at her rather than the water.

She tilted her head when he lowered his, his lips finding the side of her neck.

"I've wanted you since the first moment I saw you," Coulton admitted.

If that was a line, she didn't care. It was nice to hear, because God knew her attraction toward him had been instantaneous as well. She shivered as his tongue drew a path from her ear to her shoulder. Her nipples budded and her pussy clenched with need.

"Turn around," he commanded.

Ainsley twisted in his arms without hesitation, lifting her hands to his broad shoulders.

Ordinarily, she felt threatened by large men because the issue of size left her at a disadvantage. She was five foot four, and she weighed a hundred and ten pounds soaking wet. She might be scrappy, and she might swing a hell of a bat, but there was only so much she could do to defend herself against someone larger and stronger. As last night had proven.

She wasn't threatened by Coulton though. Even now as his hands drifted lower, cupping her ass, she didn't feel an ounce of fear. She shifted onto her tiptoes, allowing him to lift her so that she could wrap her legs around his waist, her back supported by the cool glass of the window.

Ainsley moaned, a low sound coming from the back of her throat, when Coulton pressed his crotch against hers, letting her feel the large bulge beneath his jeans.

As their bodies melded together, they looked at each other. She expected Coulton to resume the kissing, but instead, his gaze remained locked on hers.

"You're so beautiful," he said, his expression matching his tone, almost making her believe he meant it.

"You don't have to say things like that." She ran one hand down his chest as she gave him a playful grin. "I'm definitely going to sleep with you."

She expected Coulton to laugh, so she worried when he scowled instead.

Too many times, it felt like she and Coulton spoke different languages. Though when she considered that, she realized she was using the wrong word because it wasn't a language barrier so much as a cultural one. While she didn't know a great deal about his upbringing, she'd heard enough to know it was quite different from hers. As such, their reactions never seemed to quite line up.

"That's not a line, Ainsley," he insisted. "You *are* beautiful."

Don't fall for it.

Guys only say stuff like that because they want to get in your pants.

This Ainsley is wiser…stronger…

This is just going to be one night.

Tomorrow she was walking away. She had to.

Rather than reply, she lifted her face, placing several kisses on his jaw, his beard scratchy yet soft at the same time.

Coulton began kissing the side of her neck again, until he found her earlobe. He nipped at it playfully, teasing her earrings with his teeth, and she squeaked.

"Are we going to move this party to the bedroom?"

Coulton rested his forehead on hers. "Still trying to decide. Sort of like the idea of stripping you naked and fucking you against this window."

"That," she said breathlessly. "Do that."

He chuckled but made no move to release her or take off her clothing. "Or maybe I should bend you over the back of the couch, drive into you from behind while those gorgeous tits of yours bounce against the cushions."

"Changed my mind," she whispered. "That one."

"Or I could always carry you to my room, tie you spread-eagle to my bed, and go down on you until you come on my tongue a dozen times, begging me to take you."

"Shit. Too many decisions."

He grinned wickedly. "Who said I was going to let *you* choose?"

Well, that was ridiculously hot. And also a challenge.

Ainsley tightened her grip, scaling the mountain of him, just as she'd fantasized about, until her lips brushed the shell of his ear. "All of it. I want all of it."

"As you wish." Coulton released her ass, slowly guiding her

down his body until she was standing on her own two feet again.

After that, it was on.

He quickly divested her of her shirt and bra, her jeans and panties only seconds behind. Then the two of them worked together to undress him, Ainsley unfastening his jeans as he tugged his shirt over his head.

She was momentarily distracted by his chest. She'd seen him shirtless last night, but she hadn't been in the best frame of mind to fully appreciate the view. Right now, she was going to take her time and savor. After all, she needed to catalog and file this away for future spank bank material.

Coulton placed his hand on top of the one she rested against his pec. "I love your hands on me. Can't wait to feel these fingers wrapped around my cock."

Of her three previous lovers, none of them had been dirty-talkers in bed, their sex language limited to grunts, curses, and the occasional call out to a deity.

The pictures Coulton drew in her mind were as sexy as the way he was cupping her breasts, his forefingers and thumbs rolling her tight nipples.

He had a way of engaging all the senses, something she'd never experienced. He was a visual masterpiece, and she didn't know what cologne he wore, but she wouldn't be surprised if it was made of pure pheromones. His breath was hot against her neck, his chest felt like velvet steel, and his dirty talk was a fucking symphony. When he kissed her, she tasted the slight tang of the beer he'd drunk at the tavern. It was barely there, but when his tongue stroked hers, Ainsley could swear she was getting drunk.

"Don't stop," she complained, when Coulton disengaged.

He grinned as she tried to pull him back to her. "Two seconds," he said, quickly dropping his jeans and boxer briefs. He must have kicked off his shoes when they entered the condo because, just as he promised, in mere seconds he was completely naked.

And she was awestruck.

"Jesus Christ," she whispered, as her gaze slid down to his cock and stuck there. Coulton was oversized…everywhere.

"You know what I want," Coulton said, reminding her of the comment about her hand on his cock. "Touch me," he urged.

Ainsley reached out, offering him a teasing brush of her fingertips, barely stroking the head of his thick cock. Her pussy clenched at the thought of him stuffing all of that inside her. She was going to feel this tomorrow. Maybe even into next week.

"*Really* touch me, wildcat," he demanded, his voice darker, all semblance of gentleness gone. She liked that. She wasn't the type of girl who wanted soft or slow missionary with a bunch of sloppy kisses.

She wanted exactly what Coulton offered. Dirty, hard sex with a demanding alpha, who knew exactly how to get her off and didn't need her to draw a diagram of how to find her clit and G-spot.

THIS was why Ainsley had come tonight. She'd lived a lifetime of shitty days, dealing with assholes, while working a job she didn't want but couldn't leave.

She'd earned tonight, goddammit.

Coulton hissed when she gave him exactly what he asked for, gripping his cock with both hands, squeezing the hard flesh as she stroked him.

His fingers closed around a handful of her hair, tugging on it until it stung, until her head was pulled back, her face lifted toward his.

"Harder," he said through gritted teeth, before he pressed his lips to hers.

This was no kiss. This was primal possession, feral control, an outright claiming. While he destroyed her lips, Ainsley tightened her grip, drawing her hands up and down his dick with so much force, she was scared she was hurting him.

Until Coulton growled. "Good girl," he praised.

Sweet fucking hell.

Ainsley jerked Coulton harder still, her head flying back against the glass when he lifted her breast, sucking her nipple into his mouth. Her grip slackened in the face of his outright assault on her breasts. Her back arched as she tried to give him better access—to suck, bite, lick—because yes, fucking please.

Her breasts were a huge erogenous zone for her, one her past lovers failed to recognize.

"God!" she cried out.

Coulton released her nipple with a pop, his eyes black with desire, pupils blown. "My name, wildcat. Only say my name."

Ainsley had never been a fan of nicknames, because the ones tagged to her were always insulting and meant to wound. Painsley. Cunt. Bitch.

Wildcat, however, she could get behind.

"Fuck, yes," she cried, when he increased the suction on her nipples, stars exploding behind her closed eyelids. Ainsley had been wet since the moment Coulton invited her back to his place, but right now, she was literally dripping, her arousal sliding down her inner thighs.

"My name," he demanded. "Open your eyes and look at me when you say it."

Resistance was futile. She blinked several times, fighting to clear her vision. "Coulton," she said on a gasp, when he bit one of her nipples as he pinched the other. The sharp sting of pain shimmered down her spine, her pussy pulsating with need.

He continued to abuse her breasts in the best possible way, until she was whimpering, hungry to be fucked.

"Please," she said, her voice hoarse from her cries.

Coulton's hands slipped under her ass again, lifting her until her opening was even with his waist, his thick cock resting between the drenched lips of her pussy.

"Guide me inside," he demanded.

Ainsley grabbed him, placing the head of his dick right where she wanted it.

Coulton pressed in until the tip was buried, then froze.

She remembered at the same time he did. "I'm on birth control."

Coulton didn't say more, taking that information as permission, which it was. He slammed into the hilt as she screamed, his cock buried deep, her pussy stretched tightly around it.

"*Goddamn,*" Coulton groaned. "You feel so good."

"Fuck me," she said, when he held steady. She needed him to move. Now.

"Take a second. Let your body adjust."

"Coulton," she whined.

He teased her earring with his tongue, then his lips pressed to her ear. "I'm going to fuck you hard, Ainsley. Going to give you everything you want. But only as soon as you're ready. Because I made a promise. You're safe with me, and I'm not going to hurt you."

She blinked rapidly, shocked when her vision was suddenly clouded by tears.

She knew what he meant, knew he meant he wouldn't hurt her physically. Her head had interpreted it correctly.

But her heart. That fickle organ heard his words a different way. The wrong way.

Every man she'd ever known had hurt her.

Every.

Single.

One.

So the idea that Coulton wouldn't…

That isn't what he meant, Ainsley.

So much for her wiser, stronger heart.

"You're crying." Coulton ran his thumb under her eye, frowning. She caught the shimmer of wetness there.

"You aren't hurting me," she quickly reassured him, when he started to lift her off him, her words coming out louder and harsher than she intended as she wrapped her ankles around his waist tightly, refusing to let him go.

Her words had two meanings as well.

Physically, she wasn't feeling any pain.

And as for emotionally, he wouldn't hurt her. Because she wouldn't let him. *Couldn't* let him. She'd had enough heartache to last her a lifetime.

He studied her face for a beat or two longer, and she sensed his hesitancy.

"I swear," she added.

Coulton nodded, kissed her, then gave her exactly what he'd promised.

Ainsley's back slammed against the window as Coulton took her with the kind of passion she thought was restricted to the pages of dirty romance novels. He didn't hold anything back, and neither did she, meeting him halfway, thrust for glorious thrust.

She came within minutes, her body disintegrating as she was blinded by a white-hot flash, the sounds around her muted by the deafening pounding of her heart.

Coulton was mere seconds behind her, jerking roughly as he came, jets of hot come splashing against the walls of her pussy.

As the last remnants of their orgasms faded, Coulton stilled, his grip on her ass tight enough that he was adding new bruises to the ones she'd gotten last night. These, however, felt like a gift, a badge of honor.

The two of them remained there, fighting to regain their breath, their strength.

Coulton was the first to move, slowly releasing her, even while holding her steady.

"Okay?" he asked.

Ainsley nodded. "So fucking okay."

He smiled, then kissed her. "Ready to move to the couch?"

She laughed. "So fucking ready."

* * *

Ainsley opened her eyes, squinting through the darkness. It only took her a second to recall where she was, and then a second more to figure out what had woken her from the deepest sleep of her life.

No. Not what.

Who.

She peered down her naked body, grinning when she spotted Coulton kneeling between her outstretched thighs. He ran his tongue along her slit again, and she hummed, arching her back like a well-loved kitten.

Coulton lifted his gaze to hers. "We haven't finished our list."

Ainsley shivered with expectation and need. After their sex against the window, they'd retreated to the couch, alternating between making out and cuddling for a half hour before Coulton lifted her, draping her over the back and fucking her from behind through not one, not two, but three orgasms.

Three.

Ainsley still couldn't quite believe this night was real. Amazing things like this didn't happen to her.

Which meant she had to be at home, in her own shitty bed, having the greatest sex dream in the history of dreaming.

If so, she never wanted to wake up.

Coulton stroked her again, his tongue making the long journey from her anus to her clit, and she closed her eyes, blinded by stars.

From the couch, they'd made their way to Coulton's master bath. His tub was even bigger than the one in the guest room, and it had jets. He'd run them a bubble bath, the two of them soaking together in silence, speaking only through touch and kisses.

They'd fallen asleep after the bath, but it looked as if Coulton had gotten his second wind and was ready for round three.

Ring the bell, she thought. Because she was ready too.

Coulton drew a circle with the tip of his tongue, going round and round her clit, teasing her mercilessly. If he hadn't already proven he was thoroughly well-versed in the female body, knowing exactly what to do, she'd think him a lame lover like her past three.

"Need instructions?" she taunted, loving the way his eyes darkened whenever she dared to challenge his alpha male.

Rather than reply, Coulton nipped her clit with his teeth, applying enough pressure to make her squirm. She'd long ago given up trying to understand why pain was such a turn-on for her. For a while, she wondered if it was the result of something from her childhood. If it was, she'd never managed to connect the dots, and in the end, she decided she didn't care, accepting that she was just wired that way.

"Any other critiques?" he asked, releasing her clit.

She wanted to come up with some smart-ass reply, but Coulton had fucked every brain cell she had to a state of exhaustion. So all she managed to do was give him a breathy huff of a laugh.

Coulton winked, then lowered his head, getting more serious about the task at hand. His large palms held her thighs open, pushing her to his soft mattress as he used his lips, teeth, and tongue like a pro.

"Oh my God!" she cried out, when he pushed two fingers inside, fucking her with them while he used his tongue on her clit with a deadly precision.

"My name," he demanded.

"Coulton," she yelled. "I'm going to…going to…"

Her body jerked as if electrocuted, every muscle in her body tensing, then releasing.

"Holy shit," she gasped.

She expected Coulton to smirk—he deserved it—but instead, he slowly started thrusting his fingers inside her again.

Ainsley realized just how badly her past lovers had been, merely phoning it in, now that she had Coulton to hold next to them as the gold standard. Tiger had never gone down on her, claiming in his charming eighteen-year-old boy way that it was "gross."

Jagger seemed to hold the same opinion, only giving her the weakest of efforts before demanding quid pro quo.

Montgomery was the first to show her the potential of the act, and while he'd done it, he'd never brought her to orgasm that way. Instead, he used it as a way to get her aroused, something that sadly happened quickly enough he never lingered below her waist for more than a couple of minutes.

"Coulton," she whispered.

He looked up at her. "A dozen times," he reminded her.

She shook her head. Twelve of those and she'd be dead. Then she remembered something else he'd said. She lifted her unbound hands, wiggling them jazz-style.

Coulton's expression turned serious. "After last night…I wasn't sure…"

She stared at him, her heart doing that stupid flip-flop thing that told her she was doing a shitty job at remaining aloof.

He just kept saying sweet things. Making her feel safe and protected. Giving her an awesome nickname.

Wiser…stronger…

What a crock.

Ainsley appreciated his concern, and while the idea of bondage had sounded hot when he said it, she knew he was right. She was still struggling with the feelings of helplessness she'd experienced last night, so the thought of being restrained…

"Thank you," she murmured, letting him know he'd been right to cross that off the list.

For tonight.

Ainsley quickly tried to erase those last two words because—dammit—tonight was all she was giving herself.

Mercifully, Coulton saved her from her wayward thoughts when he added a third finger to the two still inside her and flew her back to paradise—first class.

After the third orgasm, she was shamelessly begging him to fuck her.

He climbed over her body, his thick, hard cock bumping against her stomach.

"You want this?" he taunted.

She nodded, not even bothering to be coy or play it cool. "Yes," she hissed. "Please, Coulton. Please fuck me."

He gave her a hot, deep kiss. "Well, since you asked so nicely."

Coulton gripped his cock, guiding it—uncovered—to her pussy.

She'd never let her former lovers fuck her without a condom. In high school, she wasn't on the pill, so Tiger always wore one. With his infidelity still fresh in her broken heart, she'd demanded Jagger use one. Then Montgomery had been the one to insist on using condoms, even after she offered to go without. His reasoning for that had become apparent at the end.

Ainsley gasped when Coulton pushed in, right to the hilt. After so much foreplay—and sex—she was more than prepared for him and his deep, powerful thrusts.

He lowered his upper body, supporting it with his elbows on the mattress by her sides. They were closer this way, his face inches from hers. They'd done stand-up sex and doggie style, tearing into each other like they'd die if they didn't come.

This time was slower, closer. More intimate.

Especially when he started kissing her as he rocked inside her.

All her senses were on overload again, until all she could see, hear, taste, smell, and touch was Coulton. He was overwhelming her in all the best ways, and despite coming...well, she'd lost count of how many times she had come, he brought her back to the precipice again, more quickly than she would have expected.

"I'm there," she said, her voice more air than sound. "Come with me."

Coulton nodded, his lips traveling over her cheek, along the side of her neck. With one more hard thrust, he bit her shoulder and Ainsley fell from the cliff. And Coulton, bless him, jumped into the abyss with her.

* * *

Ainsley lay awake an hour later in the darkness of Coulton's room, her eyes darting toward the clock on his nightstand. It was nearly four in the morning, but she refused to let herself get too comfortable here.

Coulton had delivered on all three of his sexual promises, so the smart thing to do would be to cut and run. Sleeping together would only muddy waters that were already as murky as the Mississippi.

Glancing to the side, she studied his face. He looked so peaceful and boyish with his hair mussed and hanging over his forehead, almost covering his eyes. He was on his stomach, his face turned toward her, his eyes closed, and his arm was wrapped around her waist.

Ugh. Time to stop looking.

She slowly and carefully lifted his arm, trying to wiggle her way to the side of the bed.

He stirred, his grip tightening as he drew her body against his.

"Where are you going?" he asked sleepily.

"Home."

"No. It's too late. Spend the night."

"I wasn't sure..."

Coulton came more fully awake. He cupped her cheek, looking at her with something like...

God, was that what affection looked like?

"Stay," he insisted.

"Are you sure?"

He gave her a sweet kiss on the cheek. "You're staying." He cemented that proclamation by turning her until he was the big spoon to her little one, sighing softly, as if all was right with his world.

Ainsley had never experienced that feeling, but she couldn't help but share the sentiment. Because right now, in this moment, her world felt very, very right too.

* * *

Ainsley stretched her arms above her head, wincing slightly as unused muscles reminded her of exactly what she'd gotten up to last night.

She grinned, squinting as a strip of bright light shone through a crack in the curtains. A quick glance at the clock told her it was just after nine a.m.

Ordinarily, she didn't even roll over until eleven.

But this morning, like yesterday, she had incentive to move.

Because she could smell bacon.

Again.

A girl could get used to this.

She sat up, touched when she noticed that Coulton had retrieved her clothes from where she'd stripped them off in the living room, folding them and leaving them on a chair near the bed.

She got dressed, then stepped into the bathroom, trying to finger comb the bedhead look from her hair, fluffing it as best she could.

Then, she followed her nose to the kitchen.

Coulton frowned when he saw her standing in the doorway. "Why are you dressed?"

She laughed. "Because mornings are usually when the one-night stands end." Ainsley had meant her comment as a joke, but damn if Coulton's frown didn't deepen to a scowl.

"Last night wasn't a one-night stand," he informed her.

Now it was her turn to frown. "What was it?"

"Our first night together. First of many."

She shook her head, ready to reassure him that was *not* what it was, but his next words distracted her.

"And you ruined my surprise." Coulton gestured to a tray on the counter next to him. It held a glass of orange juice, as well as chocolate croissants and strawberries. He added a pile of bacon to another plate and placed it on the tray as well. "Breakfast in bed."

Her eyes widened. "For me?"

He laughed. "Of course, for you. Unless you left a few friends back there in bed."

She wanted to respond to his joke, but her throat was suddenly very tight. Because no one had ever done anything so nice for her. "I…" she said, her words failing her.

Coulton studied her face, then walked over to her, cupping her cheek with one of his large hands. "Another first?"

He'd been shocked by the fact she'd never had a bath, but surely he couldn't feel the same way about breakfast in bed… could he? Because she didn't know anyone who'd ever had a tray with the most delectable treats she'd ever seen delivered to them in bed.

"You and I have lived two very different lives," she finally managed to choke out.

"I guess we have."

"Which is why last night should just be a one-night stand, Coulton," she forced herself to say. The more time she spent with him, the more danger she faced in terms of having her heart broken again. Montgomery had said sweet things too. Things she'd allowed to work their way into her heart before it became obvious they'd all been lines, things he'd said simply to get her into his bed. "I don't fit into your world, and you sure as shit don't want to fit into mine."

Coulton gave her a quick, hard kiss. "Agree to disagree on that. Hey. I was wondering. Is the tavern ever closed?"

His subject changes were giving her whiplash.

"On Mondays."

Coulton glanced toward his refrigerator. She followed his gaze and realized he'd tacked up his monthly schedule with a Stingrays magnet.

"Great. No game that day. Just afternoon practice. I'll swing by your place at six."

"Why?"

"Because I'm taking you out." Ainsley clearly sucked at hiding her confusion, because he quickly added, "On a date."

"A date would be a bad idea," she said softly. What she should have said was "no," but that word apparently was missing from her vocabulary whenever she was with Coulton.

"It's a great idea," he amended.

She crossed her arms, fighting to keep this thing between them casual. "You realize you don't have to wine and dine me for sex."

Coulton sighed. "Not taking you out because I want sex. Taking you out because I want to spend time with you. So I'll pick you up at your apartment at six."

"What if I just meet you somewhere?"

Coulton shook his head. "Nope. I'm picking you up."

A date.

With Coulton.

This was a major step in the wrong direction.

And yet, she knew she was going to take it.

"Okay. Fine."

So much for saying no.

CHAPTER SIX

COULTON WHISTLED HAPPILY as he tied his tennis shoes.

Monday had finally arrived. He'd had an away game in Philadelphia on Saturday that had eaten up his weekend and kept him from seeing Ainsley since their amazing night together.

He'd spent every second since dropping her off at her place replaying Thursday night and Friday morning, over and over. After securing her agreement to a date, he'd coaxed her into taking all her clothes off and crawling back into bed, where they fed each other bacon, strawberries, and croissants before burning off the calories with the world's greatest workout.

Sex with Ainsley was off the charts. He'd had some good sex with Evelyn, but Ainsley took it to the next level. She was adventurous and fit, and her kinks lined right the hell up with his. Evelyn had preferred a gentle touch, and on the rare occasions when he'd let his rougher side out, sucking her nipples too hard or nipping her neck or shoulder, she'd complained about him hurting her.

Ainsley, on the other hand, seemed to crave the pleasurable pain he offered. Then she went one better and gave him the same. Because, like her, he loved the sting of her nails digging into his skin or the way she pinched his arms, holding on for dear life as he fucked her into the mattress.

"Jesus, man. You keep grinning like that and people are going to wonder about your mental state," Tank teased.

"Thank God, it's finally fucking Monday," his teammate Victor added. "Maybe now he'll calm the fuck down over this new chick."

Coulton had filled his buddies in about Ainsley on the bus ride to Philadelphia. They'd been happy for him in terms of breaking his long dry spell, and Blake, a Baltimore local, had been amused that he'd met her in a dive bar in Cherry Hill.

"I have no intention of calming down," Coulton said, laughing. "I'm crazy about this girl."

Tank groaned. "Fucking hell, man. You're starting to sound like Preston. You know you can sleep with a woman without dating her for a hundred years."

Preston, their team romantic, had been swearing for nearly a year that he'd met and lost his soul mate at a holiday party, the man comparing every woman he'd met since then to Chelsea. Unfortunately for Preston, all those other women had come up short.

Tank persisted. "Now that you're back in the land of the fucking, why don't you play the field for a little while? Because you let way too much time pass getting over that last woman."

Coulton wanted to insist that he hadn't spent the entire two years since his split with Evelyn, nursing a broken heart. But it was hard to win that argument, given his lack of dating since then.

He'd genuinely thought Evelyn was the one, so it had shaken him for a few months when she'd called and told him it was over. Coulton hadn't been a big fan of the long-distance deal either, but he'd thought they were making it work. Sort of.

In hindsight, he respected Evelyn's strength when it came to doing the hard thing and moving on.

"I don't need to play the field," Coulton said. "Why would I look for someone else when Ainsley is so awesome?"

Blake gave Coulton a friendly squeeze on the shoulder. "I'm glad you've found someone you like."

Up until a few weeks ago, Blake would have been firmly in Tank's camp, suggesting Coulton not be in such a hurry to tie himself down. However, his teammate's tune was starting to change, thanks to the woman across the hall he'd decided to co-parent a puppy with. Erika and Blake had been neighbors and best friends for years, but it looked like that relationship status might be shifting into something more serious. Coulton hoped that was true because he really liked Erika, who'd become a member of their friend group, joining them for pizza and game nights.

Coulton hoped Ainsley would fit just as well with his friends, though he wasn't sure how to draw her in, considering she worked six nights a week. Money was obviously a big issue for the family, and since she got zero help from her deadbeat brother, she was left to earn all the money to pay the bills.

He'd spent a good bit of the weekend wishing he could find a way to lighten her load, but they were nowhere near that level in this…relationship, he labeled it. Screw what Tank thought. He'd gone out with enough women in the past two years to know when something special was staring him in the face.

"I'm fucking out of here," Victor grumbled, pulling on his leather jacket. "Got a hot date myself."

"Really?" Tank brightened, actually believing Victor, the grumpiest homebody of them all.

Coulton enjoyed shooting his friend down when he said, "Say hi to Pip from us."

Tank scowled. "Your date is with your niece?"

Victor smirked. "Promised to take her to Build-A-fucking-Bear." Victor's four-year-old niece, Phillipa, had her uncle tied around her little finger. "See you tomorrow."

Coulton rose. "I'm out too. Picking Ainsley up at six. Catch y'all on the flipside." He flashed them the peace sign as he left the arena and headed to his truck in the parking lot, anxiously anticipating the night to come.

He typically wasn't the kind of guy who showed much emotion, his teammates calling him the Gentle Giant due to his easygoing nature and mild-mannered disposition. However, neither of those laid-back attributes was present when it came to Ainsley.

With her, he'd experienced a wide array of strong emotions. It had started out as an overpowering attraction, followed by outright fury the night of her attack. That had morphed into a bone-chilling terror as he considered what could have happened to her. From there, he had to deal with frustration over not being able to protect her. And since Thursday night, he'd run the gamut from happiness to impatience over being away from her to right now, when he was so fucking excited, he could barely contain himself.

The second he climbed into his truck, his phone rang. Smiling at the caller ID, he answered it, his dad's voice coming over the speakers.

"Hey, Dad."

"Haven't had a chance to talk to you since Saturday. It was a great game, son."

It hadn't been, at least not from Coulton's perspective. He was his own biggest critic, so he counted every puck he let get by him as a personal failure. Despite their win against Philadelphia, he'd let in two goals that he really should have saved. Not that his father, who was his number one fan, would agree. Win or lose, Chase Moore always found something positive to say about the game and Coulton's performance.

"Thanks. It was a little too close for my comfort though."

Their win came in overtime, so it was hard earned. They discussed the game for a few minutes more.

"How is Slade doing in school?"

"He's doing good. Real good."

Coulton spoke to his parents a few times a week, and they also had what he called the Family of Three text thread. As an only child of an older couple who had given up hope on getting pregnant when he came along, Coulton had spent his entire life wrapped securely in his parents' love.

They hadn't had a lot of money when Coulton was a kid, his dad working in an automotive factory, his mother an aide in a kindergarten classroom, but they'd been rich in love. When Coulton expressed an interest in hockey, his parents never blinked twice when signing him up, even though it was an expensive sport. Instead, Dad had started delivering pizzas during his off-hours, while Mom did seamstress work on the side. They'd found a way to help him pursue his dreams.

The first thing he'd done after signing with Vancouver was buy his parents a house. It had always been his mother's dream to have a yard with a flower garden. Being able to hand his parents the key to that house after all the sacrifices they'd made for him had been one of the best moments of his life. Mom had cried when they'd walked through the bright, airy house, located in a suburb of Detroit. And while his father hadn't shed any tears, they'd been evident in his voice when he'd hugged Coulton and thanked him.

Dad had since retired from the factory, but Mom still worked as an aide, claiming she didn't know what she'd do with herself if she didn't see "her kids" every day.

"Hoping we can see Slade when we're in town for Thanksgiving," Dad added. Because of Coulton's busy schedule, all holidays that occurred between the months of October and May were celebrated in Baltimore and around the Stingrays games. Then, each summer, he spent a week back home in Detroit with them.

His parents had met Slade last Christmas during their visit, when they'd accompanied Coulton to drop off presents for the boy and his family.

"I think we can make that happen," he assured him. "He was just asking about you and Mom the other day. Wondering when you were coming back. I think you made quite an impression on him when you gave him that Detroit Tigers jersey."

"Had to make sure he was rooting for the right baseball team."

"Yeah, about that," Coulton joked, both of them perfectly aware of Slade's undying love for the Orioles. They chuckled.

"So what else is new?" Dad asked.

Coulton hadn't had a chance to tell his parents about Ainsley yet.

"I met a woman."

"Finally," Dad exclaimed excitedly. "Tell me all about her."

Coulton grinned. "Her name is Ainsley Hall, and she runs a bar in Cherry Hill, close to where Slade lives."

"That's a pretty rough area, isn't it?"

"It is, but Ainsley's lived there her whole life. The bar she runs, Mick's Tavern, reminds me of Moxie's. That's the reason I stopped in."

"How long have you been going out?"

"Tonight is our first official date."

"Tonight. Well, how about that? I hope your mother and I can meet her over Thanksgiving too."

While Coulton liked that idea, he was certain Ainsley, who seemed determined to keep pushing him away, would be less thrilled about it. Clearly, there was something holding her back from getting close to him, but he wasn't going to let that deter him. The more he got to know her, the more he liked her.

Every now and then, he'd catch a glimmer of fondness in her eyes whenever she looked at him that told him this thing between them was worth the effort. When he considered her upbringing, it wasn't surprising that she had trust issues. He was also starting to get a sense that her past relationships played a part in that prickly exterior she wore in an attempt to protect herself.

"Looking forward to seeing you guys. It's been too long." Coulton hadn't seen his parents since August.

"Agree. Your mother has already pulled the suitcases out of the attic and planned her wardrobe. As always, she will be overpacked."

Coulton laughed. There was nothing his mother loved more than loading up a suitcase. "I'll text you tomorrow," Coulton promised. "To let you know how the date goes."

"Have a good time, son."

Coulton disconnected the call as he pulled in front of Ainsley's building. He was a few minutes early, but that was by design. He suspected Ainsley would meet him on the street. It was hard getting her to talk about herself, so he was going to steal an inside look. He was curious about where she lived, and he prayed her apartment wasn't as decrepit as the outside of the building suggested.

Plus, he wanted to meet her father. His opinion of Mick was pretty damn low right now, and he couldn't help but hope the guy wasn't as big an asshole as he sounded. He wasn't holding out *much* hope, but he was an optimist at heart.

Locking his truck, he walked into the apartment building. The interior hallway was dim and smelled like a sewer.

Climbing three flights of rickety stairs, he lifted his hand, about to knock, when the door flew open. Just as he expected, Ainsley was there, in her jacket, her keys and phone in hand.

"You didn't have to come up here," she said quickly.

"Who's at the door?" a gruff voice called.

"Just a friend," Ainsley yelled back. "I told you I was going out."

Coulton peered over her shoulder into the apartment, overwhelmed by the stench of stale cigarette smoke.

"You don't have any fucking friends," her dad huffed back.

That pronouncement was backed up with a loud, hacking cough that sounded dangerously wet and unhealthy.

"I'd like to meet your dad," Coulton said.

Ainsley's eyes flashed with panic, quickly followed by stubbornness.

"Please," he added, when it looked like she was going to shove him back into the hall.

After a moment, she sighed, resigned, and moved back to open the door wider.

Coulton stepped inside.

The condition of Ainsley's apartment was worse than the outside of the building, something he hadn't thought possible. There were old water stains on the ceiling and along one wall that indicated there'd been a leak upstairs at some point. The carpet was stained in so many places, Coulton couldn't tell what the original color had been. The paint on the wall was peeling and the furniture was older than him.

Sitting on a tatty recliner was Ainsley's dad. Mick was dressed in a white wifebeater that was stained with something that looked like orange Cheetos dust. His stomach peeked from the bottom where the hem had ridden up and because his gray sweatpants hung low on his hips. He wore socks on his feet, though both had sizeable holes, which his big toes had pushed through. His complexion was almost gray, which couldn't be good, and he was hooked up to oxygen.

Despite the fact the man wasn't well, he managed to shoot Coulton the dirtiest look he'd ever received.

"Who the fuck are you?" he asked in breathless gasps.

"Coulton Moore," he said, introducing himself. Ordinarily, he'd hold his hand out to shake when meeting his date's father, but Mick didn't look like the handshaking type.

"Moore," Mick muttered to himself, and Coulton got the sense he was trying to place the name.

"This is my dad, Mick Hall." Ainsley was obviously ready to

get the hell out of the apartment. Not that Coulton could fault her for that.

"Nice to meet you," Coulton said, receiving the same befuddled look from Mick that he got from his daughter whenever he said something polite.

"So…" she started, turning toward the door. "We really need to—"

"Get me a beer before you go," Mick demanded.

Ainsley drew in a slow breath. "Mick. You shouldn't—"

The man exploded. "Get me the fucking beer, Ainsley! Don't need a sermon about not drinking with my meds. Like I give a fuck." By the end of his tirade, he was struggling to breathe, but he persisted, banging his fist on the arm of his recliner.

Ainsley stormed to the kitchen, returning with a can of Busch Light. She slammed it down on the side table, then turned toward Coulton. "Ready?"

Coulton nodded.

Before they made it to the door, it opened, and her brother walked in.

"You gotta be fucking kidding me," Ainsley muttered under her breath.

Eli smirked when he looked at her bruised face. "Found yourself another winner, I see, Painsley," he said, gesturing toward Coulton.

"Excuse me?" Coulton said through gritted teeth. He'd been hoping to run into her brother ever since the attack in the bar. He didn't consider himself a violent person, but damn if Eli Hall didn't bring out the beast in him.

Eli barely spared him a glance. Obviously, her brother didn't recognize him from their run-in at the tavern. Then, as Coulton took a closer look, he noticed the red-rimmed eyes and blown pupils. The asshole was stoned out of his mind.

"Word of advice. Hide your scissors around her," Eli slurred, chuckling over the idea that Coulton had hit his sister.

Coulton didn't give a shit if the man was high or not. He

grabbed him by the shirt, shaking him until Eli managed to—at least partially—focus on him.

"You again," her brother said, when he finally recognized him.

"Me," Coulton said hotly. "You think it's funny that she got hurt?"

"Coulton," Ainsley started, but he shook his head, pissed as hell about how her brother and father treated her. No wonder Ainsley always looked equal parts confused and shocked whenever he did or said something nice. She sure as shit didn't get any kindness here, despite the fact she was the only one working her ass off to keep the family afloat.

"I would never hit a woman." Coulton shoved Eli into the wall. "But I have no problem teaching assholes like you a lesson or two about how women should be treated."

"Seriously, Coulton," Ainsley tried again. "He's a lost cause."

"*You're* to blame for those bruises." Coulton tightened his grip when Eli tried to pry his fingers off.

"I didn't lay a fucking hand on the stupid cunt!" Eli protested. "Tell him, Ainsley."

How the hell Ainsley had turned out as amazing as she had after spending a lifetime with these two assholes was beyond him.

"Those thugs you sent to the tavern the other night did this to her."

Eli blinked a couple times, as his drug-addled brain tried to process those words. "You pay 'em the money?" Eli asked.

Coulton shoved Eli against the wall again, hard enough that some of the peeling paint fell off, showering the man in white flecks. "Are you serious? All you care about is the money? They beat your sister up! They were going to *rape* her."

"They stole *my* money, you fucking idiot," Mick said, clearly considering that the more serious issue.

Ainsley's hand was still on his forearm. "Coulton," she said softly. "Please. Let's just leave."

He looked at her, forcing himself to calm down. It took some effort, but he didn't want to upset her, so he released her brother.

"They got their money?" Eli asked Ainsley again. Obvious, she'd been right when she said her brother was laying low, hiding from the thugs.

"Not all of it."

Eli ran a hand through his thinning hair. "Fuck."

Mick belched, then breathlessly barked, "They got two hundred dollars of my money, you worthless prick."

His son rolled his eyes. "So fucking sue me, Mick."

Mick put the leg of his recliner down, leaning forward, though it took some effort. "What the fuck did you say to me?"

Eli laughed. "Come at me, old man. I ain't afraid of you. You're already huffing and puffing. Why the fuck don't you do us a favor and just die already?"

Jesus. What the hell was wrong with these guys?

Apparently, Eli had been right about Mick's posturing, because the old man made no attempt to rise. His breathing was labored, his gray face now blotchy and red from even that limited amount of exertion.

"Fucking useless kids," Mick muttered darkly.

"Come on." Ainsley tugged on his arm. "Let's get out of here, Coulton."

Mick had been scowling at Eli, but he turned his attention back to them when she said his name. His eyes widened. "Wait. Did you say your last name was Moore?"

Coulton nodded.

"You're the goalie for the Stingrays," Mick said.

"Huh?" Eli grunted.

"I thought your name sounded familiar." Mick looked at Ainsley. "How the fuck did *you* land this guy?"

"The same way she lands 'em all," Eli sneered. "The whore spread her legs."

Coulton took a step toward her brother, ready to tear the prick from limb to limb, but Ainsley stepped between them.

"We're leaving," she said.

"I don't think we are," Coulton replied, fists clenched. "Not until he understands he can't say shit like that."

Ainsley placed her hand in the center of Coulton's chest. "He's not worth it. Trust me."

"If you think I'm going to let him talk to you—"

"Please!" Ainsley said almost desperately. "Can we just get the hell out of here?"

Coulton glanced from Mick to Eli...and he realized Ainsley was right. These men weren't deterred by fists or words. They were evil, selfish pricks, right to the core, and there was nothing he could do or say to them that would make a damn bit of difference in the way they treated Ainsley.

He covered the hand still on his chest, wrapping his other arm around her waist. "Okay. Let's go."

They'd just crossed the threshold when Eli called out, "Hey, how much do goalies make?"

Coulton ignored him, and the two of them walked out of the apartment, Mick and Eli erupting into a shouting match before the door even closed behind them.

Ainsley preceded him down the stairs, holding herself stiffly. She was silent until they stepped out onto the street.

She stopped right outside the door. "Maybe we should just forget this."

"What? Why?"

"Coulton. I told you before. We come from two very different worlds. That up there?" she said, pointing upward. "That dumpster fire is just another Monday night." She closed her eyes wearily.

He cupped her cheek, waiting until her gaze met his. "They're assholes, but that's on them. Not us. So we're just going to say fuck 'em and have an awesome time."

She gave him a hint of a smile. "Fuck 'em?"

"Fuck 'em." He reclaimed her hand, leading her to his truck. Opening the passenger door, he waited until she was buckled in before closing the door, circling the front, and climbing into the driver's seat.

"Where are we going?" she asked, once he'd pulled out onto the street.

"It's a surprise." Given what he'd just witnessed in her apartment, he was glad he'd gone the extra mile for tonight's date. When he'd set it up, he'd been hoping to knock a few more items off her list of "never" experiences. Now, he was grateful for the chance to spoil her, to show her what she was worth. Because he hated the way Mick and Eli continually tore her down, treating her with complete disrespect.

She narrowed her eyes. "I hate surprises."

He chuckled. "This is a good one. Promise."

Coulton turned on the radio and hit an upbeat playlist on Spotify, hoping that happy music would help erase the shit show they'd just left from her mind.

When Ainsley started humming along to "Brown Eyed Girl," he grinned, then glanced in her direction as he pulled into the parking lot of the marina.

"What are we doing here?"

"I noticed you like looking at the water when you're at my place. Thought maybe you'd enjoy a closer view."

"Cool. It's a nice night for a walk," she said as they got out of the truck.

Coulton shook his head, wrapping his arm around her shoulders. "We're not walking." He pointed to the yacht in the third slip. "I borrowed my friend's boat. We're going on a cruise down the Patapsco River."

The look on Ainsley's face was worth every second he'd just endured with her family.

"What?"

Coulton guided her toward the slip, but when he started to help her aboard, she dug her heels in.

"Wait. Are you serious?"

He nodded, but she still didn't move. Coulton was amused

by the suspicious look on her face. "This isn't a boat, Coulton. It's a yacht."

"Pah-tay-to, pah-tah-to."

"You can't be serious. People don't just loan out their yachts," she said.

"Of course, they do." He remained on the deck with his hand outstretched.

Her suspicion took some time to fade. "We can really get on?" she asked, as she stepped onto the deck, glancing around guiltily like they were breaking some law.

"Yes, wildcat. We can get on. They're expecting us."

As if on cue, the captain appeared, approaching them with a wide smile. "Coulton Moore?"

He nodded. "That's me. And this is Ainsley Hall."

The captain shook both of their hands. "Captain Rogers. It's a pleasure to have you on board tonight. How about I give you a quick tour and then we can shove off."

Captain Rogers was a friendly man with a good sense of humor and an obvious love for the water. Ainsley hung on every word he said as he shared a few anecdotes about his time in the Navy, and her eyes nearly popped out of her head as he showed them the entire yacht, from the indoor saloon to the spa deck to the outdoor dining area.

Once the tour was complete, the captain left them below deck in the saloon, both of them with a glass of wine in hand, before he excused himself to start the cruise.

"I can't believe someone let you borrow their yacht." Ainsley remained in the middle of the room, looking around like she was afraid to touch anything. "Must be a really good friend."

"The boat belongs to Lucas Whiting."

"The billionaire?"

Coulton wasn't surprised she recognized the name. The Whitings were to Baltimore what the Kennedys were to Martha's Vineyard.

He nodded. "He's a generous donor for Big Brothers Big

Sisters and a huge hockey fan. Our paths have crossed at a few charity fundraisers and at Pat's Pub."

At her curious glance, he went on to explain, "Pat's Pub has become the place the Stingrays go after games to either celebrate or drown our sorrows. Lucas is married to Pat's granddaughter, Kaitlyn, so we've thrown back a few pints there together. He's a great guy, and he was more than happy to let us borrow the yacht for our date."

"Why would you do this?"

"I wanted to do something special for you."

"Yeah. But you didn't have to go to all this trouble," she insisted. "In case you didn't already know, I'm kind of a sure thing." She gave him a self-deprecating smile, and while he wanted to return it, the visit with her family was too fresh in his mind. Ainsley had too many people in her life constantly tearing her down. He wanted to build her up.

He ran a knuckle gently down her bruised cheek. "You've had a rough week, Ainsley. You deserve a break. And I didn't do this as a way to get you into my bed. I did it because you're worth it."

The incredulous look she shot him proved that, while she seemed like a confident woman most of the time, her opinion of herself was on shaky ground, no doubt impacted by the cruelty of her dad and brother. "You don't know me very well," she murmured, frowning.

He wanted to argue that he'd learned so much in those sad, soulful eyes of hers, but he let her comment stand because it served his purpose. "Then let's take tonight to get to know each other."

"Why?"

Now it was his turn to frown, confused. "Why?"

"I just don't understand why you're doing this."

And there were those trust issues again. Ainsley was constantly waiting for the other shoe to drop, expecting him to reveal some ulterior motive.

"I know you don't, and I'm not exactly sure how to convince you I'm here because I'm interested in you. Fascinated by you, actually," he said softly. "So can I ask you to trust that there are no strings attached to this, no powder kegs waiting to blow?"

She sighed. "I don't exactly excel at trust."

"I understand that, but will you try? For me?"

Ainsley studied his face for several moments, chewing on her bottom lip, then she nodded. "I'll try."

"Good." Coulton tapped his glass against hers, the two of them sealing that concession with a silent toast. "There's a chef on board, cooking us dinner, which," he glanced at his watch, "should be ready in an hour or so. I thought we could have a drink or two down here, then head up to eat and enjoy the view from the deck. Sound good?"

"I…" Ainsley shook her head, still flabbergasted. "This is all too much. How much money is this costing you?"

Coulton sighed, then pointed to himself. "Rich hockey player, remember? And it's not too much. You work your ass off to support your unappreciative family. I thought it was about time someone did something nice for you."

Finally, he saw a bit of that protective shell she encased herself in begin to crack. Especially when she softly said, "Thank you."

Ainsley wasn't much of a crier. He'd learned that the hard way, watching her after the attack in the tavern, and even earlier this evening when Mick and her brother were pelting her with brutal insults. However, right now, he thought he saw a sheen in her eyes, and it moved him.

Pain and cruelty didn't make her cry, but kindness did?

The yacht began to move, so the two of them walked over to the couch and sat down.

She twisted to face him, her leg bent. "So, what should we talk about?"

"Since this is our first official date, I suppose we could work our way through the usual list of get-to-know-you questions."

"There's a list?"

He laughed. "I've never looked, but twenty bucks says I could google it and find at least fifty first-date conversation starters."

"It's been a while since I've been on a date, so I wouldn't know."

"Oh yeah? How long has it been?" Coulton asked, grateful she'd given him an opening. He was curious about her relationship history.

"Just over two years."

While he hadn't been in a relationship almost the same amount of time, he'd at least re-entered the dating game. "That *is* a long time. Bad breakup?"

"I…" Ainsley looked around the saloon, shifting on the couch uncomfortably.

Coulton reached out and grasped her hand. "You said you'd trust me," he reminded her.

"I said I'd try," she retorted. She was always going to make him work for things, but he didn't mind at all. In fact, he loved a challenge.

He narrowed his eyes, and it looked like she was going to relent. However, his request for trust seemed to strengthen her resolve in a different direction—an uncomfortable one.

"Maybe it's better to just get this past-history part over with. Then you'll see why this thing between us…"

She didn't finish, didn't need to. She clearly believed his interest in her was finite, that it was going to wane. And now he was coming to understand it *was* her former relationships convincing her of that, more than anything else. It was time to prove to her there was nothing about her past that could drive him away.

"Tell me," he urged.

Ainsley glanced around at their surroundings and gave him a sheepish look. "We probably shouldn't do this on a boat."

"I think it's the perfect place. You're a flight risk."

She laughed, though the mirth didn't reach her eyes. "Yeah. That's not the problem. What I meant was, *you* won't have a way to escape. You'll be stuck on here with me."

"Ainsley. I like you. I have no idea what you think is so bad that I would walk away from you, but I'm asking you to give me a chance to get to know you. The real you."

She snorted. "Be careful what you ask for." Then, she pulled her hand out of his, clasping hers together tightly in her lap. Coulton was tempted to tug her hand back, overwhelmed by the desire to touch her, to find a way to set her at ease, but in the end, he decided only his reaction to whatever she said next would do that.

"I've only dated three guys. The first one was in high school. Tiger," Ainsley started.

"Tiger?"

"That was honestly the name his mother put on his birth certificate," she clarified. "We went out most of our senior year. He was a cheating asshole throughout, sleeping with God only knew how many other girls, some of whom were my friends."

Aaaaaand now he was starting to understand her trust issues.

"Worst part is, of the three guys I've been in relationships with, Tiger was the best of the bunch."

"Ouch," he said, his comment having the desired effect.

Ainsley smirked. "Yeah. Ouch. Second boyfriend was Jagger, an alcoholic who was out of work as much as he was in it. He also made my dad and Eli look like choir boys."

Coulton scowled, recalling Eli's comment about Ainsley picking another winner. "He hit you?"

Ainsley shook her head. "Only once. He preferred to inflict his pain with hateful words. If he'd hit me, well, I wouldn't have stuck around for that. I left Mick's house and moved in with Jagger to escape that shit, so I refused to jump out of the frying pan into the fire. I'm not stupid. Just...poor, which has always limited my options."

Ainsley had mentioned that her dad beat her before, but it didn't make it any easier to hear. Now that he'd met Mick, he was even more determined to get her the hell out of that apartment once and for all. It was apparent Ainsley didn't want to be there, either, but she couldn't afford to move out.

He couldn't begin to imagine how horrible her childhood had been, but rather than tackle that subject, he continued with the current topic. Because he wanted to know more about this asshole, Jagger. Mainly, what his last name was and where Coulton could find the prick.

"But Jagger did hit you?"

She nodded. "During our last fight, he backhanded me. He was drunker than I'd ever seen him. I'd hit my limit on his bullshit. Told him I was leaving him."

"Good for you."

She lifted one shoulder. "He was really pissed. Probably because he was out of work at the time and I was paying the rent, buying the groceries, taking care of everything."

"What happened after he hit you?"

Ainsley chewed on her lower lip. "You heard my brother's comment about hiding scissors."

Coulton nodded. "I thought he was stoned and talking nonsense."

"Oh, he was stoned, but…" She looked away from him, and Coulton could tell they were reaching what she considered the make-or-break part of the story. "We really should have had this conversation onshore. You're trapped with me." She gave him a weak laugh, trying to pass her words off as a joke, but he could see she meant what she said. She expected him to walk.

"Tell me about the scissors."

"Jagger wasn't going to stop with just one smack. He was enraged, and I needed to get the hell out of that apartment or he would've seriously hurt me. We were in the kitchen and I was backed against a counter, too far away from the knives, which were in a drawer on the opposite side of the room. But there was a pair of scissors on the counter behind me. So when he came at me again, I grabbed them and stabbed him in the shoulder. I guess the pain was bad enough that he sobered up. He called the cops and had me arrested."

Coulton scowled. "You were arrested?!"

She scooted back a bit, mistaking his anger. He halted her, reaching for her upper arms.

"No. No. I'm sorry," he said, quieter, hating that she was skittish as a newborn kitten. "It was self-defense, Ainsley."

She blinked a couple of times, as if trying to decide if she'd heard him correctly.

"*He* was the one who should have been arrested," Coulton stressed.

"I…I know. But I wasn't really thinking clearly because…I *had* stabbed him. He lost a lot of blood, and I panicked, thinking maybe I'd hit a major artery or something. The ambulance took him to the hospital and the cops took me in, booked me. I spent the night in jail. Next morning, my court-appointed attorney showed up. He said the same thing you did. It was self-defense."

"Did they let you out?"

She shook her head. "Not right away. It took my lawyer a few days to convince the judge to let me out on my own recognizance because it was my first offense. It was lucky he did, because there was no way Mick was coughing up bail money."

Yet another reason for Coulton to hate Mick.

"The day of my trial," she continued, "I showed up at the courthouse, only to discover that the prosecuting attorney had decided to drop the charges at the last minute. While I didn't have a record, Jagger did. He'd been arrested four times for assault, drunken bar brawls, shit like that. I guess the prosecutor decided I really *had* acted in self-defense. So…I was free to go."

"Good for the prosecutor. Even though I don't think you should have been arrested and charged in the first place."

Ainsley shrugged, but he caught the slight smile on her face. "Thanks."

He scooted toward her, wrapping his arm around her shoulders, pulling her close, and giving her a quick kiss on the top of her head. No more distance, he decided, pleased that she'd opened up and shared what was clearly a difficult time in her life. "Don't know if you've noticed, but I'm still here."

She laughed. "Yeah, well, it's that or diving into the river, so…"

"Tell me about guy number three." Coulton caught the quick flash of pain in her eyes before she shuttered it away, and he began to suspect that this was the guy who'd hurt her the most. Which, when he considered the first had cheated on her and the second had hit her, didn't bode well for what he was about to hear.

"Montgomery," she said, lacing the name with a healthy bit of disdain.

"Is that a first or last name?"

"First. He was part of the prosecuting attorney's team that dropped the charges against me. A junior prosecutor. He was born with a silver spoon in his mouth, rich, refined, clean-cut, handsome. He caught up to me as I was leaving the courthouse."

"Why?" he asked.

"He said he was impressed by me. Called me a badass for fighting back against Jagger. I was flattered and shocked that he was flirting with me. Guys like him," she paused, her gaze resting on his face, as Coulton heard the unspoken *and you*, "don't usually look at girls like me. Montgomery was a smooth talker, very good with words."

"Most lawyers are," Coulton observed.

"Yeah. I guess they are. Anyway, he invited me out for coffee, and I accepted. We went out, and by the end of the afternoon, we were back at his condo." She gave him a rueful grin. "Like I said, he was good with words."

"You started dating?"

"I thought we did."

Coulton frowned. "He had a different opinion?"

"My relationship with him was sort of uncharted waters for me. Tiger and I were teenagers, so you know what that's like—making out in friends' basements and hanging around fast-food places. Jagger was my first adult relationship, but we were both poor as shit, so our dates were limited to Mick's Tavern or chilling in his bedroom. He'd shared an apartment with four other guys when we first started dating. We only lived together the last year, which was when it all fell apart spectacularly."

"It was different with Montgomery?"

"Monty had a good job, a great apartment, and a lot of money. For months, we met up a few times a week, either for coffee or dinner. Then we'd always end up back at his place. He was sweet to me—saying nice things, buying me little gifts, giving me flowers. I wasn't used to any of that. I thought… I thought those things meant he had feelings for me."

"He didn't?"

She shook her head. "After six months, it occurred to me that I'd never met any of his friends or work colleagues, and I'd never even spent the entire night at his place because he always had to be up early for work. One night, we were lying in bed, and I told him I wanted to take things to the next level. I'd seen a note on his calendar about his mother's birthday party, and I asked if I could go with him and meet his family."

Coulton could already tell he was going to hate where this was going.

"Monty refused." She paused. "No. It was worse than that. He *laughed*."

"Laughed?"

"He said I wasn't exactly the kind of girl a man took home to meet his parents."

Coulton wasn't even sure how to reply to that, because what the fuck?

Ainsley was putting on a good front as she told him the story, but he still caught a glimmer of pain in those sad eyes of her.

"What the fuck is that supposed to mean?" he finally asked.

She gave him that damn shrug, trying to act casual about something that had very clearly hurt her.

"When I asked him what kind of girl I was, he pulled off the mask, lost the silver tongue, and said, 'The kind you fuck.'"

"What's Montgomery's last name?" Coulton growled through clenched teeth.

Ainsley smiled, though it didn't quite reach her eyes. "I thought we were in a relationship, that we had something real, but it turned out, I was nothing more than a booty call. After that, I lost my shit and slapped him."

"Good for you."

She shook her head. "He didn't like that. At all. Or the fact I told him we were done. He had this snakelike-lawyer demeanor. The dude was seriously determined when it came to winning, always bragging about the cases he'd won, losing his shit whenever he didn't get a guilty verdict. Apparently, that same competitiveness drifted into his personal life, because he refused to accept the idea of me dumping him.

"So…that was when he went for the jugular. He said he'd been planning to break things off with me because his girlfriend, Emma, was returning from Europe. She'd been overseas, studying abroad for a year. I was just warming his bed while he waited for the girl to return who you *did* take home to meet your parents. Said the fact I was poor made me an easy, cheap lay. The kind who didn't require more than a hot meal to get me to…" She swallowed heavily. "Spread my legs."

Coulton tugged Ainsley tight against him, cupping the back of her head as she pressed her face to his chest. He didn't know why he felt the need to hold her like this, because she wasn't crying.

Even though she could use a good cry.

"He was an asshole," he murmured against the top of her head.

"Maybe so, but that fact doesn't negate that I was an idiot. I had my head turned by his pretty words and face. I should have known a guy like him…"

She straightened up as she looked at him, but she didn't say anything more.

She didn't need to, because she'd told him all he needed to know.

Primarily, that he had his work cut out for him.

CHAPTER SEVEN

AINSLEY WOKE up the next morning and smiled.

She was in Coulton's bed again. After sharing her relationship history, she'd expected him to bolt. Because Jesus, she'd stabbed boyfriend number two.

But he hadn't walked away. Instead, he'd gazed at her with something that looked strangely like respect. When she considered all the reasons why she was attracted to Coulton—and the list was growing—it occurred to her the fact he never pitied her was very close to the top. He looked at her like she was strong, a survivor. On rare occasions, she felt those things about herself, but most of the time, it just felt like she was going through the motions, more numb than powerful.

Talking about Montgomery had ripped the scab off a wound that wouldn't heal, and for a little while, she'd remembered exactly why she needed to protect herself around Coulton. Of course, that newfound self-preservation hadn't lasted through dinner last night, because her resistance when it came to the sexy, far-too-charming goalie was zip, zilch, nil, non-fucking-existent.

They'd dined on the best food she had ever put in her mouth, even though she wasn't a hundred percent sure what half of it had been. The waiter had described each course—there had been courses!—which included seared foie gras with red onion marmalade, caramelized figs and pan toast, rack of lamb with a macadamia nut crust and a fancy sauce, roasted red potatoes, mint pea timbale, carrot puree, and a crème brûlée.

It had been incredible, delicious, and then, after dinner, they'd done just what Coulton had suggested. Stood at the railing, watching the world pass by as they sailed over calm water and listened to contemporary string music piped through the yacht's sound system. Coulton had drawn her into his arms during an instrumental rendition of "Total Eclipse of the Heart," the two of them swaying on the deck, and for the first time in her life, she'd wished time would freeze.

Right there.

Right then.

Once they returned to the marina, he'd asked her to come home with him, and she'd said yes without a second's hesitation. Because seriously…he'd taken her out on a yacht, wined and dined her, then slow-danced with her! It was like something ripped out of a romantic movie.

Ainsley glanced toward the window, the curtains closed to keep out the sunlight, and tried once again to regret that she wasn't being as careful as she should.

She'd fallen for three of the worst men on the planet, so opening herself to that kind of heartbreak again would be the height of stupidity. And while Tiger and Jagger had hurt her, it had been Montgomery, with his sweet words and thoughtful gifts, who'd crushed her heart so thoroughly, she didn't think she'd ever recover.

It had taken her some time to realize that Montgomery hadn't just claimed her heart. He'd given her the hope of a better life. Hope that she could have a life outside of Cherry Hill and Mick's Tavern. That she wouldn't always be hungry, tired, scared, alone.

That was why his cut had been the deepest.

Coulton placed a soft kiss on her bare shoulder when he woke up.

She didn't acknowledge it. Instead, she said, "Your hand is on my tit."

Coulton gave her breast a squeeze. "Hmm. How did that get there?"

Ainsley laughed, especially when he flexed his hips, his very hard cock pressed against her ass.

"Someone's wide awake," she joked.

Last night, they hadn't made it more than a handful of steps inside his condo before Coulton pushed her against the wall, kissed her senseless, then stripped her down and took her, fast and furiously. From there, they'd progressed to the bedroom, where they knocked quite a few sexual positions off their list. In addition to missionary and doggie style, they added cowgirl and sixty-nine to their repertoire. At one point, as she was begging for mercy and more at the same time, Coulton joked that it was a marathon, not a sprint.

"Sweet dreams?" he asked.

She chuckled. "You fucked me into a state of dreamless exhaustion."

"Mmm. I think I wouldn't mind doing that again," he said. "Are you busy tonight?"

Ainsley's heart fluttered at the thought he wanted to see her again, even as the skeptic inside told her to get her head in the game.

Rather than commit to any future sexcapades, she rolled in his arms, the two of them lying on their sides and facing each other. She reached out to run her fingers over his face.

"I like your beard," she confessed.

Coulton rubbed the scruff on his chin. "I do too. Never had a beard before Baltimore."

"Why not?" she asked, curious. "It suits you."

He lifted one shoulder casually. "Evelyn wasn't a big fan of facial hair."

"Ah." It was the first time he'd mentioned his ex since that initial morning in his kitchen. They'd spent a lot of time talking last night, but too many of those conversations had been one-sided, Coulton asking the questions and her answering them.

So much for playing her cards close to her chest. She'd told Coulton things about her relationships and childhood that she'd never shared with anyone. Maybe because he was a great listener. Or because he seemed genuinely interested. Or because of that lack of pity in his replies.

Most likely, it was all of those things combined.

But now, it occurred to her there were a million things she wanted to know about him too. Like basically everything. "Did you always want to play in the NHL?"

If Coulton thought her question had come from left field, he didn't let on. "I think every kid in the world dreams of growing up to be a famous singer or actor or professional athlete. I was no exception. Of course, I was blessed with a generous helping of common sense, so while I wanted to play professionally, there was that little voice in the back of my head reminding me it wasn't a realistic goal."

Ainsley reached out to place her hand on Coulton's waist, thrilled when he mimicked the touch. "But you must have found a way to ignore that voice," she pointed out. "Because look at you now."

"I don't know if I ignored it as much as I didn't let it hold me back. It was there more for protection than as a barrier."

She frowned. "I don't understand."

"I didn't stop going for my dream because it was unachievable. But, if I hadn't succeeded, I had that little voice to reassure me that it was okay if I failed, because my goal was a hard one. As long as I tried my best and did everything possible to achieve it, then I could still hold my head up high if I didn't make it. I think it's human nature to dream big, Ains. It's fun to win, but it's also important to be able to accept losing without letting it destroy your self-confidence or happiness."

Ainsley pondered that, letting it sink in. "That's a cool way to look at it."

"What about you?" Coulton asked. "What did you want to grow up to be when you were young?"

Ainsley wasn't sure how to respond to that question. Probably because there wasn't an answer. Or at least not a good one.

"I don't remember."

Coulton narrowed his eyes. The guy was scarily good at recognizing when she was lying. "Try."

"I didn't really think about what I wanted to be as much as where I didn't want to be," she finally said.

Coulton reached over her shoulder, his finger tracing the skin where her birdcage tattoo was. "You dreamed about escaping?"

"When I was younger, yeah. Whenever Mick would smack me around or lock me in a closet, I would dream about the day when I could get out, away from him and Eli and all of it. But that dream died in high school."

Coulton frowned. "Why?"

"By that point, I was old enough to understand that I didn't have the luxury of dreaming."

"Explain that to me," Coulton insisted, running his fingers through her hair.

She tried to concentrate on her response, but when he touched her—something he did a lot—it was hard to focus on what she was saying over how he was making her feel.

"I was a mediocre student, Coulton, so it wasn't like I was going to ever go to college. I didn't have the grades to get a scholarship, and *without* a scholarship, I didn't have the money. I don't have a driver's license because we've never owned a car, so my employment options were limited by public transportation. I applied to work as a cashier in a local grocery store when I was in high school, but Mick flipped his lid. Said if I was going to work, it was going to be for him, because he'd had enough of me freeloading on the rent and food."

Coulton had an expression she was starting to call the Mick

scowl. "He's your fucking *dad*. Those things are his responsibility."

She rolled her eyes. "Do I really need to point out our different upbringings again?"

"No. I'd rather you didn't," he said darkly. "Not sure I can stand to hear it anymore."

Ainsley pushed forward, planting a quick kiss on Coulton's lips, touched by how angry he was on her behalf. It was a novel experience for her, and she liked it way more than she should.

"Anyway, that was when I started working in the tavern," she continued.

"Pretty sure you weren't old enough to be a bartender."

She smirked. "I started out washing dishes, serving the crappy food, cleaning the place. Not that it helped much, because the tavern has always been a pit, disgusting as shit. And don't even get me going on the bathrooms. The only thing that would improve that place would be some gasoline and a match."

"So you've been working at Mick's since high school?"

She shook her head. "No. I thought I'd managed my escape from Mick and Eli with Jagger. I moved into an apartment with him and found a job as a waitress at a chain restaurant near the Inner Harbor. The tips were good enough that I could pay the rent and buy groceries, but not enough that I could save anything for a rainy day. Savings accounts are a rich person thing," she said, giving Coulton a playful grin. Ever since he'd discovered she'd never had a bath, she'd started making him a list of "rich" things, something that seemed to amuse and upset him in equal measure.

This jest did the same, as he smirked and shook his head in unison. "Why did you quit the restaurant job?"

"Refer back to me stabbing Jagger. I missed three shifts in a row without calling because I was locked up. The manager had a zero-tolerance policy, so when I went back to explain… Well, let's just say my boss didn't think being in jail for stabbing someone made me a person he wanted to retain."

"So you moved back in with Mick?"

"The day after I got out of jail, I didn't have anywhere else to go."

"Where had you planned to go when you left Jagger?"

Ainsley sighed. "Another waitress from work said I could sleep on her couch until I found a place I could afford on my own. It wasn't a great plan, but I'd been desperate to get away from Jagger. That offer dried up when my job did. Because again…me stabbing a guy really seemed to be a sticking point for everyone at the restaurant. That left me only one option."

"Mick."

She nodded. "It was either go home or sleep on the street. He was a smug fucker about it too. He'd been pissed when I quit working at the bar and moved out. He made me beg, then he saddled me with a shit-ton of shifts as a way to pay penance. I didn't have a choice because I knew I was going to get hit with a bunch of legal fees, and at the time, I was at least eighty percent sure I was going to jail. I'd been too terrified to think about the long term."

Coulton gave her a soft kiss on the forehead. "Jesus, Ainsley. I can't begin to imagine how scary all of that must have been for you."

She shrugged, trying not to let him see how much his affectionate kiss and kind words were impacting her. She really needed to learn how to manage her expectations with Coulton, because nothing good was going to come of this. It never did.

"Does your asshole father even fucking pay you?" Coulton asked hotly.

"Of course he does. I'm not an idiot. I wouldn't work for free. It's just…not a lot. The money we make from the tavern these days goes into one account, and that's what we use to pay all the bills. It used to be more, but with his medical issues," she sighed, "whatever's left at the end of the month is split between me and Mick, and lately…"

She stopped talking, her eyes darting around Coulton's

very clean, well-furnished, bougie-ass condo, and her pride kicked in. It was hard for her to admit just how poor she was. Not that she had to. Coulton had seen the truth up close and personal when he'd picked her up for their date. She'd been absolutely stunned he hadn't taken one look at the shithole she called home, turned on his heel, and gotten the hell out of there.

Coulton looked only slightly appeased by her response. "If you could be anything you wanted and money wasn't an object, what would you be?"

Ainsley opened her mouth to respond, then closed it again because she didn't have an answer to that. She hadn't lied when she said she didn't dream. Dreams were built on hope, and that was something she'd lost a long time ago.

Coulton called his little voice common sense.

She called her voice reality. And while she'd always thought it was there to protect her, now she was wondering if it had also held her back. She hated to think she'd been making excuses for not trying, but now that she considered it…

God. Coulton was really getting into her head. Every time she had tried to better her life, she'd gotten knocked right back down on her ass. And while that sucked, when the hell had she stopped getting up?

The idea that she'd settled—or worse, given up—didn't sit well with her.

"Honestly," she said. "I don't know what I'd do."

She expected Coulton to press the subject, but something on her face must have told him she was telling the truth. "Do me a favor," he said, squeezing her hip. "Give it some thought."

"Ooookay," she said, shooting him a funny look, because why? Rather than ask, she just agreed. She'd already said way more than she was comfortable with. "I will," she lied.

"Can I ask you one more thing?" Coulton gave her a cheeky grin, one that said he knew he was pushing her.

"Sure. Why hold back now?" she joked, even though this

conversation had well passed the limit in terms of her comfort zone.

"Why do you stay with Mick? You got a job at a restaurant once. Why not do it again? There are other places to live in Baltimore."

Ainsley bit her lower lip. That question was harder to answer than the one about her dreams. She blew out a long, slow breath. "I…don't know."

Coulton wasn't letting her get away with that lame response, so he waited her out.

"You missed your calling," she said disgruntledly. "You should have been a shrink."

He chuckled but didn't take the bait, lifting one eyebrow as he waited for her reply.

Ainsley hadn't known the answer to the dream question, but she knew this one. Even if she hated it. "He's a shitty dad, but he's still my dad," she said. "He's mean and cruel and a total bastard. I know he doesn't love me. Hell, he doesn't even like me, and the only reason he keeps me around is to use me, but, apart from Eli, he's the only family I have. When Mom left, saddling him with two brats…"

Coulton narrowed his eyes.

"Mick's words, not mine," she hastened to add. "He didn't ditch us. I know that's a low bar, but I had some friends from school who were growing up in the foster system. They were constantly getting shuffled around from place to place, and some of those homes were…well…they were really dangerous. Especially for the girls. Better the devil you know, I guess." She shrugged. "Shortly after the Jagger ordeal, Mick first got the COPD diagnosis, and he started struggling at the tavern. Now, he can't work, and I don't know. I feel like…"

"You can't ditch him," Coulton finished for her.

She looked away, closing the lid on that subject. She'd started this entire conversation hoping to learn more about *him*, and as always, Coulton turned it all back around to her.

"Can I see your drawings?"

Ainsley had only shown her artwork to one other person because they were deeply personal to her. But the second he asked, she realized how much she wanted him to see them. "Yeah. You can. Wait here."

She climbed out of bed and quickly walked to the living room, where she'd left her messenger bag. Grabbing the sketch pad, she returned to the bedroom, climbing back under the covers. Coulton was already sitting up, reclining on a pillow. He'd even set up a spot for her.

For the next hour, she flipped through page after page as Coulton studied her drawings, asking about her inspiration and complimenting her work. He even recognized which pictures she'd had inked on her skin.

"I'd love to have any of these tattooed on me," he said, as she reached the last page. "You're so talented, Ainsley."

She smiled, touched beyond words. "The only other person to see my artwork is the guy who did my tattoos. He said the same thing, said they'd be awesome inked on skin."

"Thank you," he murmured, drawing her attention back to him. "For sharing that with me. I know it's not easy for you. So…how about a reward?" he asked, as he rolled her to her back, climbing over her.

"Reward, huh? Pretty sure of your skills there, aren't you?" she teased, grateful he was able to read her moods and so good at giving her easy outs.

"You were in this bed last night. You know exactly what my skill level is." Coulton wiggled his eyebrows suggestively.

"God, I want to call you a cocky ass, but…" She had to give credit where credit was due. "All those damn orgasms would prove me a liar."

Coulton gave her a kiss on the cheek. "Since you were too wrung out from my mad skills, I'm going to show you what I dreamed about."

As he slipped his cock inside her, she reconsidered her stance on certain types of dreaming.

Because wow.

Coulton rocked inside her, his pace and depth increasing with each return until her vision turned white, her nails digging into his shoulders. While she'd read about passion in the silly romance novels her mother had left behind, she'd never experienced it up close and in person until him.

He held nothing back as he kissed her, nipped at her chin, pulled her hair, and whispered dirty, dirty things in her ear. He fucked her with a relentless force that made her tremble in the best possible way.

Coulton continued pounding through her first orgasm, pausing for only a minute during her second, before joining her in her third, the two of them exploding brighter than fireworks on the Fourth of July.

Ainsley tried to still her breathing in the aftermath, her hand flat on Coulton's chest, the hard thud of his heart matching hers.

Then, he turned to look at her, giving her that affable grin that was almost boyish, and she couldn't help but return it. When was the last time she'd smiled this much?

When his grin faded too soon, morphing into something that looked like regret, she wondered what she'd done wrong.

"I'm heading out this afternoon," he said. "Four days on the road. Flying to Vegas, then on to San Jose."

"Oh." She understood that traveling was a big part of his job, but that didn't stop the uneasiness that pressed in on her at the idea of him being gone. She didn't subscribe to that *absence makes the heart grow fonder* bullshit. She belonged to the church of *out of sight, out of mind.*

Surely during his time away, Coulton would come to his senses and see this thing between them wasn't destined to go the distance. For all she knew, he was just slumming, like Montgomery. She wasn't a fool; she knew women hovered like flies around shit when it came to professional athletes. Maybe she was just his current Baltimore booty call, and he planned to indulge with other women while jet-setting around the country. She hated to think that way, but him using her for sex made a hell of a lot more sense to her than anything else.

Coulton sat up, giving her a bird's-eye view of his muscular back and sexy ass as he bent down and picked up his pants from the floor where he'd dropped them last night.

"I'll call you as soon as I get back," he said, even though that traitorous part of her that couldn't trust instantly doubted him. "And I'll text while I'm gone."

"Okay. Cool," she replied, striving for casual.

"How about some breakfast?" he asked. "I make a mean French toast."

She forced a smile and nodded, hanging out in the kitchen while he made her a restaurant-worthy breakfast.

All the while, she couldn't help but feel like the bottom was about to drop out from under her.

* * *

Ainsley refilled a pitcher, then delivered it to a table of grizzled old men, fighting over who the best quarterback in the NFL was, as if anybody really gave a shit.

What a difference four days could make, she thought miserably.

On Tuesday morning, she'd been flying high on yachting and amazing sex, but like Icarus, she'd ventured too close to the sun.

Because unluckily for her, she had plenty of people in her life more than ready to knock her down a peg or thirty.

Coulton had texted a lot the first couple of days he was gone, and she'd been as giddy as a teenager whenever her phone pinged. They'd engaged in some very fun, naughty sexting the first night, and she'd been thrilled that he was thinking about her while on the road.

She should have known better than to get carried away. The

last two days had been total radio silence, which meant she'd spent forty-eight hours rereading all their previous texts, trying to figure out what had gone wrong, then kicking her own ass for acting like such a stupid idiot.

If he didn't want to talk to her, then fuck him.

Anger was an easier emotion for Ainsley than sadness, so she grabbed hold of her fury, letting it burn long and hot. All the while, she justified again all the reasons why she should have steered clear of the sexy goalie. Rich guys, in her experience, were all the same. Coddled little mama's boys who took one look at her tats and piercings and pegged her as a bad girl, one they could sow their wild oats with before settling down with a nice girl.

Montgomery—and now Coulton—had seen her as an easy mark. And the part that really pissed her off was, they'd been right. She was. All they had to do was say a few nice things, buy her a freaking decent meal or a trinket, and—because she was so light on kindness in her life—she'd been putty in their hands.

Well, screw that.

And screw Coulton Moore.

Fuck it. Screw everybody.

Mick, in typical form, wasn't helping the situation, reminding her over and over she wasn't good enough for anyone to love. Not for Jagger. Not for Montgomery. And definitely not for Coulton. In the past, she'd either ignored Mick's bullshit or fought back, defending herself. This week, she couldn't summon the energy to do either. After a lifetime of his verbal abuse, she thought her thick skin impenetrable.

She was wrong.

Because this week, Mick's cruel words hit hard. It didn't help that his health was declining. The worse he felt and the harder it was for him to breathe, the meaner he got. She wasn't sure how much longer she could live with him without losing her mind completely. Ainsley was slowly suffocating, at home and at work, but guilt wouldn't let her leave. Mick truly was helpless, and without the money she brought in, he would also be broke.

Coulton had asked her to dream about a different future, and without realizing it, she had started to do so, imagining a world where she lived somewhere safe and warm and clean. Where she worked as a tattoo artist. Without admitting it to herself, she understood now that her countless sketch pads and years' worth of art was her way of building a portfolio.

Or it had been.

Until a few years ago, when Mick, in a fit of anger over some slight she couldn't even remember, stole her sketch pads while she'd been out and burned them all. All her art, reduced to ash. It had taken her nearly six months before she could even stomach picking up a pencil to start drawing again. Nowadays, her sketch pad was always in her bag, always on her person.

Ainsley rubbed her eyes wearily, wishing she could tuck the bad memories away, but Coulton had opened Pandora's box, and the lid wouldn't close again.

To make matters worse, she'd gone the extra mile on dreaming and had included Coulton in that perfect, fictional future. Her gut had told her things between them were over, but she hadn't wanted to listen, so she'd ignored it.

Ainsley reached behind her for her sketch pad. It was a slow night. Usually drawing helped, but tonight she wasn't feeling particularly inspired. She flipped to the last page, sighing as she studied her current drawing. She'd started it after the first night she'd spent in Coulton's bed. It was a portrait of his face, and while it wasn't finished, there was enough there to make her heart ache with longing. She wasn't sure why she tortured herself by drawing him.

"You think Coulton will make an appearance tonight?" Petey asked. "The Stingrays aren't playing."

Ainsley shrugged. "Don't know. Don't care."

She'd hadn't told anyone—not even Maren—she had gone on a date with Coulton, and now she was glad. Telling Maren about the romantic cruise or Coulton's affectionate kisses or the way he made her a breakfast of fluffy French toast served with real butter and maple syrup would have only make her look like even more of a loser, now that shit had gone south.

Ainsley looked around the tavern, checking on the patrons. Everyone had a full glass, so she decided it was a good time to hit the bathroom. Locking the register, she pocketed the tiny key, then quickly slipped into the back. Since she was working alone tonight, she made it fast, unwilling to leave the tavern unmanned for more than a few minutes.

When she returned, she caught the backend of Eli slipping out the door.

"Was that Eli?" Ainsley asked Petey.

Petey, when engrossed in a game, was worse than useless. He barely spared her a glance. "Huh?"

Ainsley walked over to the older man, blocking his view of the television. "Was that Eli who was just in here?"

It took Petey a second to direct his focus to her face. Finally, her words sank in. "I don't know. I was watching the game. Didn't know you weren't behind the bar."

Ainsley returned to the cash register, a pit in her stomach starting to form. Turning the key, she hit the button to open the cash drawer.

Empty.

That motherfucker!

Since the drawer hadn't been jimmied or broken, and considering Eli had gotten in and out so quickly, there was only one way he could have opened it. There were two keys to the register, and since she had hers…

She pulled her cell from her back pocket, dreading this call.

"What?" Mick barked.

"Where is your key to the register?" she asked.

"Why?"

"Where is it, Mick?"

"On my fucking key ring, where it always is. Did you lose

your goddamn key? Because if you did, I swear to sweet fucking Jesus, I'll—"

"I have mine." She cut him off before he could make his threat. "Go check your key ring."

Ainsley pulled the phone from her ear as Mick let loose with a string of breathy curses. She let him rage, since she also heard him put down the leg to the recliner. Given the fact he was losing steam and no longer able to yell at her due to a lack of air, she figured he was walking to his bedroom. He kept his keys in a bowl on the nightstand.

When she heard him mutter, "Where the fuck is it?" her suspicions were confirmed.

Eli had obviously been waiting outside the bar for her to leave her station.

"Eli was just here. The register's empty."

Despite his inability to breathe, Mick still managed to launch into one hell of a breathless tirade. Mercifully, eighty percent of his ire was directed at Eli, but it still wasn't going to make for a pleasant evening at home later. Especially when he asked where she'd been, and she said the bathroom. Apparently, she should have a better grip on her bodily functions. Good to know.

"How much did he get?"

Ever since the attack, Ainsley had stopped leaving a lot of cash in the register, shifting the majority of it to the safe. "Maybe a hundred bucks."

While it wasn't a lot, it was more than they could afford to lose, considering they were also down the two hundred bucks Mario and Luigi stole last week. At this point, Ainsley was starting to worry they wouldn't be able to cover the rent.

"I'm going to kill that motherfucker," Mick said, with enough rage that Ainsley believed him. Mick's health was declining every day, and she couldn't help but think a man with limited time left and nothing to lose was a dangerous combination. "If he shows his face here, I'm going to blow his fucking brains out."

"I gotta go. Customers," she lied, left uneasy by Mick's threats, especially since he'd bought a gun a couple of years ago for home protection after someone had kicked in the door to their apartment and stolen their TV. Ainsley had seen Mick pissed off before, but lately, his anger had progressed to the next level.

She didn't dare tell Mick that she'd shown up this morning to discover someone had painted the words "slut" and "cunt" on the front of the building. While she couldn't prove it was Mario and Luigi, they obviously weren't the type to let an unpaid debt—or an ass-kicking—go unanswered.

She would have to find a way to get the graffiti covered without letting Mick know, because he sure as hell didn't need any more ammo against Eli.

Ainsley bowed her head, trying to stretch the kinks out of her neck, exhaustion kicking in hard. The past four days had been a good wake-up call. Because this was as good as her life got, and all the dreaming and wishing in the world wouldn't change that fact.

"I'm heading out," Petey said, handing her a tatty ten to cover his beers. She handed him his change, unsurprised when he didn't add anything to the tip jar, then she gave him a half-hearted wave as he left.

She glanced down the bar at the two old guys slumped over the counter. They'd come in together, but you wouldn't know it, given the fact they'd said less than four words to each other. She could probably shoo them along and close early, but what was the point? It wasn't like there was anything better waiting for her at home. In fact, given Mick's current mood, she was tempted to call Maren to see if she could crash on her couch tonight.

Needing to keep herself awake, she picked up a dishcloth and started working her way around the tavern, wiping down tables that weren't dirty simply to have something to do.

She'd just finished wiping down the last booth when the door opened, and she turned, grateful for customers.

She frowned when Coulton walked in.

He smiled when he spotted her, but it faded quickly when he caught her less-than-pleased expression.

Walking across the tavern, he paused a few feet in front of her. "Hi, Ainsley."

She scowled. "Coulton."

He reached out, intent on taking her hand, but she pulled it away, transferring her dishcloth to it to stop him. She didn't bother to hide the fact she was pissed off, but he didn't seem to care as a ghost of a smile crossed his lips.

"Mad at me?"

She scoffed. "Why would I be mad at you?"

"I broke my phone, Ainsley. Second night on the road. I didn't have your number memorized, so I had no way to reach you. Tried the bar's landline, but it didn't go through."

She glanced over her shoulder at the busted phone she'd been meaning to replace. Then she lifted one shoulder casually. "You don't have to call me or text. I don't expect that."

He tilted his head. "You don't?"

She rolled her eyes like his question was completely ridiculous, even though that response cost her something. She might not expect it, but she'd wanted it.

Time to shut this thing down. She didn't like the way she'd felt the past two days when her texts went unanswered. It proved it was time to pull on the reins. Hard. Because she was letting herself fall for him. "We hooked up a couple times, Coulton. That's it."

"Felt like more than hooking up to me."

Ainsley scoffed. Pretty words. That was all they were. She was a sucker for them, but that needed to stop now.

"Well, you're wrong. It was just sex. You helped me scratch an itch, so I'm good now. Won't need your services again," she said in her bitchiest tone, holding her breath as she waited for him to reply with some nasty barb before walking out.

Coulton studied her face for a moment, looking at her in that way that made her think he could see right to her soul. It was unnerving and intimidating and…hot.

"It wasn't just sex to me," he insisted.

Now, as always, his response threw her for a loop, because who said something like that? Who put themselves out there like that? The man had no sense of self-preservation.

"I…" She hesitated, uncertain how to respond to him.

"Who did the graffiti outside?" he asked, changing the subject.

"I don't know."

His look told her he suspected the same assholes she did. His next question confirmed it. "Did those guys come back?"

She shook her head. "No. They're probably still licking their wounds. Pretty sure I broke Luigi's arm."

"Hope you did. Are things okay with Mick? Eli?"

Ainsley had spent the past two days listing all the reasons why she was finished with Coulton Moore. She hadn't expected to see him again, but since he was incapable of taking a hint, she was going to have to spell things out for him. "What's the deal with the Spanish Inquisition, Coulton? Mick and Eli and those assholes are none of your business. You and I are *not* in a relationship. I'm not interested in being your booty call or your girlfriend or whatever the fuck this is, and I don't do clingy guys, so back off."

Coulton snorted.

Actually fucking snorted.

"God, you're adorable when you're mad. Like a wet kitten with her back up."

Ainsley was slammed with two emotions, both striking her simultaneously. Fury—because what the fuck kind of comment was that? And happiness—because no one had *ever* called her adorable…and she didn't hate it. Not at all.

"Adorable?" she gasped, unable to come up with a witty response.

"Close the bar, wildcat," he said, in that deep, dark tone that got her nipples hard and her pussy wet.

"No. I can't just close whenever I want. Someone's gotta pay the bills."

He glanced around the tavern pointedly. She didn't bother to follow his gaze because she knew what he saw. The only two people in the place were the same old guys sitting at the counter, and they'd been nursing their beers for the better part of an hour.

Rather than respond, Coulton walked over to the men and offered them both a fifty if they left. Needless to say, they took the cash and got out.

Coulton followed them, closing the door, and locking it. Then, he turned off the lights, leaving them in near darkness, the dim streetlamp outside casting them in silhouette.

"What the hell kind of big-baller play was that?" she asked, a million butterflies fluttering in her stomach. "You just wasted your money. I don't know what you expect to happen here, but let me go ahead and clue you in. It's a big fat nothing."

He moved until he stood close to her again. "Let's start over," he said, in a soft voice devoid of anger. What the hell was *wrong* with this guy? She was being a total cunt. Why wasn't he getting pissed off and leaving?

"Start what over?"

He reached out again, moving faster this time, and snagged her wrist. He took the dishcloth from her hand and tossed it onto a nearby table. Using his grip, he tugged her until her breasts brushed his chest.

"I missed you, Ainsley," he murmured, his lips a breath away from hers. "Thought about you every night."

"Well, I didn't—"

Coulton closed the distance, kissing her roughly, hungrily, wiping the lie from her lips with his own.

No, he wasn't merely wiping it away. He was obliterating it.

Ainsley would like to meet the woman who could resist this

kind of passionate, all-encompassing, incredible kiss, though she was pretty sure she didn't exist. Her lips softened and her tongue met his as she returned the kiss.

Coulton paused for a moment, his lips tickling hers as he spoke. "You can push me away as hard as you want, wildcat. I'm not going anywhere."

"Why not?" she asked, before she could think better of it.

He pulled away from her. Not far. Just enough that he could see her face clearly. "You really don't see it, do you?"

"See what?"

"How incredible you are." He didn't give her the chance to respond, not that she would have known what to say anyway. Coulton had found an entire vocabulary of words no one had ever used to describe her. Incredible. Adorable.

He took her lips again in another forceful kiss, twisting her as he did so, pushing her, step by slow step, until her back was pressed against the bar. With one hand, he pulled off his T-shirt, draping it over one of the stools, like he was one of those old-timey gentlemen placing their coats across a puddle for women to step over.

Then he unfastened her jeans and panties and tugged them down until they landed around her ankles. She only managed to kick one leg free before he lifted her and placed her bare ass on the shirt-covered stool.

Between the darkness and the sheer curtains over the windows, it was unlikely anyone could see them from the street. Not that she gave a shit at the moment.

Coulton drew down the zipper on his own jeans and pulled his cock out. She'd seen it several times, but that still didn't quite prepare her for the sheer girth of the man. Even now, after he'd rocked her world countless times, she suffered that split-second moment of doubt that the massive thing would fit inside her.

He wasted no time, proving just how much he'd missed her. Sliding his fingers through her slit, he grinned cockily at the wetness he found there.

She scowled, though there was no heat behind it. The man kept putting himself out there for her, so she figured she owed him one—or twenty. "Fine. I might have missed you. A little bit."

Coulton's smile was wide and bright and so gorgeous it took her breath away, though that reaction was brief and washed away when he lined his dick up with her opening and slammed inside.

His thrusts mimicked his kisses, as he took her with a power and a need that mirrored her own. Ainsley dug her nails into his upper arms, her hips sliding forward and back as she matched his rhythm and pace.

"God," she cried out, when he slid a hand between them, his fingers stroking her clit until she saw stars.

"Come for me, wildcat. Then you're coming back to my place, so I can convince you once and for all that this isn't just a hookup."

If she wasn't on the precipice of an orgasm, maybe—ha ha—she'd find a way to resist that invitation, but all she could do right now was hang on for dear life.

"Coulton!" she screamed, climaxing hard enough her teeth rattled.

He followed her over, not bothering to drag it out, as was his usual style. "Fuck, Ainsley," he gasped, his jaw clenched as his own climax raced through him. "I missed you."

He'd said those words several times, but this time, she let herself hear them.

And more than that, she let them soak in.

CHAPTER EIGHT

COULTON WOKE before Ainsley the next morning. Pushing himself to his elbow, he studied her face as she continued to sleep. This was the only time he saw Ainsley with her guard down. Her face was peaceful, her lips curved in an almost smile.

He swore his heart had cracked in half the night she'd told him she didn't let herself dream. While he had replayed their first date countless times in his mind over the last four days, cursing every single minute he was on the road and away from her, it was that conversation about her lack of dreams that kept coming back to him.

He lightly ran his hand over her hair, careful not to wake her. He'd expected her anger last night. God, he had cursed a blue streak when he broke his phone and realized he couldn't call her. He'd driven his teammates insane with his constant bitching and climbing the walls, aware of exactly how Ainsley would interpret his silence.

He'd made her write her number down on a piece of paper on their ride to his place from the tavern last night. That slip of paper was now a permanent resident in his wallet.

She'd definitely intended to send him packing when he first arrived at the bar, and while he'd felt the slightest bit of trepidation about that, he also couldn't help but be thrilled by her ire. Because it meant she was starting to care about him too.

Every step forward with Ainsley was followed by two steps back, but he didn't mind. He meant what he'd said to her. She was incredible and worth the effort. The time away had only solidified his belief that there was something truly special between them. Something worth fighting for. So Coulton was determined to stay the course, to win her trust…and, God willing, her heart.

Ainsley stirred, her eyes opening slowly. She stretched her arms above her head, the action shifting the sheet low enough that he could see her tits. She wasn't shy about her body, so she made no effort to cover herself.

Instead, she gave him a smirk. "Are you watching me sleep, perv?"

Coulton laughed. "Yep." He bent down to kiss her, but Ainsley turned her head at the last second, covering her mouth.

"Morning breath."

Coulton pulled her hand away. "Don't care." He kissed her, then forced her lips apart, showing her just how little he minded.

Ainsley sank into the kiss easily, her hands wrapping around his shoulders. "You're so big," she murmured when their lips parted.

"Maybe you're tiny."

She laughed softly. "Tiny is just a nice word for too skinny."

He liked this early morning version of Ainsley. Apparently, she needed a cup of coffee in her before she managed to re-erect her walls.

Coulton ran his hand along her side, aware of how thin she was, just as he suspected the ribs he felt were a product of hunger, not dieting or genetics. He looked forward to feeding her breakfast, because shit—there was nothing hotter than listening to Ainsley moan after each bite of food. He'd been hard enough to drive nails into concrete that night on the yacht, as she closed her eyes in bliss during each course.

"What are your plans for the day?" he asked.

Ainsley frowned, and those walls that didn't exist when she was asleep flew back up. "Why?"

"Because I want you to meet my Little Brother."

"Thought you said you were an only child," she joked.

"I mean Slade."

"Jerome's cousin?"

Coulton nodded, recalling Jerome and Ainsley's friendship. "Do you already know him?"

Ainsley shook her head. "No. Jerome and I just had friends in common back in school, so we weren't super close. When we hung out together, it was usually somewhere around school or at someone else's house."

"And where exactly did you go when you skipped algebra to get stoned?" he asked, with a shit-eating grin.

"Jerome has a big mouth," Ainsley grumbled, though he could tell she didn't care. "You ever get high?"

Coulton shook his head. "No. My rebelliousness in high school was limited to stealing beer from my dad's stash and drinking it in an orchard on the outskirts of Detroit with a bunch of my buddies a few of times."

"Wow. You were a wild child," she teased. "Your poor parents."

"Most of my time outside of school was spent on the ice, either at practice or in games, or on the road for travel team. Guess my entire life has been pretty one-note."

"Nothing wrong with that," she said. "Just proves how committed you were to your goal. Meanwhile, I got into all sorts of trouble because I was bored."

"That's why I think the Big Brothers Big Sisters program is so important. Slade was falling into bad habits, hanging out with the wrong crowd. You're going to love him."

Ainsley gave him a knowing look. "Back to that, are we?"

Coulton laughed. "Yep."

She sighed. "I don't know much about kids."

Coulton rolled his eyes. "He's not a toddler, Ains. He's nearly twelve years old, and he has more personality than twenty people combined. He's freaking hilarious and likes to think he's a ladies' man, so he'll probably spend the entire afternoon flirting with you."

Ainsley's lips tipped up at the corner. "Sounds like he takes after Jerome. That guy thought he could charm every girl out of her panties."

"Could he?"

Ainsley snorted. "Fuck no. But it was funny as shit to watch him try. Jerome is a good guy. I'm kind of sorry I didn't keep up with him."

"Do you see many of your friends from high school?" Coulton asked.

She shook her head. "Not many. I mean, a lot of us are still in the neighborhood, but life took us in different directions. Three of my best friends had kids before we even graduated, so they're busy doing the mom thing. A bunch of the rest of us are working all the time."

"Jerome gets together with some buddies to play video games when he's not at work."

Ainsley lay on her back, sinking into the pillow. "I don't have time for stuff like that."

"Maybe you should make time." Coulton knew she would dismiss the idea out of hand—and she did—but something had to give. Ainsley worked twelve to fourteen hours a day, six days a week, running a bar out of obligation rather than for the love of the job. It was a miserable existence, and though Coulton wasn't quite sure how to help her break the chain, that didn't mean he didn't want to try. "In the meantime, today is your day off, and I want you to spend it with me."

"The whole day?"

He nodded. "Yeah. I promised to take Slade ice-skating. You ever been?"

She raised one eyebrow at him, letting that be her answer.

"Rich-person activity?" he asked.

She tapped the end of her nose to let him know he got it in one.

"So, I'll teach you."

She looked skeptical, but she wasn't saying no, which Coulton took as a good sign.

"Wait. Don't you have a game tonight?"

He grinned, tickled that Miss I Hate Hockey knew his schedule. "I do. I want you to come. The team has a box reserved for family and friends of the players. You can watch the game from there, then come out afterward to meet my teammates."

She was shaking her head before he'd even finished speaking, but Coulton wasn't accepting no as an answer. He cupped her cheeks with his palms and kissed her before she could verbally refuse.

"Please?" he said, after a long, deep, and very thorough kiss.

"I don't think—"

"Ainsley, you can keep putting up roadblocks, but I promise you, I'm going to knock every single one of them down. I want you to meet my friends."

"Why?"

"Because they're important to me, and so are you."

She didn't seem to have an answer to that, so Coulton forged on.

"So it's decided. We'll have breakfast here, then pick up Slade for ice-skating and lunch. Then I'll leave a ticket for you at the box office for the game. You okay to get to the arena? Because I can get someone to swing by and pick you up."

Ainsley smirked. "It's decided, huh?" She rolled her eyes, then gave in. "I can get to the arena on my own."

"Excellent. I love it when I get my way." Coulton punctuated that proclamation with another kiss. He'd meant to keep it short and sweet, but Ainsley had other ideas as she slid one leg around his waist. Coulton accepted the unspoken invitation by climbing over her and dragging the kiss out…then down. His lips slid along the side of her neck until he reached her breasts. He sucked on one nipple while he pinched the other. Ainsley hooked her ankles together at the base of his back, his hard cock pressed between them.

"I can't fucking resist you," he murmured, lifting his hips until the head of his cock was right where he wanted it.

"Need you," she gasped, her head thrown back as he sucked on the sensitive skin of her throat.

Coulton slipped inside, not stopping until he was buried deep. Then he raised his head, his eyes locked with Ainsley's. Their gazes held as he started to thrust, neither of them looking away. He had no idea how she said so much with those sad, beautiful eyes of hers. Even now, fear and doubt still lingered there. What would he give to banish those feelings once and for all?

He suspected Ainsley saw very different things than he did when she looked at herself in the mirror. It was a shame, because if she looked deeper, she'd see the things that were pulling him in, drawing him closer.

Determination and strength. And, while she would deny it, every now and then, he saw a glimmer of hope for a better life. She might say dreaming was pointless, but there was still a part of her longing for more, and he wanted to be the one to give it to her.

Ainsley started to turn her head when the connection between them grew too strong, his thrusts powerful, relentless.

He cupped her cheeks, holding her steady. "Don't look away," he demanded.

She narrowed her eyes briefly, discomfort mixed with stubbornness. It faded quickly, however, softening, resembling that peace he'd seen on her face before she woke up.

"You're so beautiful," he murmured.

Ainsley's pussy clenched, tightening around him until his vision became cloudy. He was falling hard for this woman. It was probably too quick, but he didn't give a shit. Everything about her appealed to him in ways he'd never experienced. Not even with Evelyn. His feelings for his ex paled in comparison to the emotions Ainsley evoked inside him.

She revealed a side of him he didn't realize existed as he sought to protect her, spoil her, claim her. He'd never once looked at a woman and thought "mine," but as he stared at Ainsley, he was overwhelmed by a possessiveness and a need he was helpless to contain.

"Coulton," she said on a gasp, when he brushed her G-spot. "I'm coming."

"I'm with you," he said. "Together."

Several more thrusts and he felt her tip over, her pussy clamping around his cock so hard, he was helpless to stop from following her into the void.

They remained still, their bodies and eyes connected, as they fought to catch their breath. Coulton was overwhelmed by the desire to say three little words to her, but he held them back. Ainsley wasn't ready to hear them, wasn't ready to believe them.

So he would wait.

Shifting to his side, he fell heavily to his back next to her. "Shower and breakfast?"

She nodded. "Sounds good."

"And then Slade and ice-skating."

She groaned at that part of his list, but he wasn't letting her back out. Pushing himself up, he climbed off the mattress, reaching out to tug her toward him. He gave her a quick kiss as she stood.

"Come on. I'll scrub your back if you scrub mine."

She laughed. "Deal."

* * *

"I knew this was a bad idea," Ainsley said as she clung to him, struggling to find her footing in the ice skates. Meanwhile, Slade was skating circles around them, offering advice on how best to teach her.

Coulton was tempted to point out that six months ago, Slade had been in the same boat as Ainsley, a newcomer to ice-skating.

Although Slade had learned a lot faster. The three of them had been on the rink for nearly an hour, and Ainsley was still fighting to merely balance on the skates.

"What the hell must be wrong with someone that makes them think, 'Hey, you know what would be fun? Strapping sharp blades to our feet and sliding around on ice.'"

Coulton laughed. "You're thinking too hard. Haven't you ever roller-skated? Rollerbladed?"

"Those all classify as rich-people activities," she pointed out, blowing a strand of hair out of her face.

Slade got a kick out of Ainsley's comment. "Golf is a rich-people sport," he said, adding to her list. "And that game they play in the fields with sticks."

"Lacrosse," Coulton said. "So what's a poor person's sport?"

"Basketball," Ainsley and Slade replied in unison.

As Coulton had said, Slade had taken to Ainsley in an instant. Hell, Coulton had spent a good part of the day feeling like a third wheel as Ainsley and Slade talked about all things Cherry Hill. They'd attended the same schools, so Ainsley asked what teachers were still teaching. Then, they argued over which corner deli was the best. She'd even regaled Coulton and Slade with some funny stories about Jerome in high school.

"Okay. Let's try this from a different angle." Coulton shifted until he was standing behind Ainsley. "Instead of clinging to my arm, I'm going to hold you up with my hands on your waist. I'll push you forward, while you work on moving your feet correctly. Okay?"

She gave him a dubious look that he ignored.

Coulton held on to her as promised, slowly moving across the rink.

Slade—the show-off—skated backward in front of them,

offering words of encouragement. "You got it, Ains. Now, put more pressure on your right foot because you gotta make the turn."

After a couple of laps around the rink, Ainsley finally seemed steadier, and when he released her waist, his hands hovering close to catch her if needed, she managed to propel herself forward and even managed to make a turn.

"I'm doing it!" she said excitedly.

Slade started clapping. "You're doing awesome! Look at us skating like rich people."

Ainsley stumbled slightly when she laughed at Slade's joke.

The three of them continued to skate for another hour, Ainsley's confidence growing with each lap she completed. With her able to support herself, Coulton and Slade started doing tricks to entertain her, spinning circles, racing each other up and down the ice, and skating backward.

"Next time, I'll bring a stick and puck," Coulton said to Slade. "I think you're ready to learn how to play hockey."

Slade rolled his eyes. "You can teach me, but I still want to play baseball."

Coulton grumbled, his obvious disdain for Slade's chosen sport, cracking up his skating partners.

He looked at his watch and sighed. "We're going to have to leave now, or we won't have time for lunch." He was prepared for Slade to beg for more time, because the kid was never ready for the fun to end, but when Ainsley said she was starving, Slade grabbed her hand, leading her to the edge of the rink and helping her to the bench where they'd left their street shoes.

The rest of the afternoon passed too quickly for Coulton, who was genuinely enjoying Ainsley's and Slade's antics. They continued their list of rich-people things—the food edition—while they scarfed down greasy cheeseburgers and fries. Because it was game day, Coulton's meal was a lot healthier and boring, salad and a grilled chicken breast.

When the meal was over, they piled into Coulton's truck, and he drove to Slade's apartment building first.

"Thanks, Coulton," Slade said, leaning over the backseat to give him a fist bump. "You gonna keep coming out with us, Ains?"

Ainsley looked equal parts surprised and pleased by Slade's question. "I don't know. I guess we'll have to see how things go."

Coulton snorted. "She'll be back."

Ainsley narrowed her eyes, but there was no anger behind it. Mainly because Slade started giggling. "You better watch your back, Coulton. Ains is a Cherry Hill girl. No man's ever gonna tell them what to do."

"Yeah, Coulton," Ainsley piled on. "You hear that. I'm Cherry Hill."

Slade offered Ainsley the same fist bump, then climbed out of the car. Coulton waited until the boy was inside before pulling away from the curb.

"He's awesome," Ainsley said, as Coulton headed for her apartment.

"Yeah. He really is. You were great with him," he said. "You're going to be an awesome mother someday."

Ainsley shook her head. "That's never going to happen."

He frowned. "What's never going to happen?"

"Me and kids."

"You don't want to have kids?" Coulton definitely wanted a family.

"I wouldn't put a kid through having me as a parent. Jesus. I'd be terrible."

"Why do you think that?" he asked.

"It's not like I had the greatest role models, Coulton. My dad is an abusive asshole, and my mom split."

"So what? Those things aren't genetic, you know. Truthfully, I think your parents—without meaning to—have probably guaranteed you'll be a fantastic mom. Because you know exactly what not to do. And I know you, wildcat. There's no way you'd ever treat a child the way you were treated."

She didn't reply to that, but he could tell his words had resonated.

As he pulled up in front of her building, he parked by the curb and turned off the engine.

Ainsley twisted to face him.

"Ticket will be at the box office for you," he said.

"It's kind of been a long day."

Coulton reached over the console and placed his hand on her leg. "You're coming to the game."

Ainsley sighed. "I just think it's too soon for me to meet your friends. Maybe we should pace ourselves."

"You were worried about meeting Slade and look how well that turned out."

"Yeah," she said, "but he's just a kid. And from Cherry Hill, so he gets me."

Coulton chuckled. "My friends are going to get you too. Trust me when I say you're just the right kind of smart-ass for Tank. And my buddy Victor is going to give you a run for your money when it comes to dropping the F-bomb."

She grinned. "Fine. I'll come to the game, but can we wait to decide about the after-party until…later?"

He decided to let her think that was an option, mainly because he was worried she might still bail on coming to the game. "Sure. Now…what are you doing for Thanksgiving?"

"Working at the tavern," she replied. "Why?"

"I was hoping you would have dinner with me and my parents."

"Pass," she said quickly. "Hard fucking pass. Jesus. I just said we needed to pace ourselves."

Coulton lifted one brow. "And I didn't agree."

She rolled her eyes, then watched him curiously when he reached for his keys, pulling one off the ring to hand to her.

Ainsley didn't budge. "What's that?"

"The key to my apartment."

Her eyes widened. "What the hell are you giving me that for?"

Coulton shook the hand that held the key, trying to get her to take it from him. "I'd feel better if you had it. If you ever need a place to stay." His gaze traveled beyond her, taking in the dilapidated apartment building.

Ainsley shook her head. "No. It's way too soon for that. We don't know each other well enough for you to give me the key to your place."

"Bullshit. Would you just take the thing? It would make me feel better," he added.

"Why?"

"Because I don't like you living with Mick and Eli. They're sadistic pricks. Plus, those two assholes who beat you up are still out there. My building, unlike this one, has a security system that would make it impossible for them to get to you if they decide to come looking."

"They'll come to the tavern if they're looking. Not here."

Coulton took in a long, slow, deep breath, and closed his eyes. "That doesn't make me feel any better, Ains." Tired of arguing about it, he reached out, grasped her hand, forced her closed fist open, then dropped his key on her palm. "I'll text you the code to the building."

"I'm not staying there," she stubbornly insisted.

"Think about it. You'd have access to the bathtub. You could watch movies on the big screen. You could sleep in my bed. You said it's comfy."

"You don't fight fair."

"Never said I did. You can even play with Sofia."

She grimaced. "Stooping to using that adorable hamster against me?"

"Is it working?"

She grinned. "Truthfully? You had me at bathtub."

He laughed, then leaned forward to give her a kiss. "It would make me feel better knowing you were at my place when I'm out of town."

The baffled look she shot him was classic Ainsley, and it told him he still had his work cut out for him. Not that he was surprised. Ainsley had spent her entire lifetime being let down by everyone who was supposed to care about her. He probably wasn't making things easier by moving them at this breakneck pace, but like her, he was a fish out of water. He couldn't make himself slow this down if he tried, because he wanted everything with her, and he wanted it right now.

"Yeah, well. I meant what I said. I don't have any intention of using it, but I guess if there was an emergency, it would be good to have. Oh, and for the record," she added. "Giving me the key to your place is not slowing things down."

Coulton leaned forward, tipping her face up with a finger under her chin. "Thank you for taking it." He placed a soft kiss on her lips, then pressed his forehead to hers.

"Please don't hurt me," she whispered quietly.

"I won't," he vowed, her soft, desperate request breaking and claiming his heart simultaneously.

And in that moment, he stopped pretending.

He was in love with Ainsley Hall.

Now he just needed to get her to fall too.

CHAPTER NINE

AINSLEY STOOD up and cheered as Coulton stopped Washington from scoring a goal. She'd been resisting the urge to pinch herself all night, because she couldn't believe she was here, sitting in one of the bougie boxes with a great view of the ice. Maren, a huge fan of the sport, would be pea green with envy when Ainsley told her about this tomorrow at work.

She was struggling to recall why she'd ever hated hockey. The sport was wildly exciting, and now that she knew how hard it was to skate on ice, she was even more impressed by Coulton's agility despite his large stature.

The guy was incredibly talented and strong and sweet and sexy as fuck.

She'd given up all hope of holding the man at bay, of protecting her heart.

It was simply impossible.

"What a save!" Erika exclaimed.

Dr. Erika Nelson had introduced herself the second Ainsley arrived, explaining she lived across the hall from Coulton's teammate, Blake Mills. Apparently, Coulton had texted Erika this afternoon, asking if she'd introduce Ainsley to the others in the box.

Ainsley was touched by his thoughtfulness, because she had been quite nervous about sitting in a box filled with strangers. Five minutes with Erika and every drop of anxiety had vanished, since the woman was so damn friendly and nice.

"So…you and Coulton," Erika asked, as the first period started to wind down.

Ainsley wished she'd thought to ask Coulton what he'd told his friends about them. Had he said they were just friends or that they were dating? Did he make it sound like a casual thing or something more? Hell, *she* wasn't even sure exactly what they were. She'd been too afraid to ask. Or…trigger shy might be the more accurate term. The last time she'd asked a boyfriend what their relationship status was had been with Montgomery, and he'd let her know in no uncertain terms how little she meant to him. She wasn't ready to open herself up to that kind of rejection again if Coulton was just fooling around.

"Yeah. Um. It's sort of new. We've only gone out a few times, so I'm not sure there's a label to attach to it or anything."

"I'm glad he met someone. The poor guy has been on his own for too long."

"Coulton told me about his breakup, and that he'd dated his last girlfriend for a long time. It makes sense it took him time to get over her."

Erika tilted her head. "I guess so. We had a heart-to-heart about it one night after too many tequila shots," she said with a laugh. "I have to admit, I didn't get the sense that Coulton had been head over heels in love with Evelyn. It felt more like a comfortable relationship."

Ainsley frowned. "Is that a bad thing?"

"No, not at all. Being comfortable with someone is great." Erika glanced toward the ice, her gaze following Blake as he slid from one side to the other with the puck. "But passion should be a part of it too, right? Coulton said that toward the end of his relationship with Evelyn, they'd started to feel more like siblings than a couple."

"Oh. Yeah, that's not good." He hadn't mentioned that to Ainsley, but they hadn't exactly spent a lot of time talking about Evelyn. Probably because Coulton had an uncanny ability to constantly turn their conversations back to her.

"But this is just me, talking out of turn. What I'm really trying to say is, Blake told me that Coulton's been a different person the last couple of weeks since he started dating you."

Ainsley liked the word *dating*, even if she wasn't sure it fit. Regardless, there was another word that stood out more. "Different?"

Erika grinned. "Happy, Ainsley. He's really happy."

Ainsley smiled, Erika's comment having the same effect on her. She seriously hoped she was making Coulton happy, because God knew she'd smiled more in the past few weeks than she had in the last decade. The man was breaking down her defenses, and she didn't mind it as much as she should.

She was starting to trust him, and while, yes, that scared her spitless, the fear wasn't enough that she wanted to stop seeing him.

"I'm going to grab another beer," Erika said, shaking up her empty can. "You want another?"

Ainsley shook her head. "I'm good."

As the buzzer sounded to end the first period, Ainsley stood and stretched, looking around the arena.

She was in the team box, which was open and connected to several other boxes on this level. Turning toward the box to the right, she froze when she saw a familiar face.

No. Fucking. Way.

She wasn't sure what she'd ever done to piss off Karma, but that bitch had it out for her. Bad.

Ainsley started to duck her head in order not to be seen, but she didn't move quickly enough.

Her gaze locked with Montgomery's, and she watched a plethora of emotions cross his face in rapid succession. Surprise to confusion to curiosity to annoyance to—fuck her—that slimy smile that she'd stupidly mistaken as charming during the early days.

He stepped over to the railing that separated the boxes. He was still in his outdoor jacket, his hair windblown, so she assumed he'd just arrived at the game.

"Ainsley," he said.

She was tempted to flip him the bird, then turn around and ignore him, but there were too many people in the box that were friends of Coulton's teammates. She wanted them to like her, so she thought it best to move closer to Montgomery so that she could keep this conversation quiet, civil, and—please God—short.

"Hey, Monty." She looked over his shoulder, studying the box he was in, which was filled with just men.

Montgomery followed her gaze. "Bachelor party for one of my colleagues at work," he explained. "I got held up in court, so I'm a little late."

"Oh."

Then Montgomery gave her box the same once-over. "You know this is the team's box, right?"

She resisted the urge to roll her eyes. What the fuck did he think? She'd snuck in? "I'm aware."

He waited for her to say more, but she didn't owe this prick any explanations.

"You look good," he said, his eyes traveling down her body in a way that made her skin crawl. "Really good."

She didn't respond to that creepy compliment. "Well. I'll let you get back to your party." She was in no mood to make small talk with the asshole.

Before she could step away, Montgomery quickly reached out, grasping her wrist. She gave his hand a very pointed look before shooting him a warning glance. Montgomery took the hint and released her.

"I was just thinking about you the other day," he said.

"Cool," she said dismissively, glancing over her shoulder,

wondering if Erika would be able to understand if she shot her a "rescue me" look. They didn't know each other well, but that look was pretty universal amongst women.

Unfortunately, Erika was talking to a couple of the wives of Stingrays players, the three women laughing as they stood near the snack table.

"How have you been?" Montgomery asked.

"Busy," she replied, not bothering to look in his direction. She wondered how much longer before the second period began and they could all resume their seats to watch the game.

"Are you dating anyone?" he asked, looking around the box as if trying to decide if she was there with one of the men.

She whipped her head around, giving him a dirty look. "My personal life is none of your business."

Montgomery gave her one of those condescending sighs meant to make her feel like she was being unreasonable. "I guess you're still mad at me."

"I'd have to give a shit about you to be mad," she retorted. "I feel absolutely nothing for you."

"I handled things badly, Ainsley," he said in a voice that almost sounded sincere. "I was under a lot of stress at work and, well, I wasn't exactly happy about Emma returning from overseas. The truth is, our parents are the ones who pushed the relationship between us, and it's never been an easy one. That year she was gone was the first time I'd felt free in ages."

Ainsley wasn't sure why the hell he was telling her any of this. "Okay," she said, because it seemed like the simplest reply. "Well, I should—"

"Emma doesn't get me. Not like you did."

Ainsley couldn't help but scoff. Was he fucking kidding her with this bullshit? "I promise I didn't get you either."

"But you did. Things were so easy with you. We had fun together," he said, before leaning closer. "Especially in the bedroom. Emma is a prude when it comes to—"

"This is a good place to end the conversation," she hissed,

fighting to keep control of her temper as well as the volume of her voice. There was no way Montgomery thought she'd go back to him after the cruel shit he said to her, did he? Did he also think she'd be sympathetic about his rich-bitch girlfriend not putting out?

"Ainsley, wait." He reached out again but stopped just short of grabbing her arm. "I'm saying all of this wrong. I just wanted to say I'm sorry. Letting you go was a big mistake, and I'd like to try to make it up to you if I could."

"Are you asking me out?"

Her question was one of shock, not interest, but Montgomery interpreted it the wrong way. "We could go out for drinks, maybe dinner."

Ainsley shook her head. "Aren't you still dating Emma?"

"Well, yeah. But I'm planning to break things off soon."

And she was going to start shooting lasers from her eyeballs. Once a cheater, always a cheater. Obviously, Montgomery was still operating under the assumption she was a gullible, easy fool.

"I'm not interested in going out with you," she said, grateful when Coulton and his teammates returned to the ice.

"Ainsley, please. Just drinks. I'd love the chance to apologize."

"You already did," she said, cutting him off. She didn't bother to say she hadn't accepted it because she hadn't, and she wouldn't.

"I guess what I'm really asking for is another chance."

She laughed. "Nope. No chance."

Ainsley should have known her response would be the equivalent to waving a red flag, because Montgomery morphed into counselor-mode, ready to launch into all his counterarguments in order to drive his case home.

Fortunately, she was saved by the return of Erika.

"Hey, look what Coulton just had sent up from the shop downstairs for you," the kind doctor said, holding up a jersey, laughing when she flipped it around so Ainsley could see Coulton's name and number on the back. "He's clearly marking his territory," she teased.

Ainsley laughed as well, handing her beer to Erika so she could slip the jersey on over her shirt. "This is awesome."

"Coulton Moore," Montgomery muttered. "You're dating the goalie?"

She ignored him completely as Erika glanced from her to Montgomery and back again. Ainsley had no intention of introducing them or giving her ex the chance to keep this conversation going.

"Let's grab our seats," she said, turning away from Montgomery, wishing she and Erika had claimed seats on the other end of the box. Instead, they were in the middle, still too close to Montgomery's box for her comfort.

Especially when the asshole claimed the chair on the end of the row, next to the half-wall between their boxes. Only two people and an empty seat separated them, and he obviously wasn't finished with her, given the way he kept looking in their direction.

Erika must have noticed, because she leaned close to Ainsley. "Do you know that guy?"

Ainsley sighed. "We went out a couple of years ago. He's a major douchebag."

"Ah," Erika said. "Shitty exes are the worst. Must be killing him that you're dating Coulton."

"I hope it is." Ainsley giggled, then she shut Montgomery out of her mind, all her attention focused on the ice. During one time-out, she saw Coulton glance in their direction. She raised her hand and waved, thrilled when he waved back.

Then, because she couldn't help herself, she looked at Montgomery, who'd caught the exchange. He looked pissed off, which pleased Ainsley more than she could say. Not because she wanted to make him jealous, but more because the petty part of her wanted him to suffer.

When the second period ended, Montgomery called out her name, intending on starting their conversation again, but she ignored him, walking to the back of the box for another beer and hanging out with Erika, who was all in on helping her avoid her ex.

"That guy is not taking a hint, is he?" she asked, glancing over Ainsley's shoulder. Ainsley didn't bother to turn around.

"He's the typical guy," she said. "Obviously, I've just become the toy he didn't want until someone else started playing with me."

Erika nodded slowly. "I get that."

For the rest of the game, Ainsley continued to ignore Montgomery, who finally gave up and started hanging out with the guys in his box. As the third period started to wind down, the bachelor party heated up, most of the men—Montgomery included—drunk and loud.

As the last buzzer sounded, she and Erika rose, cheering loudly as the Stingrays won two to one in a game that had been more of a nail-biter than she cared for.

"Hey, Erika," one of the Stingrays' wives called out. "Are you girls going to Pat's Pub for the after-party?"

Erika nodded. "Yeah."

"Awesome. We'll see you there."

She and Erika put their coats on. "Did you drive here?"

Ainsley shook her head. "No. I got an Uber."

"Want to ride with me to the pub? The guys still need to do their postgame workout and shower. They'll be at least another hour, probably more."

"That would be great, if you don't mind."

"Not at all." Erika looped her arm in hers. "I've had a great time hanging out with you tonight."

Ainsley smiled because she felt the same. She was very short of girlfriends. Tonight had been one of the first time in ages when she'd had a woman anywhere near her age to talk to, and it had been nice.

So nice, she let herself be pulled into the meet and greet with Coulton's teammates without a moment of hesitation.

* * *

"I love the way you look in that jersey," Coulton said, placing his hands on Ainsley's shoulders when he arrived and giving her a kiss on the top of her head.

She looked up at him from her spot at the table. She, Erika, and several other wives and girlfriends had asked for a large table upon arrival. The bartender, Padraig, had helped them pull several tables together, making sure they'd have enough seats for the players when they arrived.

Ainsley patted the empty chair next to her that she'd saved for him. "That was an amazing game."

Coulton grinned, dropping down next to her. "Careful, wildcat, or you might give people the impression you like hockey."

She shoulder-bumped him. "Smart-ass. You're never going to let me live that down, are you?"

"Maybe in a decade or two," he teased.

Ainsley's heart skipped a beat at the thought of the two of them still being together in a decade. Then she gave herself a mental headshake because it was obvious his words were simply a joke.

She grabbed a pitcher from the center of the table as Padraig arrived armed with frosty mugs for the new arrivals. Coulton and the bartender spoke for a few minutes about the game. It was obvious they knew each other, and Padraig was a huge Stingrays fan. Typically, bars weren't her chosen place to go to on her day off. Simply because she spent too much of her life in Mick's Tavern. But Pat's Pub was the polar opposite of Mick's. Clean and warm and inviting.

With the arrival of the players, the quiet conversation she'd been enjoying with just the women erupted into a full-fledge celebration, and Ainsley was right in the midst of it all, laughing and talking and…fitting in.

She'd spent too much of today stressing out over meeting Coulton's friends. Wasted time, she realized, as she looked around the table. Erika winked at her from a few seats away, then turned back to start talking to Blake, who was sitting very, very close to her. Erika had mentioned that she and Blake had adopted a puppy together, and while she made it sound like they'd done so as friends and neighbors, Ainsley had gotten the distinct impression that Erika's feelings for Blake weren't as platonic as they seemed.

"I'm going to grab a couple more pitchers," Coulton said at one point, leaning forward to give her a kiss on the cheek.

Her libido had been on simmer ever since he'd arrived at the pub, because Coulton seriously seemed incapable of sitting next to her and not touching her. Not that she was complaining. She loved the way he rested his arm along the back of her chair, toying with her hair or gripping her shoulder to tug her close. He'd given her no less than fifty sweet kisses on her cheek, forehead, behind her ear, and on her lips. She'd never been with a man who was so open about his affection. Ainsley hadn't ever considered that was something she would like, but when the man was Coulton, she discovered she liked it very, very much.

"Okay," she said. "I'm going to run to the bathroom while you're gone."

They rose at the same time, Coulton heading for the bar, her toward the back. Before she got halfway across the room, a large party arrived from what she'd learned was Sunday's Side. Earlier, Erika had explained that Pat's Pub took up only half of this large building in Fell's Point, the other half a restaurant owned and operated by the same family, the Collinses.

Ainsley groaned when she recognized several of the men who'd been in the same box as Montgomery.

She saw him before he spotted her, but it was obvious he'd

come into the bar looking for her when she watched him scan the room, then smile when his eyes landed on her.

She didn't return it because, dammit, his presence was the thunderstorm to her parade.

"Ainsley," he said, approaching her.

"Why are you here?"

His grin faltered in the face of her antagonistic tone. "My buddy, the bachelor, is the world's biggest Stingrays fan. When he overheard that the players were going to be hanging out here, he begged us to move our after-party to Pat's. We just had a late dinner at Sunday's," he said, jerking his thumb toward the restaurant.

Glancing toward the table she'd just left, she realized several of the guys in Montgomery's group had walked over to talk to the players.

Montgomery leaned closer, and she caught the smell of bourbon on his breath. Dinner appeared to have muted his drunkenness, but only a little. "I'm not sorry I ran into you again. I was hoping to convince you to go out for that drink with me."

"No," she said, not bothering to offer a reason.

"Are you really dating Coulton Moore?"

She nodded. "Yes."

Montgomery gave her a sympathetic look. "Oh, Ains. Are you sure it's really dating? I mean, look at all those women over there." He gestured to the gaggle of puck bunnies, who'd been hovering on the perimeter of their group ever since the guys arrived. "The man's a professional athlete with women throwing themselves at him twenty-four seven. There's a difference between hooking up and dating."

"You'd know all about that, wouldn't you?" she spat at him.

He sighed. "I deserve that. But the truth still remains, I'd hate to see you get hurt."

Ainsley couldn't decide if she should laugh at the irony of his warning or punch the dickhead in the throat for being such a clueless bastard. The one thing she refused to do was point out that he'd hurt her, because she wouldn't give him the satisfaction of knowing just how badly he'd knocked her down.

"I'm a big girl, Monty," she said instead. "And I'm perfectly capable of taking care of myself."

Montgomery smiled. "That's one of the things I loved best about you. You are a total badass," he said. "Unlike Emma, who has a complete meltdown if she breaks a nail."

Ainsley closed her eyes briefly, praying for patience. So far, she thought she'd been making a good first impression with Coulton's friends. She'd hate to lose that advantage by kicking Montgomery in the nuts. Though given they were hockey players, they'd probably love it.

"Good to know," she said sarcastically. "Now if you'll excuse—"

"Please, Ainsley. I know I fucked up. You were always so easy to be with and you never made a bunch of demands. I made a mistake, but I'm willing to do whatever it takes to make it up to you."

Ainsley shook her head. "No," she started, more than ready to walk away from him.

As always, he talked over her. "We set the sheets on fire. God. You and me…we were combustible in the bedroom. Surely you must miss that. Why don't you ditch this crowd? We can go back to my place and—"

"*Hell* no," she said, loudly. "You and I are history, and I have no intention of repeating it."

Out of the corner of her eye, she spotted Coulton on his way from the bar. He tilted his head curiously when he saw her with Montgomery. Dropping the pitchers off at the table, he walked over to her.

"Hey, Ainsley. Everything okay?" Coulton asked as he approached. Then, bless his soul, he looped his arm over her shoulders, tucking her against his side.

She leaned into him, soaking up his strength.

Montgomery, who was just shy of six feet tall, looked like one of the seven dwarfs standing next to Coulton.

Rather than wait for her to make the introductions, her ex took charge, thrusting out his hand. "Montgomery Miles."

Coulton clearly recognized the name, because the temperature surrounding them dropped at least fifty degrees as he scowled.

"Coulton Moore." He accepted Montgomery's hand, and given the slight wince on her ex's face, she'd say her sexy goalie's firm grip was a little too on point.

"Ainsley and I were talking about what a great game it was," Montgomery lied.

Coulton nodded, the smile she was used to seeing on his face uncharacteristically absent.

Montgomery, the idiot, tried to shift closer to her. "Have to admit, I didn't realize you were a hockey fan, Ains. Always got the impression you didn't care for the sport."

Ainsley sucked in a deep breath, ready to eviscerate her ex for being such a douchebag, but Coulton beat her to the punch as he pulled her tighter against him, grinning. "I showed her the errors of her ways," he said to Montgomery, even though he was looking at her.

She laughed, placing her hand flat against Coulton's broad chest. "Oh, you think so, do you?" she teased.

Coulton chuckled. "I know so."

"I don't know. After spending so much time with Slade this afternoon, I'm starting to think I might prefer baseball."

"So how did you two meet?" Montgomery interjected, unhappy at being cut out of their conversation.

"At Mick's Tavern," Coulton replied coolly.

Montgomery laughed, mistaking Coulton's reply for a joke. When neither of them joined in, he sobered up. "Seriously?"

Montgomery had only been to Mick's once, early in their relationship. He'd offered to pick her up for their date. It was the first and last time he made that offer, because he'd been too worried about someone stealing or messing with his precious car. After that, all their time was spent at his place, and she'd had to make her way to and from there by public transportation or rideshare.

Coulton ignored Montgomery's question. "I've got a couple of friends at the bar who'd like to meet you," he said to Ainsley.

"I'd like that," she said, accepting his hand as he quickly guided her away from Montgomery.

Once they were out of earshot, she grinned. "That was an aggressive handshake there, hotshot."

Coulton growled. "I should have broken his fingers."

"Bit rude of us to walk away like that," she added, though her tone and smile let him know she was grateful for the save. "Without saying goodbye and shit."

"I don't like that fucker."

This was hands down Ainsley's favorite conversation ever. "Me either. FYI? You are getting sooooo lucky tonight."

Coulton laughed loudly, then turned her toward him, cupping her cheeks in his hands. "God, you're gorgeous. And I can see I'm not going to be able to leave you alone for fear that every other guy in here will try to snatch you away from me." He placed a quick, hard kiss on her lips, then continued dragging her toward the bar to meet his friends.

Another hour passed as she and Coulton bounced around the bar, socializing with his teammates and various members of the Collins family. He'd even introduced her to Lucas Whiting, so she had the opportunity to thank him for letting them borrow his yacht, and she'd been pleasantly surprised by how nice the billionaire was, part of her expecting him to be a major snob.

A cheer captured their attention, and they watched Tank taking shots with four puck bunnies, two of whom were hanging off him.

Coulton rolled his eyes.

"You realize you could have your pick of any woman in here

tonight," Ainsley pointed out, hating that Montgomery had planted that seed and she'd let it take root.

"Don't want any of them. I'm already here with the smartest, sweetest, sexiest girl in the bar."

Ainsley looked around as if searching for someone. "Really? Where is she? I'd like to meet her," she joked.

Coulton wrapped his arms around her waist and gave her a gentle kiss that lingered. "We're going to have to work on your ability to take compliments."

"Yeah. I think we are," she admitted begrudgingly. "I don't have a lot of experience with them."

Coulton's eyes softened. "I know you don't. But I intend to change that."

In that moment, Ainsley swore she must be hovering several feet in the air, her feet no longer touching the floor.

The entire night had been surreal and fun and a welcome relief from her real world, where she spent too much time with miserable, grumpy assholes.

"Damn, I still need to go to the bathroom," she said, pulling away from him. "Never made it there the first time. Fucking Monty."

As the night progressed, the crowd in the pub had grown until the place was so packed, Ainsley had lost sight of Montgomery completely. She was hoping that meant he'd left.

"How about I settle up the tab and we head home?"

"Home?" she asked, in no hurry to see the night end.

Coulton tapped her nose playfully. "Home. My place."

Ainsley nodded in agreement, secretly *wishing* his place was her home. She shoved that thought away quickly because there was such a thing as dreaming too big. Tonight had been amazing, but she had to keep her expectations reasonable. She recalled Coulton's little voice, the one that kept him from getting too disappointed if he didn't get what he wanted. She needed that voice right now, she thought, as she slowly made her way through the swarms of people to the bathroom.

She stood in line for a few minutes, cursing herself for not excusing herself earlier. By the time the bathroom was available, she was all but crossing her legs.

Once she was finished, she washed her hands, then fluffed her hair. Coulton had told her countless times how pretty she was. So many times, in fact, she was starting to believe it, starting to see herself through his eyes.

She'd always thought herself too thin, her cheekbones high and sharp. She didn't have the full lips or long lashes or bright blue eyes or wavy blonde hair that seemed to be the standard as far as puck bunnies went. But she realized she liked that she wasn't a cookie cutter of every other woman in here. She was unique, and Coulton liked her for who she was, not what she looked like.

Walking out of the restroom, she was surprised when she felt a rough tug on her upper arm. She twisted as Montgomery pulled her farther down the hallway, away from the main room of the pub.

Ainsley jerked her arm out of his grip. "What the fuck is your problem?"

"You look so hot tonight," Montgomery said, slurring his words.

"You're drunk," she said.

Montgomery didn't hear her as he continued, "Come home with me, Ains. I promise I'll rock your world."

She laughed. There was only one man who'd ever rocked her world, and it wasn't Montgomery Miles. "For the last time, I'm *not* interested! Go home to Emma."

She turned to leave, but Montgomery grabbed her again, his hands on her waist. "Don't be like that. You know you want me."

Ainsley twisted around, trying to dislodge him and failing as Montgomery pulled her against him. Bile rose to her throat when she felt his erection through his pants.

With her hands on his chest, she pushed him hard. Hard

enough that his grip slipped. When he tried to recapture her, she took off the kid gloves—kneeing the son of a bitch in the nuts.

Montgomery gasped as he lurched forward, his hands covering his balls. The forward motion, pain, and alcohol worked against him, and he fell to his knees. "Fuck!" he cried out through gritted teeth.

She quickly stepped away, even though he was in no condition to retaliate. Ainsley hadn't made it more than a few feet before she backed into a wall of muscle.

"Easy there, wildcat. I'm here."

She glanced over her shoulder at Coulton, who was shooting daggers at Montgomery with his eyes. "You beat me to him," he said, sounding equal parts impressed and disappointed.

Ainsley chuckled. "I owed him that."

"You did, but that doesn't mean I didn't want to be the one to teach him a lesson for grabbing you. I saw it from halfway across the bar and had to fight my way through the crowd to get to you."

She soaked in his warm embrace, her pussy clenching when she felt his hot breath near her ear as he bent lower. "Watching you take him down was the hottest thing I've ever seen," Coulton murmured.

Given the fact her back was still pressed to his chest and she could feel his erection against her ass, she took him at his word.

"FYI," he added, tossing her own words back at her. "You are getting *so* lucky tonight. But you're going to have to do something for me first."

"What's that?" she asked.

"Be my shield. There's no way I can will this hard-on down, so you're going to have to cover the five hole for me."

Ainsley giggled as Coulton turned her toward the pub, both of them ignoring Montgomery, who was lying in the fetal position, groaning, and cussing the two of them out.

Coulton kept his arm wrapped around her waist, holding her

in front of him as they said their goodbyes and made their way to his truck.

"What was the deal with Montgomery back there?" he asked, as they pulled out onto the street, heading for his condo.

"So much shit that pisses me off," she said.

"Like?"

"Like his girlfriend is apparently frigid, and when he realized there was someone else who wanted me, he thought I must be worth a second look. And because he believes me to be easy and a pushover, he thought he could wave his hand and I'd go running back to his bedroom."

"Jesus. I'm glad you kneed him in the nuts."

She giggled. "Me too."

Coulton pulled into a parking spot near his building, then grasped her hand as they walked across the street to the entrance.

The moment they crossed the threshold to his condo, he closed the door, then turned her, pushing her back against it.

He hadn't lied about his erection not going anywhere, because he was still rock-hard and ready to go.

Coulton's lips slammed against hers as his hands worked quickly, divesting her of her jeans. She followed his lead, unfastening his belt and ripping it from the loops. Then she tackled the button and zipper of his pants, reaching in to tug his cock out of his boxer briefs.

Coulton groaned as she wrapped her hand around his thick dick.

Her jeans and panties fell to her ankles. "Kick them off," he commanded, as they came up for air. "But leave the jersey on. I like you wearing my name."

Ainsley wasn't sure if he intended the double entendre, but she let herself pretend he did.

Coulton's hands landed on her bare ass, lifting her so she could wrap her legs around his waist, his pants hanging low on his hips. They were both too worked up, too ready to take the time to undress properly and make their way to the bedroom.

Ainsley reached between their bodies, guiding his cock to her opening. Once there, Coulton finished the journey, shoving inside with one hard, fast thrust.

"God," Ainsley cried as he took her, pounding with a force that should hurt, but instead set every part of her body aflame. "More!"

Coulton bent his head, his lips gliding along the side of her neck before he bit her shoulder through the material of his jersey. "Never going to get enough of this. Of you."

Ainsley locked her ankles at the small of his back, using the wall behind her for leverage as she tilted her hips on each of his returns. The slight shift in position meant he was stroking her G-spot, and within a half dozen more thrusts, she was there.

She clenched her eyes shut as a million nuclear bombs exploded inside her, his continued fucking detonating one after the other until she thought she'd pass out.

Or maybe…

When she lifted her eyelids, she realized Coulton was no longer moving, his grip on her ass still firm.

She blinked a few times. "Did I black out?"

Coulton grinned widely. "Yep. Just for a few seconds."

He was clearly pleased with himself.

Hell, she was pleased with him too.

"You're going to remind me about this a lot, aren't you?" she asked sardonically.

He chuckled. "All the fucking time."

Ainsley sighed blissfully, then realized he was still inside her and rock-hard. "Think you can do it again?"

He wiggled his eyebrows.

If there was one thing she'd learned about Coulton Moore, it was that he couldn't resist a challenge.

And…for the first time in her life, she was a very lucky girl.

CHAPTER TEN

"COULTON!"

Coulton pulled up short when he walked out of the elevator and spotted Evelyn waiting in the hotel lobby for him.

Shit.

"Evie," he said, giving her a hug. The Stingrays had traveled to Vancouver yesterday for tonight's away game. Evelyn had texted him when he was on the plane, asking when he'd be arriving and if he had time to get together. For the first time ever, he let her text go unanswered, hoping he could get in and out of Vancouver without seeing her. Things between him and Ainsley were too new, too tenuous, and he didn't want to do anything to risk upsetting her.

Usually, he was the one who made contact with Evelyn whenever Baltimore traveled to Vancouver, but this time, he'd been too wrapped up in the arms of a beautiful bartender to remember to reach out.

"Thought I'd surprise you," she said as they parted.

"I, uh…I was just going to have some breakfast." Coulton gestured toward the hotel restaurant. "Then I need to get ready for the game."

"That's okay," Evelyn said, not picking up on his reticence.

"I'm used to these hit-and-run visits. And as luck would have it, I haven't eaten yet."

"Great," he murmured, unwilling to hurt her feelings, but wishing he was anywhere but here.

Ordinarily, Coulton didn't mind the nights spent on the road, but the last couple of weeks, he'd started to resent them. Especially since traveling with the team meant leaving Ainsley.

Monday night had been one of the best of his life, as Ainsley —despite her earlier hesitation—had fully embraced the night out with his friends. His teammates had all made a point yesterday to tell him how awesome she was, including Tank, who, up until he'd met Ainsley, had insisted that Coulton not tie himself down so quickly.

Falling asleep with her in his arms after they'd left Pat's Pub had felt so right, it had been next to impossible to climb out of bed the next morning. But he'd had no choice, as he had an early flight. Ainsley had woken up with him, watching as he packed his bag. She'd started to get dressed so she could leave when he did, but he'd convinced her to crawl back under the covers and sleep in. Then he'd spent most of the flight imagining her in his space, eating breakfast in his kitchen, drinking the coffee he'd left in the pot for her, showering in his bathroom, using his bodywash and shampoo.

The idea of her wearing his scent when she went to work, making him way too happy…and hard.

So yeah. Leaving her yesterday had sucked, and the only consolation he could find was that at least this was a short trip. He'd be back in Baltimore tomorrow morning, and even though it was Thanksgiving and his parents would be there, he was bound and determined to see her at some point during the day. There was no way in hell he could wait until Friday.

He grinned to himself, perfectly aware he was acting like a teenage boy with his first crush.

Coulton and Evelyn followed the hostess across the restaurant as she led them to a table. Along the way, they passed several of his teammates, as well as McKenna, who traveled with them. Most of his buddies had met Evelyn before during their away games in Vancouver, but this time, he noticed the looks of surprise on both Blake's and Victor's faces when they saw him with his ex. They knew he was still friends with her, so their reactions reiterated what he already knew. Having breakfast with his ex was a bad idea.

"Why don't we join my friends?" he suggested, prepared to use his teammates as a buffer.

Evelyn rejected the idea. "Nope. They get you all the time. It's my turn." Once they were seated, Evelyn leaned back, studying him for all of ten seconds before she said, "You've met someone."

Coulton snorted. "How the hell can you tell that just by looking at my face?"

"You wear your heart on your sleeve, Moore. Plus, if that smile gets any brighter, I'm going to have to put my sunglasses on. Who is she? Tell me everything."

Coulton rolled his eyes, but there was no denying Evelyn. When she wanted to know something, she was like a dog with a bone.

"Her name is Ainsley Hall. She's a bartender. Well, actually, she runs her family's tavern. And she's amazing. Beautiful and smart, a talented artist," he tacked on, recalling the drawings in her sketch pad.

Evelyn clapped her hands, delighted. "Oh my God. I'm so happy for you. How long have the two of you been going out?"

"I met her at the beginning of the month and…" He sighed. "I gotta be honest, I'm feeling a little guilty for sitting here with you."

"Ah," Evelyn said, the light finally going on. "Guess I see why you didn't text me back. And why you wanted us to sit with the guys."

"I'm falling for her, Evie. Hard. I know it's fast, but…"

"There's nothing wrong with fast, Coulton, especially if she's the one."

"I really feel like she is," he admitted. The fact that he could talk to his ex-girlfriend about his new relationship like this drove home something he'd come to realize over the past two years since their breakup. He and Evelyn had always been better friends than lovers. Not that they didn't love each other, but he'd never felt the same passion, the same heart-racing, cock-thumping need for Evelyn that he felt for Ainsley.

"You gotta invite me to the wedding," she demanded.

"Jesus. Let's not get ahead of ourselves. Neither one of us has even said the L word, and I'm not sure Ainsley is quite as sure about me as I am of her."

"No woman could be with you and not love you," Evelyn reassured him. "It's just not possible."

"You have to say that," he pointed out. "You're one of my best friends. She's had some rough breakups, so she's struggling to believe this could be real."

"So you put in the work until she gets there."

"Okay. I will." He'd already decided to stay the course, wooing Ainsley until she had no choice but to fall head over heels with him. Then he intended to spend the rest of his life loving her right back.

"Let me know when it gets to the engagement ring stage, because I want to help you pick one out. I have impeccable taste."

Coulton shook his head, but damn if he wasn't sitting here imagining himself standing at the front of an aisle, watching Ainsley walk toward him in a long white dress.

"You'll be the first to know," he promised. "Now, what about *your* love life?"

"I'm seeing someone too. It's been a few months, and he's a great guy. I'm trying not to get too carried away, but I have high hopes. He's a doctor at Mount Saint Joseph Hospital."

"Sounds awesome."

"Now, let's clean up the mess I just made."

"What mess?" he asked, as Evelyn raised her arm to wave the waitress over.

"We'd like to join that table," she said, pointing to where Victor and Blake sat.

Coulton grinned. "Thanks."

Coulton, Evelyn, and his teammates spent an hour eating and joking around. McKenna stopped by as they were finishing up their breakfast. He introduced her to Evelyn, explaining they were old friends and that she lived in Vancouver.

"Can I take a picture?" she asked the group.

The four of them pushed their chairs closer together for the shot.

"Thanks," McKenna said.

Once they'd paid the tab, he and Evelyn hugged goodbye, and he headed upstairs to get ready for that night's game.

As he buttoned his shirt, he couldn't help but wonder what Ainsley was doing, and if she was missing him as much as he missed her.

* * *

Coulton rubbed his eyes wearily, shifting in a fruitless attempt to get comfortable.

"Tough game," Preston said, leaning back against the headrest of his seat. Because tomorrow was Thanksgiving, they were taking a red-eye back to Baltimore so that they could be with their families for the holiday.

"Yeah." They'd lost in overtime, something Coulton would usually struggle with because he'd been the one to let the puck hit the back of the net, but tonight, he had bigger things on his mind.

"Hate trying to sleep on planes," Preston bitched.

"Me too."

If he was smart, Coulton would close his eyes and at least try to get some rest during the flight, but he didn't bother. For one thing, his frame wasn't made for modern airplanes, and even with the extra legroom in economy plus, there was no way he could get comfortable enough to sleep.

For another, he was doing battle with himself as he considered Ainsley.

"Heard you saw Evelyn." Preston hadn't been in the hotel restaurant, which meant Victor or Blake had mentioned it.

"She showed up at the hotel to surprise me."

"Yeah, that's what the guys said," Preston replied.

Coulton hadn't mentioned seeing Evelyn to Ainsley yet, wanting to tell her in person, so he could reassure her that he had no feelings for his ex whatsoever. Ainsley wasn't friends with any of her ex-boyfriends, so he wasn't sure she believed it was possible for two people who used to date to have a platonic friendship.

It didn't help that Ainsley was still waiting for this thing between them to fail. Because of that, there was no way he'd keep any secrets from her. He was going to be honest and up front with her about running into Evelyn, determined to do whatever it took to prove he wouldn't betray her trust. Ever.

"I'm going to tell Ainsley I ran into Evelyn," he reassured his friend, not wanting Preston to think he was keeping secrets.

"Good. Honesty is the best policy."

"It is," Coulton agreed. "And you know me, I'm a straight shooter. I care way too much about Ainsley, so the idea of losing her is… Well, I don't want to lose her, but we're still in the early days. She's been hurt before, so she's holding me at arm's length, waiting for me to screw up."

"That's rough. You think she'll react badly to you seeing your ex?"

"I don't know. I told her Evelyn and I were still friends, and even though I usually see her when we're in Vancouver, I'd intended to skip that visit this time. Ainsley is still a flight risk, so I don't want to tell her about Evelyn showing up to surprise me until I'm standing right in front of her."

"So you can bar the door in case she needs convincing?" Preston asked, only half joking.

Coulton nodded miserably. "Something like that."

He would come clean to her the second he saw her again. Tell her about Evelyn, and then pray she believed him when he told her that he and his ex would never be anything more than friends.

When the seat belt sign flashed off, McKenna rose, walking back to him and Preston.

"I'm working on social media posts for tomorrow, and you guys are the last two on my list to talk to. I'm asking all the players what they're thankful for."

Preston replied first, giving Coulton a couple minutes to consider his answer, and while he suspected it was cliched and common, he simply used the tried and true. "I'm thankful for my parents, my teammates, my Little Brother, Slade, and friends —old and new."

He didn't include Ainsley's name, even though he wanted to, because he wasn't sure how she would feel about that. She was a private person and, despite the fact he was head over heels, he didn't know how she felt yet.

"Perfect," McKenna said, tapping on her phone. "That's all I need." She made her way back to her seat, as Preston turned toward him.

"No mention of Ainsley."

"You think I should have named her?" Coulton asked. "Because God knows I want to scream from the mountaintop that she's mine. But she's pretty private and I didn't want to call her out without talking to her. Putting her name on social media could open her up to some scrutiny from the media and rabid puck bunnies."

Preston shuddered because they both knew there were

women out there who took their hockey hero fantasies way too far.

"Probably a good idea to talk to her first. And I'm glad you've finally crossed over to the dark side," Preston said with a shit-eating grin.

Coulton grinned. "Yeah, Romeo. I did."

"I'm happy for you," his friend replied, even as his own smile faded. While Preston had found the woman he believed to be the one, they'd parted after just one night. The rest of the guys on the team gave Preston a hard time for falling in love in a single evening. Hell, Coulton used to be right there with them, but now he understood. The first night he met Ainsley, he'd felt a connection he couldn't fully explain, but the more time he spent with her, the more it seemed as if he'd known her his whole life. His soul had recognized her right from the start.

"You got plans for Thanksgiving dinner tomorrow?" Coulton asked.

Preston nodded. "Yeah. Tank and I are going to have dinner with Victor, his sister, and Pip."

Most of Coulton's teammates—like himself—were Baltimore transplants, so it wasn't always possible to spend the holidays with family. Fortunately, the Stingrays had formed their own family, always there for each other so no one had to spend a holiday alone.

"Your folks coming to visit?" Preston asked.

Coulton nodded. "Yep. They got into town earlier this afternoon. They have a key to my place, so I suspect my mom has already filled the fridge with all the feast essentials, and at the crack of dawn, she and my dad will be awake and putting the turkey in the oven."

"Sounds great." Preston sighed tiredly before leaning his head back and closing his eyes.

Coulton did the same, but sleep was elusive. Instead, his tired mind jumped from one subject to the next, even though they all had a common denominator.

Would Ainsley be angry he'd seen Evelyn?

Was she safe?

Was she already asleep?

Had she eaten enough today?

Could he convince her to close the tavern and join him and his parents for Thanksgiving dinner?

And most importantly, how long should he wait before dropping the L-bomb on her?

* * *

Ainsley sat in the hard chair, listening to the *beep beep beep* of the machine the doctors had hooked Mick to. She rubbed her dry eyes, blinking several times to clear the grit blurring her vision. After a glorious night of rest in Coulton's bed Monday, she'd returned home to her usual nightmarish life. Mick had looked like shit, but he'd insisted she open the tavern Tuesday and last night, claiming she wasn't going to use him as an excuse to sit on her lazy ass.

Arguing with Mick was always pointless, so she'd gone to work as usual. Given last night was the night before a holiday, everyone and their brother had been at Mick's Tavern, drinking themselves into stupors. Because Maren was out of town—she spent every Thanksgiving with Nat's parents in Fairfax—she'd been manning the bar alone. She was on her feet for ten hours straight, and while she'd tried to call Mick a few times, he hadn't answered. Ainsley hadn't worried too much about that, since he rarely answered her calls.

Grateful when last call rolled around, she'd limped home on sore feet, her only plan when she got there to drop into bed and sleep.

So much for that.

She glanced at the time on her phone. It was nearly five a.m., and that sleep hadn't happened yet. Actually, it was looking like she was just going to have to chalk up last night's rest as a total loss.

One night without sleep wouldn't kill her.

Maybe.

Glancing at the bed, she was relieved to see at least Mick was finally sleeping. When she'd returned home last night, she'd found him on the floor, wheezing for breath, his chest making a disturbing crackling sound. She knew he was in bad shape when she'd called 9-1-1 and he didn't protest. Of course, he'd been out of it, delirious with pain and struggling to breathe.

They'd done a series of tests upon their arrival before setting him up in this room in ICU. An hour earlier, the doctor had pulled her into the hallway to tell her all they could do at this point was make him as comfortable as possible. He'd prescribed a morphine drip and offered her a sympathetic smile when she'd asked how long Mick had.

"It could be days, or it could be hours," the doctor had replied.

He was dying.

Her dad was dying.

She'd known this day was coming for the past year, but now that it was here, she wasn't quite sure how to feel.

Ainsley had never been close to her father, thanks to a lifetime of abuse and neglect. He'd made it his life's mission to make sure his kids knew he'd never wanted them, and he resented Mom for dumping them on him. She'd spent the last hour sitting next to him, trying to recall some good memories. Sadly, they were few and far between.

There was the one year he'd remembered her birthday. Things had been going well at the tavern and in a burst of generosity, he'd bought her a birthday cake from the grocery store. She was turning nine, and she could still recall how sweet and delicious that cake was. Ainsley had intended to savor it, only allowing herself a small piece each day so she could make it last.

In the end, she'd only gotten that one piece, because Eli had swiped it from the refrigerator, he and his friends devouring it, despite her protests.

Then there was the night Mick had come home and found her in her room, crying. She'd discovered Tiger's cheating, and the two of them had just broken up. She'd been devastated and certain she'd never fall in love again. Mick had patted her on the shoulder and told her there were more fish in the sea. It hadn't been much, but that comforting touch and those words—the nicest he'd ever said to her—had bolstered her.

She thought there must have been other times he was kind, but she was struggling to remember them. Her tired brain—pissed off due to the lack of sleep—taunted her, telling her there were no more good memories.

"Everything okay in here?" a nurse asked softly, walking in and checking on Mick.

Ainsley nodded, and the nurse gave her a soft smile, looking at her as if she would fall apart in the face of losing her dad.

The horrible truth was, her initial emotion when the doctor told her Mick was dying had been relief.

That made her feel like a terrible person, which was the reason why she was sitting here by his bed at five in the morning, desperate to remember something—fucking *anything*—good.

A grunt from the bed captured her attention. Mick was awake and scowling at her.

He pulled the oxygen mask from his mouth. "What are you doing here?" he asked in a breathless whisper.

"Sitting with you."

His expression grew even darker. "Get out."

"Mick," she started, wondering if she should let him know just how dire his situation was. "The doctor said—"

"I'm dying," he said on a raspy gasp. "I want to do it alone. Get the fuck out." Mick put the mask back over his mouth and turned his head, letting her know she was dismissed.

This man had spent a lifetime hurting her, with fists and words, but this…

Just when she thought he couldn't hurt her any more, he found a way.

He always found a way.

Ainsley swallowed hard against the lump in her throat, trying to force it down. Trying to force it all down—the pain, the guilt, the sorrow, the resentment.

She'd hoped that at the end, they would find peace, but it looked like she was going to have to figure that out for herself.

She rose from the chair and walked to the door. Every fiber of her being told her to just keep walking, but when she reached the threshold, she couldn't help but turn to take one last look.

"Goodbye, Dad."

If he heard her, he gave no indication, his gaze locked on the opposite wall. She waited for a few seconds, but in the end, she had no choice but to walk away.

As she made her way to the exit, all she could think was how much she wished Coulton was there with her.

* * *

Ainsley trudged up the steps to her apartment slowly. When she reached her floor, she paused for a moment, blinking several times to make sure she was really seeing what she thought she was.

The door to her family's apartment was hanging open. And not because she'd forgotten to close it after the EMTs had carried Mick down to the ambulance. Nope. The door had been kicked in, the frame cracked, with sharp shards of splintered wood sticking out.

"Fuck," she muttered, reaching into her messenger bag, feeling around until she found the can of pepper spray. Stepping forward, she glanced into the apartment. The quiet stillness told her whoever had broken in had already come and gone, but she kept a firm grip on her pepper spray anyway as she walked inside.

Peering around the living room, she wasn't surprised to discover the television was missing, as was the old record player Mick kept around for some unknown reason, considering she'd never once heard him play a record on it. The drawer in the end table next to Mick's recliner hung open and, as she stepped closer, she cursed under her breath when she realized the gun Mick kept there was gone as well.

Excellent. They had armed their thieves.

Glancing into the kitchen, she saw a square of grease on the counter where their microwave used to sit and the refrigerator hung open, the half case of Mick's cheap beer gone as well.

She pushed the fridge door closed, then braced herself as she walked down the hallway to her room.

Ainsley gasped as she stepped inside, struggling to take in the utter destruction surrounding her. Her initial suspicion when seeing the door kicked open was that some asshole neighbor had seen her and Mick leaving in the ambulance and realized their apartment would be empty.

Now, it was obvious this was the work of Mario and Luigi. They'd finally gotten their vengeance.

And then some.

They'd taken a knife to basically everything in the room—her bed, pillows, curtains. All her clothing was in the middle of the floor, shredded to ribbons. Her beloved Stingrays jersey from Coulton lay on top, slashed and laying in three pieces. As she stepped closer, she wrinkled her nose at the stench, because they'd obviously pissed on everything as well.

Her picture frames, mirror, and makeup were broken, shattered glass all over the place. They'd overturned her dresser and nightstand, smashing them so that now the only thing they were good for was kindling. The handful of books she'd had on her dresser were shredded, ripped apart, and strewn across the piss-covered mountain of her ruined belongings.

It was total annihilation.

A complete loss.

Ainsley wasn't sure how long she stood there, looking at her destroyed possessions.

She'd thought Mick had delivered the knockout punch back at the hospital, but she was wrong.

This was the true KO.

Walking back to the living room, she perched on the edge of Mick's old recliner, her elbows on her knees, her head in her hands.

Briefly, she considered calling the cops, then decided why bother?

God, she was tired.

Ainsley remained there, head in hands, for…she didn't know how long. When she lifted her head, blinking in pain, her eyes drier than the Sahara Desert, she tried to clear the fuzz in her brain, tried to figure out what to do next.

Coulton.

She wanted to talk to Coulton.

Pulling her phone from the bag still crisscrossed over her body, she opened it. It was early, not quite seven a.m. He was getting back this morning, but she didn't know exactly when.

Several notifications had popped up from her various socials. One from the Stingrays Facebook page caught her eye. Coulton would be way too pleased if he knew she—the self-proclaimed non-hockey fan—had started following the team on all her socials.

She grinned when she saw a picture of Tank in his Stingrays uniform, leaning on his hockey stick in the arena, looking like a total badass. According to the post, he was thankful for ice. When she glanced at the second picture attached to the post, she shook her head. It was of him at Pat's Pub with a glass of bourbon in his hands, one of those huge single pieces of round ice chilling the liquor.

Sliding down the thread, she realized all the players had a

post about what they were thankful for. There was a picture of Blake and Erika together, holding their adorable puppy, Corky. In another post, Victor posed with a tiny girl perched on his shoulders. She assumed this was Pip, the niece Victor was thankful for. It was the greatest picture on earth, because both the young girl and her uncle were missing the same front tooth, and Ainsley couldn't help the crushing weight on her chest as she wondered how different her life would have been if Mick had carried her around on his shoulders, laughing with her when she was little.

She continued scrolling until she found the one she most wanted to see. Her heart gave a tiny lurch when she saw the photo of Coulton with his hands resting on Slade's shoulders, the two guys looking at each other with genuine affection. She might have been more moved by the shot, but she was too distracted by the second picture.

In it, Coulton sat with Victor, Blake, and a woman. Not just any woman.

Evelyn.

Ainsley wasn't proud to admit she'd done a fairly deep dive on Evelyn a week or so ago. It had been a slow night at the tavern, and she'd fallen down the Instagram rabbit hole, scrolling through Coulton's pictures, soaking in every detail. As such, she'd seen pics of his parents and cousins, loads of him and Slade and his teammates, and even farther down in the timeline, pictures of him and Evelyn. He hadn't deleted them because, according to him, they were still on good terms.

Once she had Evelyn's last name, she'd gone into full online stalker mode, checking out all the other woman's socials, curious about the kind of woman who could capture and hold Coulton's heart for five years. During her undercover Facebook search, she'd learned that Evelyn was dating a doctor.

Studying the photo again, she realized it was a recent picture, because she recognized the Stingrays sweatshirt she'd watched him pack two days earlier. And because of his beard…

He'd trimmed it more closely than he normally liked on Tuesday morning, because of *her*. Ainsley had distracted him, perching on the edge of the sink to watch him shave. He bitched when he'd cut the beard too low down on one of his cheeks. Had been forced to even the sides, after which he'd tickled her, claiming it was her fault he'd messed up because she was so damn sexy he couldn't concentrate.

His beard was wrong in this picture.

That was when another thing hit her.

His away game had been in Vancouver.

Ainsley had been so stupidly drunk on orgasms Tuesday morning, she hadn't put two and two together.

Coulton had seen Evelyn while he was away. She shouldn't be surprised by that. He'd told her he was friends with his ex-girlfriend, a concept that felt incredibly strange to her. If she never saw Monty, Jagger, or Tiger again, it would be too soon.

Then she read the post, curious about his answer to the Thanksgiving question. Coulton said he was thankful for his parents, Slade, his teammates, and friends—old and new.

There wasn't a single mention of her.

And she hated just how much that hurt.

CHAPTER ELEVEN

"AINS?"

Ainsley glanced toward the doorway, bleary-eyed, where her brother hovered. Since reading Coulton's "thankful for" post, she'd been staring at the wall, full-on zombie style for God only knew how long.

She'd passed exhaustion about thirty miles back and was now meandering aimlessly in utter numbness. Mario and Luigi could probably walk in here right now, shoot her in the chest with Mick's stolen gun, and she wouldn't feel a thing.

"Ains?"

Eli had stepped inside and was now closer to her, his bloodshot eyes crinkled with lines that suggested worry. She must look horrible if her brother, who'd clearly spent the last week sleeping on the streets, was concerned about her.

"Hey," she said woodenly. She really—REALLY—didn't have it in her to go toe to toe with Eli today.

"We get robbed?"

She snorted mirthlessly because duh. "Yep."

"Where's Mick?"

"Hospital. Dying." On another day, in another lifetime,

maybe she would have tried to break that news with more compassion, but she was out of emotions. All of them.

"Oh. Fuck."

"Yeah. Fuck," she repeated.

This was probably the most heart-to-heart conversation she'd ever had with her brother.

"Who broke in?"

Ainsley started to glance toward her room but stopped herself. She had no intention of ever stepping foot in that bedroom again. Right now, she was considering asking Eli if she could hunker down next to him in whatever alley he'd been squatting, because she was done with this place.

"Given the state of my room, I'd say Mario and Luigi found a way to get repaid."

Eli frowned, confused.

"The two assholes you borrowed money from," she clarified.

"Shit," Eli breathed.

It wasn't an apology, but it was probably as close to one as she'd ever get from him.

"Mick's really dying?" he asked.

She nodded.

"What are we going to do?"

Ainsley might be the younger sibling, but that was only in years. Maturity-wise, she'd always been the older one, the one left to deal with all her brother's mistakes, the one to make decisions and pay the bills for their fucked-up family after Mick got sick. Eli was twenty-six, but he might as well be a toddler in terms of helplessness.

"I don't know," she said. She didn't have the energy or the desire to take the next step. She was fine with sitting right here in this lumpy recliner, staring at the peeling paint, and breathing in the black mold she was certain grew behind the walls.

"You going to sell the bar?"

She shrugged. "I don't know," she said again.

Eli fell silent, running a hand through greasy hair that hadn't seen a drop of water in way too long. "You going to keep the apartment?"

"Which word is tripping you up, Eli? I, or don't, or know?"

His eyes narrowed, but only briefly before he sighed. She was in worse shape than she thought if Eli was pushing aside his go-to response to everything. Aggression.

He glanced around the apartment, his gaze fixed on the door to Mick's room. "He's really dying?"

"Yeah," she replied in a softer tone. "Doctor said it could be days or even just hours."

Eli scowled. Ainsley didn't detect a bit of sadness in his expression. Not that she expected to. She figured the only reason her brother was still in the picture was because he'd seen her and Mick as easy marks the past couple of years. Once their father was gone, she doubted she'd ever see Eli again.

Her phone pinged. It was still clenched in her hands from when she'd read the Facebook posts. Glancing at the screen, she saw the text was from Coulton. He'd sent a happy Thanksgiving gif—the one with Monica from *Friends* shimmying with a turkey on her head.

Ainsley sighed and clicked away without replying.

Eli must have caught a glimpse of her screen. "You still dating that hockey player?"

Ainsley, who'd been blissfully numb, felt the first twinge of pain at Eli's question, even though the answer to this one matched the others. "I don't know."

She didn't have the brain or emotional bandwidth to figure out anything at the moment, not even her feelings for Coulton. She didn't know why it mattered so much that he hadn't been thankful for her. It was a stupid thing, really, but she couldn't shake off the pain of being overlooked or grouped in with that new friends descriptor.

Eli remained there for a few minutes more, the silence between them lingering too long for his comfort. Ainsley had turned her attention back to the wall, her brain too tired to focus on anything else.

"Should I stick around?" he asked.

Ainsley lifted her gaze to her brother, surprised by his offer, when she could see he would literally rather be anywhere else in the world. She shook her head. "You don't have to."

"Oh. Okay. Yeah." He hesitated. "Um. Do you have a few bucks I could borrow? I'm really hungry."

Her gaze slid down her brother's tall, lanky frame. His cheeks were more sunken in than she'd ever seen them and his clothes hung on him. She reached into her bag and pulled out her wallet, handing him all the cash she had. A whopping twelve dollars. "Here."

"Thanks," he said, taking the money from her. "I guess…"

Eli stared at her, and she could tell he didn't know what to say. Clearly, he could see they were at the end of something… everything.

Unfortunately, she had experience with this part, because she knew exactly what to say.

"Goodbye, Eli."

Her brother swallowed heavily, then nodded, and—like father, like son—left without saying goodbye back.

* * *

Coulton checked his phone for the millionth time. He'd sent Ainsley a few texts since returning home. A silly gif to wish her a happy Thanksgiving, then an invitation to join him and his parents for dinner. In the last one, he told her how much he'd missed her, asking if she wanted to get together soon.

He could see she'd read all of them, so her silence was bothering him. Especially since their last text exchange from yesterday—while brief—had been playful and funny.

"Still no response?"

Coulton shook his head. Upon first arriving home, his

parents had both inundated him with questions about Ainsley, whom they were excited to meet.

He'd answered every single question, then he opened up and shared…well…basically everything. His mom and dad weren't just his parents; they were two of his best friends and, as such, he had spent a lifetime telling them everything. And because they were amazing, they responded just as he expected. They were outraged by her father's and brother's treatment of her, concerned about the fact she was working herself to exhaustion and not eating enough, and anxious to spread some of that spoiling they did of him to Ainsley.

Mom was currently in the kitchen, working on Thanksgiving dinner. Coulton had offered to help, but she knew how hard it was for him to sleep on the plane, so she'd insisted he relax on the couch and visit with Dad, who was playing with Sofia.

"I'm starting to worry," Coulton confessed.

Dad grinned. "I've never seen you like this over a woman."

Coulton didn't bother to deny he was completely smitten over Ainsley.

"She's most likely busy," Dad pointed out. "Didn't you say she was opening the tavern today?"

"Yeah." Coulton glanced at the time on his phone. "She usually opens around noon." It was close to three, so he supposed Dad could be right. Regardless, he hated that she was working through the holiday. If anyone needed a break, it was Ainsley. He was going to work overtime to convince her to close the tavern for a few days around Christmas.

"Coulton," Mom said, stepping into the living room, her phone in hand.

"What's wrong?" he asked, when he noticed her distressed expression.

"I was scrolling through Facebook while I waited for the timer on the sweet potato casserole to go off." She held her phone out to him. "Have you seen the post about what you're thankful for on the Stingrays page?"

Coulton shook his head, reaching for Mom's phone. The second he saw the photo, he rose.

"Shit."

Dad stood as well, alarmed. "What is it?"

"I didn't have a chance to tell Ainsley about seeing Evelyn yet."

Dad put Sofia back in her cage after Mom showed him the post, while Coulton looked for his car keys.

He needed to clear things up with his girl.

"Mom," Coulton said, as he started toward the hallway.

"I'll put dinner on hold," she said, perfectly aware of what he was going to say. "You go make things right with Ainsley."

He nodded, walking into his bedroom and sinking down on the bed to put on his shoes. He'd just tied the first tennis shoe when his phone rang.

His heart raced—with relief and fear—when he saw Ainsley's name on the screen. "Ains," he said, answering immediately. "Listen, about that picture on Facebook," he started. That was as far as he got before she interrupted him.

"Can you come to the tavern?" she asked, in a voice that was all kinds of wrong.

"Yes. I'm on my way right now." He finished tying the other shoe, his phone cradled between his ear and shoulder. "Are you okay?"

"I just…" Her voice broke. "I just need you."

He grabbed his keys. "I'll be there as quick as I can."

Ainsley didn't say goodbye, just disconnected the call.

Coulton raced to the door. "Ainsley just called. Something's wrong."

"You need us to come with you?" Dad offered.

"No. I've got it. I'll text you as soon as I figure out what's going on."

"We'll be here if you need us," Mom reassured him.

Coulton made the drive from his place to Cherry Hill in record time. Luckily, traffic was relatively light, as most people had already done their traveling for the holiday and were most likely tucking into their turkey feasts.

When he opened the door to Mick's Tavern, he thought perhaps he'd missed Ainsley, because the lights were off and the place appeared to be deserted. Which didn't make sense, considering the door was unlocked.

"Ainsley," he called out, walking toward the bar.

"Here," her soft voice replied, and he paused, turning to find her tucked into the corner of a booth.

Coulton walked closer, but with the lights out, the room was too dim for him to make out her face. So he returned to the front door, locking it before turning on the lights.

Ainsley's head was bowed, her hair hanging around her face like a curtain.

He lowered himself onto the seat next to her. "Ainsley," he said gently, using one finger under her chin to tilt her face toward him.

Jesus.

What the hell had happened? When he left her Tuesday morning, she'd been all smiles and flushed cheeks. Now, just two days later, he suspected a light breeze could blow her over. She was pale, except for the circles under her eyes that were so dark she looked like she had two black eyes. To make matters worse, he swore she'd lost weight she didn't have to lose.

"Angel," he said, drawing her into his arms. She sank into him almost bonelessly.

"I'm sorry I called you," she murmured against his chest.

He pulled back slightly, cupping her cheek. "I always want you to call me."

"I know your parents are in town."

He leaned his head forward, forcing her to hold his gaze. "Always call me," he stressed. "*Always.*"

She blinked a few times, before finally just closing her eyes for good.

"What happened?" he asked.

"The hospital called a little while ago. Mick died."

Coulton's chest tightened, his heart aching for Ainsley. While she'd never been close to her dad, it was clear she was in pain.

"I'm sorry."

She started to shrug but stopped, unable to brush off her feelings this time. "I'm tired," she said, her eyes still closed.

"I know you are. Do you want to talk about it?"

He half expected her to ignore his question, so he was surprised when she opened her eyes and nodded.

Coulton listened as she took him step by step through the past hellish twenty-four hours. Every word she said sliced through him like daggers, as he considered her going through the nightmare alone.

In the course of a single day, she'd lost her father, her brother, her home, and all of her belongings.

Through it all, Coulton kept his arm tucked around her tightly, trying to imbue some of his strength into her fragile frame. His wildcat had gotten knocked down, but there was no way he was letting her stay there.

"Where is everyone?" he asked, glancing around the empty tavern.

"After the doctor called to tell me…" She swallowed deeply. "After he called me, I kicked everyone out. There were only a few people here anyway." She glanced over at the bar, then ran her hand over the table in front of them. "Eli and I spent most of our childhood in this booth."

Coulton recalled Petey telling him about Mick raising his kids in the tavern.

"Mick put us here so he could keep an eye on us while he was working. This booth was where I did all my homework, ate my dinner, learned how to cuss, and drew in my sketchbooks. I sat here day after day for years."

Ainsley was looking at the table, her words coming slowly, spoken so softly, Coulton wondered if she was talking to him or to herself.

"Eli could never sit still, so he was always getting in trouble for roaming around the tavern or getting in Mick's way behind the counter. He would try to hang out with the customers, and when he got older, he was constantly sneaking drinks of beer. He was ten the first time he got drunk, and when Mick realized how shit-faced he was, he took him into the back room and whipped his ass with a belt until Eli threw up. Then he made him sit on his sore ass in this booth, not letting him stand at all for the rest of the night. You'd think that would have turned Eli off alcohol…but the very next week, he was up again, sneaking more beer."

Coulton sat quietly as Ainsley recounted several more stories, some good, most bad. He let her talk until she talked herself out. Somewhere in the midst of her reminiscences, she rested her head on his shoulder, and he tucked her close.

The one thing she hadn't done was cry.

"Ainsley," he started.

"I saw the picture of you and Evelyn on Facebook." It was the first time in nearly an hour that she'd lifted her head and looked at him.

He sighed. "She showed up at the hotel to surprise me."

"You told me the two of you were still friends." There was no accusation or anger in her tone, which in a lot of ways, made Coulton feel even worse.

"She texted when I was on the plane, headed there, asking if we could meet. I ignored it, hoping to skip seeing her. I should have just texted her back and told her no."

Ainsley gave him a sad smile. "Why would you do that?"

"I didn't want you to think there was anything going on between me and her," he answered honestly.

She nodded. "I haven't exactly made this easy between us. I struggle with trusting people, and I've taken that out on you, even though you've never let me down or lied to me. I didn't realize until today that I've given you no reason to trust *me*. No reason to trust that I won't cut and run whenever I get afraid."

"Ainsley," he started to protest. He wanted to tell her he *did* trust her, but the truth was, he'd held back on telling her about Evelyn in a text because he'd been worried about losing her.

She placed her hand flat on his chest, just over his heart. "I'm sorry, Coulton."

He held her face in his palms and placed his forehead against hers. "I'm never going to hide anything from you," he promised. "I never want to let you down."

Ainsley blinked rapidly, her eyes wet with tears she refused to shed. "I want to earn your trust," she whispered.

"You have it," he said, even as she shook her head.

"I don't. Not yet."

He started to protest, but she placed her fingers against his lips. He gripped her hand when she started to pull her fingers away, kissing the pads of her fingertips.

"The truth is I didn't answer the thankful-for question honestly. Because the main thing I'm thankful for this year is you. Just you."

She lifted her face to him, smiling, and he leaned toward her and kissed her. His lips slowly and softly worshipped hers, though he kept it tame. Ainsley was the poster child for exhaustion at the moment, and his need to take care of her overrode every other desire.

"Can I ask you for something?" Coulton knew what he wanted would be difficult for her.

She nodded.

"Let me take care of you tonight."

Her brows furrowed, that same look of confusion she'd worn all the time when they first started seeing each other reappearing.

"I know you're used to taking care of yourself, Ainsley, but for just this one night, can you hand the reins over to me and trust that I know what you need?"

She studied his face for a moment, and then—thank God—she nodded. "I called you because…"

He saw the first chink in her armor, her exhaustion giving way to pain.

"I don't know what to do. All I knew was that I wanted you. Needed you."

Coulton knew exactly how hard it was for his powerhouse of a woman to admit she was lost. "You don't need to know what to do," he said. "Just trust that I do."

He rose from the booth, offering her a hand. She slipped her small one into his without hesitation, leaning on him heavily as he pulled her into his arms. He placed a soft kiss to the top of her head.

"It's going to be okay," he reassured her. "I'm here. I've got you."

Her arms looped around his waist as a soft sob escaped. Unfortunately, Ainsley stemmed the dam immediately, cutting her grief short.

"Come on." Grabbing her jacket and oversized bag from behind the bar, Coulton led her to the street, locking the tavern and pulling down the gate.

It spoke to Ainsley's level of exhaustion that she didn't question where they were going. Or what they were doing. Instead, she simply followed his lead.

Once they were in his truck, he fired off a text to his parents, letting them know he and Ainsley were on their way back. He also told them that her father had died.

The ride from Mick's Tavern to his condo was a quiet one. When Coulton pulled into a parking spot in front of his place, he got out, crossing in front of the truck to help her out. Ainsley hesitated once she was on the sidewalk, looking at his building.

"Your parents are here," she said, as if just remembering.

"Yes."

She looked down at herself. "I haven't showered since yesterday morning. This is my second day in this outfit and I..." She ran her fingers through her hair, giving him a rueful grin. "Are you sure you want to introduce me to them?"

Coulton cupped her cheeks, giving her a soft kiss. "They are going to love you," he reassured her. "I texted to let them know we were on the way, and about Mick. Trust me when I say, me introducing you to my parents is just one of the ways I'm going to take care of you tonight."

He didn't know how to explain to her that what she needed right now was the warmth, love, and unconditional acceptance of a mom and dad. Luckily, she'd get all three of those things in droves from his parents.

She let him lead her inside, her hand in his as they walked into his condo.

Mom and Dad must have heard them at the door, because they walked out of the kitchen together.

They both gave Ainsley warm, welcoming smiles, though Coulton could see the concern etched in his mother's eyes.

"Mom, Dad, I'd like you to meet Ainsley Hall," he said, still holding her hand. "Ainsley. These are my parents, Chase and Melanie Moore."

Dad stepped forward immediately, shaking Ainsley's hand. "It's nice to meet you, Ainsley. Coulton hasn't stopped talking about you since we got here."

Ainsley slid Coulton a pleased look as he playfully rolled his eyes.

"Way to make me sound cool, Dad."

"Oh, son. That ship sailed years ago."

They laughed as Mom moved closer.

Ainsley reached out to shake her hand, but Mom brushed it off, pulling her in for a tight embrace. Mom gave the greatest hugs on the planet.

Ainsley's surprise was brief, then she wrapped her arms around Mom, sinking into the embrace.

"Coulton told us about your dad," Mom murmured, holding her tight. "I'm so sorry."

Ainsley nodded, still hanging on, jerking slightly when she realized how long she'd been clinging to his mom.

Mom—God bless her—just tightened her grip. "Take as long as you need."

Ainsley sighed, then did just that.

Coulton couldn't remember the last time he'd cried, but damn if watching Ainsley, who'd never known a mother's love, hold on to his, didn't have his eyes growing a bit misty. A quick glance at Dad revealed his father was equally affected.

"Thanks," Ainsley said, when they parted.

Mom patted her cheek affectionately. "Have you eaten?"

Ainsley shook her head. "I, um, I had some toast yesterday morning."

Mom's love language was food, food, and dessert, so Ainsley's response set her in motion. "Then you're just in time. I need fifteen, twenty minutes to finish cooking and get the meal on the table."

Ainsley started to shake her head. "No, I don't want to crash your Thanksgiving dinner."

"Ainsley," Coulton said, wrapping his arm around her shoulders. "I invited you. Several times. Remember? Besides…" He gave her a wink. "I'm calling the shots tonight."

Ainsley narrowed her eyes. "You're going to make me regret agreeing to that, aren't you?" Her teasing tone gave him hope that she was going to bounce back just fine. He hadn't liked the utter desolation on her face when he'd arrived at Mick's.

"Oh yeah. Tell you what? Why don't you grab a quick shower, and I'll find you something of mine to wear."

Mom snorted. "I can't imagine you own anything that won't swallow her, Coulton. Chase, go grab the green pajamas out of my suitcase."

Dad was en route, even as Ainsley was trying to refuse the offer. "Oh, that's okay."

Mom talked over her. "I'm here four days and I packed three pairs. I am the queen of overpacking."

Dad must have hustled, because he agreed with Mom's statement as he returned and handed Ainsley the pajamas. "She's not lying. She brought six pairs of shoes."

Mom lightly slapped Dad on the shoulder. "I told you. I wasn't sure what the weather would be, and I wanted options."

"Options," Dad muttered good-naturedly, as the two of them headed back to the kitchen.

Mom scoffed. "This coming from the man who'll have to do laundry while he's here because he doesn't have enough boxers or T-shirts."

Coulton could hear them play-fighting all the way to the kitchen. He grinned at Ainsley as he gestured in the direction they'd gone. "So…that's my parents."

Ainsley giggled. "I love them. They're so nice."

Her words meant the world to him. "Come on. Quick shower, big dinner, and then straight to bed. You could do with about twenty-four hours of sleep."

She allowed him to lead her back to his bedroom. "Maybe I shouldn't stay, since—"

"You're staying," he said, in a tone that let her know they weren't continuing that discussion.

He followed her into the bathroom, turned on the shower to let the water heat, then he started undressing her. It spoke to Ainsley's level of exhaustion that she didn't fight him, but instead, just let him pull her shirt over her head, strip her bra, then tug off her shoes, jeans, and panties.

There was nothing sexual about his actions, because that wasn't what she needed. Guiding her into the shower, he watched as she stood under the steaming water, her head bowed, her body almost limp. She was running on fumes.

So Coulton stripped off his own clothing, climbing into the shower with her.

"Coulton," she whispered.

"Let me take care of you." He shifted them so that he could wet her hair, then he reached for his shampoo. Gently massaging a lather into her hair, he relished the way she placed her hands on his chest and closed her eyes, completely giving herself over to him. He rinsed the shampoo, then repeated the process with the conditioner. Grabbing a washcloth, he squirted shower gel on it, slowly drawing it over her body.

Ainsley swayed slightly, too tired to stand, so he kept his ministrations quick and efficient. Once she was clean, he turned off the water, wrapping her in one of his big bath towels, drying her. He put the lid down on the toilet, perching her there as he dried himself. After that, he brushed her wet hair, then the two of them moved to his bedroom, where he dressed her in Mom's pajamas before pulling on lounge pants and a T-shirt. He opted for more casual clothes so Ainsley wouldn't feel self-conscious eating dinner with his parents in just pajamas.

Mom and Dad had finished putting all the dishes on the table by the time they emerged from his room.

Mom smiled when she saw Ainsley in her pajamas. "You look so adorable in those, you're going to have to keep them."

Ainsley smiled softly. "They're really comfy." Then her eyes widened as she took in the table. "You made *all* this food?"

Mom gestured to him and Dad. "Well, I had some help from my sous chefs. Come on. Let's sit down and eat."

Coulton and Ainsley claimed one side of his rectangular table, Mom and Dad sitting across from them. They began passing the dishes, Coulton loading Ainsley's plate with turkey, stuffing, mashed potatoes, green bean casserole, a buttery roll, and cranberry sauce.

"There's no way I can eat all this," she said, as he poured a healthy portion of gravy on the meat, potatoes, and stuffing.

"Try," Coulton murmured.

She immediately went for the stuffing, and Coulton couldn't help but grin because that was a solid start. He dreamed of his mother's homemade stuffing, always joking that a huge pan of that and a tub of gravy would be his last meal if he was ever on death row.

"This is delicious," Ainsley said.

"The secret to good stuffing," Mom confided, "is to cut the toast into very small chunks."

"The secret is bacon," Coulton amended.

"Hear, hear," Dad agreed, raising his wineglass.

He was grateful to his parents for keeping the conversation going. Ainsley's hunger was only surpassed by her exhaustion, so while she tucked in, moaning and closing her eyes in bliss after nearly each bite, she clearly wasn't up for talking.

So Mom and Dad did what they did best. They read the room, decided to put their "get to know his girlfriend" conversation off until later, then took up the task of keeping things light and easy by regaling Ainsley with silly stories from Coulton's childhood. Ainsley listened with great interest, laughing at all the funny parts. She even asked a question or two.

With nearly two-thirds of her plate gone, Ainsley finally hit the wall. He'd watched her try to hide three yawns in a row.

Rising, Coulton held his hand out to Ainsley. "Bedtime, wildcat. You need sleep."

Ainsley accepted his hand, offering no argument. "Thank you so much for dinner," she said to his parents. "It's the best food I've ever eaten."

From most people, that compliment would just be words, but Coulton knew Ainsley meant them most sincerely.

"I'm glad you enjoyed it," Mom said.

"Me too," Dad piped in. "Because the four of us are going to be eating the leftovers for days."

They all laughed, then Mom moved in, giving Ainsley another hug. "I'm so glad you're here with us."

"So am I," Ainsley replied. She gave Dad a wave and turned toward Coulton's room.

Coulton hung back. "Thank you," he said softly, for just his parents to hear.

"She's wonderful."

Coulton smiled. "She really is."

"Go, be with her, son," Dad encouraged. "She's just lost her dad. She shouldn't be alone. Your mother and I will clean up."

Best. Parents. Ever.

He nodded his thanks again, then walked to his bedroom.

Ainsley was standing by the bed, looking like a lost puppy.

"Okay?"

She glanced up at him and shrugged. "This morning, I was afraid I'd end up sleeping on the street."

Coulton scowled. Like he would have ever let that happen. He crossed the room, pulling back the covers, nodding toward her side. "Get in."

She did, sliding over toward him when he joined her. He loved how easily she came to him, how she sank into his chest as he wrapped his arms around her. How she'd called him when she needed him.

Her soft sigh of contentment warmed him all the way to the core, because she sounded at peace.

For the first time ever.

"This year," he murmured, "I have something pretty amazing to be thankful for."

Ainsley didn't lift her head, but he felt her hand slide over his chest to cover his heart.

"Me too," she whispered.

CHAPTER TWELVE

AINSLEY CAME AWAKE SLOWLY, wondering what could have roused her from a sound sleep.

"Shhh. It's okay."

She felt Coulton's hand rubbing her back, up and down, the touch gentle and comforting, but confusing.

Until she realized his T-shirt, where her head was resting, was wet.

Lifting her hand, she wiped tears from her cheeks.

Had she been crying? In her sleep?

She raised her head and found Coulton looking at her. "It's okay, Ainsley."

The compassion in his voice was her undoing…and a lifetime of tears poured out of her. The dam was broken, and every defense she'd ever erected to protect herself came tumbling down.

Coulton pulled her head back to his chest, his grip on her firm, unwavering.

"It's okay," he said again. And again. And again.

Ainsley sobbed harder. "I don't know what to do," she gasped, struggling to say each word. She was facing a mountain of hard decisions, and she didn't have a clue where to start.

"For right now, all you have to do is let it all go and hold on to me."

She clung to him as she nodded, because that was all she could handle at the moment. "Okay."

Her life was officially in tatters. Her father was dead. Her home gone. Her belongings destroyed. She had no money to replace what was lost. Hell, she didn't even have enough money to bury Mick.

All she had left was that stupid tavern that she didn't want.

No.

Wait.

That wasn't all.

She had Coulton.

She lifted her head as her tears stilled, her doubts calmed, and her fears…

They vanished.

"I love you," she whispered.

It was the first time in her life she'd spoken those words to another person without breaking into a cold sweat, overwhelmed by the terror that her feelings would be rebuffed, rejected.

Coulton, her steady, solid, wonderful Gentle Giant, responded just the way she expected. He smiled widely, and even gave her a breathy, joyful laugh.

"Oh God, Ains. I love you too. So fucking much."

The tears that fell now were a completely different creature, and a unique experience for her. She was crying because she was happy.

He lowered his head, his lips next to her ear, his breath tickling. "Say it again."

She giggled, then repeated those three little words. "I love you."

He pressed his forehead to hers. "Again," he demanded.

She gripped his hair, pulled his face away from hers, their gazes clashing. "I. Love. You."

Coulton kissed her. "I love you, too, wildcat. And you're going to be okay, I promise."

For the first time in her life, she believed it.

She would be okay.

Happy and loved.

Because she had him in her life.

* * *

The long weekend passed in a blur of activity. Apparently, her agreement to let Coulton take care of her and help her through her father's death extended to his parents.

Mr. and Mrs. Moore—or Chase and Mel, as they insisted she call them—had been awake and ready to guide her through the painful decisions associated with losing a parent. They'd both lost their own parents, so they had known exactly what to do, who to call, what paperwork she needed. Melanie held her hand the entire time they were at the funeral home, discussing next steps. She had opted for no funeral, just a simple cremation, even though just that was beyond Ainsley's budget. Coulton had insisted she pick what felt right without considering the cost, then he told her he'd be paying the bill.

Since Friday, she had started writing down everything he was spending—on Mick's cremation *and* her new wardrobe—assuring him it was nothing more than a loan. She was determined she would pay back every penny when she was able, even though Coulton kept saying what was his was hers, and vice versa. She tried to tell him they were way too early in their relationship to start talking like that, but he was so sure that what they had was a forever thing, she couldn't help but believe him.

"What a weekend, huh?" Coulton tucked her closer to him on the couch. They were snuggled together on his sectional, *Die Hard* playing on the TV, even though neither was watching it. She'd laughed when Coulton suggested they watch a Christmas movie, then fired up the Bruce Willis classic. Not that she disagreed with his choice because, in her mind, it was one of the best Christmas movies.

"It was a whirlwind," she said. "I miss your parents already."

Coulton chuckled. "They'll be back in a few weeks for Christmas. I have a feeling you're going to get more presents than me this year. Welcome to the Spoiled Rotten Train."

Ainsley had ridden to BWI with Coulton this morning when he dropped his parents off for their flight back to Detroit. Melanie had given her one of those strong, long, warm, incredible hugs, insisting Ainsley call her if she needed anything. She'd nodded her promise, unable to speak through the lump in her throat at the idea of having a mother to turn to for help. Coulton had already added her to what he'd originally called his Family of Three text thread. It had since been renamed Family of Four.

She kept checking it, delighted when his dad texted to let them know they'd landed in Detroit, and his mother reminded them to eat the casserole she'd left for them in the refrigerator, then provided instructions on how best to reheat it. They were run-of-the-mill texts, but they made her so ridiculously happy.

She marveled over the difference a weekend could make. Thursday, it felt like her world was crashing and burning. Now, here she sat on Sunday night, more at peace and content than she'd ever been in her life. She should probably be suffering from the worst case of whiplash, considering she had spent the last month ping-ponging between the paradise that was Coulton and the hell that had been her reality for so long.

"You think Slade's still bouncing off the walls?" she asked him.

Coulton snorted. "Not sure. That kid sure does love free candy. I half expect the owner of the Stingrays to garnish my wages to pay back what he and his cousins consumed on Saturday night."

"They sure as hell put a dent in the treats," she agreed.

Coulton had finally accomplished a goal, managing to get

seats in the team box for Slade, his aunt Barbara, Jerome, his sister, and his other cousins. Ainsley was also included in the invite, along with Melanie and Chase, so it had been a regular Coulton Moore fan club get-together. And the first piece of clothing Coulton replaced had been her beloved Stingrays jersey with his name on the back.

It had been a great game, and a very welcome distraction from Mick's death and the tavern, which she hadn't reopened, and all the other worries weighing her down.

Melanie had assured her the best way to get through her grief was to stay busy and not let herself get too overwhelmed. Coulton had encouraged her to simply take everything one step at a time, one day at a time, and it had helped.

After she'd taken care of Mick's cremation arrangements, she and Maren had begun making plans for a wake at the tavern early next week. She'd contacted her landlord and gotten out of the lease on their apartment. Maybe it had been too soon to make a decision like that, but after the break-in and the destruction of her belongings, she could never stay there again. She'd felt equal parts violated and terrified.

Ainsley worried a little bit about leaving Eli homeless, but considering he hadn't spent many nights there in the past few months, she decided it was for the best.

Coulton told her she could stay at his place as long as she needed. His exact words had been, she could "move in and stay forever." She kept telling herself once she got settled, she would look for her own place...but there was a little voice in the back of her head that kept going "ha ha" every time she thought about moving out.

"So what's next on our list?" Coulton asked.

Ainsley loved the way he always included himself, constantly reassuring her that she wouldn't do any of this alone.

"I guess the next step is to make a decision about the tavern." She'd been thinking about it a lot since Mick's death. The tavern had always been his dream, not hers.

Coulton nodded slowly. "What are you thinking?"

She knew what she should do. Keep it open, because it was the only thing paying her bills. Unfortunately, that wasn't what she wanted to do.

She must have let the silence linger too long as she wrestled with her response.

"Remember when I told you to start dreaming about your future?" Coulton asked.

Ainsley nodded. She'd been doing a lot of dreaming since that conversation. "I do."

"Did you?"

"Yeah. I did."

"And?" he prompted.

"My dream future, the one where I live happily ever after, requires two things."

Coulton raised one eyebrow, clearly curious. "What's the first thing?"

"A new job."

Coulton reached for the remote, muting the TV, then he twisted on the couch until he was facing her. "As?"

She'd never said these words aloud, and she was surprised by how vulnerable she felt. What if he thought it was a bad idea? Or a dumb one? "I want to be a tattoo artist."

Coulton, the loveable goof, excitedly pumped a fist in the air like he'd won the Stanley Cup. "Hell yes! You're too talented to keep your art all to yourself. Tomorrow, we'll do some research on how to get started."

"I've already looked into it a little bit." After she'd shown her tattoo artist her drawings, he'd tried to encourage her to apprentice under him. She'd brushed off the offer at the time, because she'd been young and dumb, and her self-confidence was still shaken after Tiger's infidelity. "I need to apprentice under a tattoo artist and get certified. I think my artist would take me on."

"I love that idea. And when you're ready, I think you should open your own shop. I'd invest in it. And I guarantee you'd have a line of my teammates beating down the door to get some of your art inked on them."

She raised her hand, trying to slow him down. "Hey, Mr. One Step at a Time. How about I just try to get an apprenticeship first?"

Coulton smirked. "If you're gonna dream, Ainsley, dream big."

"Okay. I will."

"So you're selling the tavern?"

It felt strange to admit it out loud, but if she was being true to herself, then yes. That was exactly what she wanted to do. "Yes. Even though Eli and I won't make a lot of money on the sale. Mick refinanced for a cash loan when the medical bills started piling up, and the place is a legit pit, so it's not worth much anyway."

"You're going to split the money from the sale with Eli? Hasn't he basically stolen his half of the inheritance over the years?"

Eli had stolen more than half, but Ainsley still knew splitting it was the right thing to do. Even if he did squander and gamble his share away instantly. At the very least, it would assuage her guilt over walking away from him. She'd given up any hope of ever having a relationship with her brother. Without Mick around, loosely binding them together, there was nothing left.

"It's the right thing to do. Besides, after I settle Mick's estate and pay you back for the cremation, I doubt it will amount to much."

Coulton didn't argue with her. Instead, he looked at her in that way she was becoming completely addicted to. Like he was in awe of her. "I'm glad you're selling the tavern and pursuing something that will make you happy."

She shrugged. "I'm hoping it doesn't take too long for me to start making money, so I can pay my share around here."

Coulton grasped her hand and gave it a squeeze. "I'm a rich hockey player, remember?"

She narrowed her eyes. "Your money has nothing to do with why I'm with you. I don't want you to think—"

"I don't think that, Ainsley," he interjected. "But if I want to spoil you, I will, dammit. And there's not a thing you can do to stop me. So will you please stop writing down the cost of everything I buy for you in that stupid notebook?"

That was going to be a hard promise to make. "I'll…try."

Coulton pressed his forehead to hers. "That's the best I'm going to get from you, isn't it?"

She nodded.

"Fine," he said begrudgingly. "I'll take it. So what's the second part of your dream future?"

"You." It was funny how telling him about her career choice was harder than admitting to Coulton that she wanted her happy ending to include him. For someone who'd spent too much of her adult life approaching romance like it was a war zone, and any minute a sniper could take her out, she found it surprisingly easy to talk to Coulton about her feelings.

Probably because he wore his on his sleeve, and he was not shy about sharing them with her. Telling him she loved him Thursday night had broken down every single barrier between them, and if she'd thought him a PDA aficionado before, that was *nothing* compared to how he'd been all weekend.

He was constantly holding her hand, giving her soft kisses, telling her she was beautiful and that he loved her. He'd actually asked his dad—in front of her—if he thought Christmas was too soon to buy her an engagement ring. Ainsley had laughed, thinking it a joke, until Chase assured him it wasn't too soon at all, and that Coulton better stake a claim before some other guy tried to steal her away.

Ainsley had quickly set both men straight, pointing out they hadn't even dated a month yet, and that Christmas was far too soon. Melanie complimented her efforts, then warned her that

Moore men were impossible to resist. She told Ainsley that Chase had proposed to her after just three months of dating, and that she'd said yes and never once looked back.

Coulton leaned toward her, giving her a hard, hungry kiss that matched the look in his eyes. They hadn't had sex since she'd started staying here on Thanksgiving. For one thing, his parents had been in the guest room down the hall. But more than that, she got the sense that Coulton knew how emotionally fragile she was, and he was giving her space and time to heal.

Time she no longer needed.

When their lips parted, he cupped her cheeks. "Looks like you're fifty percent of the way to your happily ever after. Because you already have me, and I'm not going anywhere."

"Coulton," she said softly.

"I mean it, Ainsley. You can insist it's too fast or too soon as much as you want, but you won't convince me because I know this is the real deal. You're the first person I want to talk to in the morning and your face is the last one I want to see when I close my eyes at night. You challenge me, you make me happy, and I love you."

She sniffled, certain she'd never heard nicer words in her life. "I feel the same way. Do you mind if we don't finish watching this movie?"

"You want to watch something else?" he asked, reaching for the remote.

"Yeah. You. Getting undressed."

Coulton turned the television off. "Okay, but only if I get to watch the same thing."

Ainsley laughed when he pulled her up from the couch, bending over in one fluid motion to toss her over his shoulder before carrying her to his bedroom.

Once they were inside, he drew her close, kissing her with a passion that took her breath away.

Ainsley had spent most of her life wishing for time to move more quickly, never happy with where she was. That was not the case when it came to Coulton. With him, she found herself constantly praying for time to stand still.

Coulton kept saying this was forever, but as he kissed her, she knew even that wouldn't be long enough.

She was breathless by the time he released her. Then he gave her a charming grin as he tugged his shirt over his head. The sight of his chest, his rock-hard abs, always had her reconsidering her medium. Drawing was all well and good, but to truly capture his beauty, she would need to take up sculpting.

Reaching out, she ran her fingers over his bare chest. Coulton grasped her hand, pulling on it until her palm rested over his heart. "This is where I want my first tattoo from you."

"The first, huh?" she asked, thrilled that he trusted her artistic talent enough to let her ink him when the time was right.

"You can use my whole body as your canvas," he said, drawing her shirt over her head, placing a kiss on her shoulder, his finger tracing one of the patterns inked there.

Ainsley reached for his belt, unfastening it before pulling it off with a flourish. Then she started tackling the button on his jeans.

Coulton stopped her, stepping away. "Thought this was *my* show."

She put her hands up, surrendering. "My bad." Then she waved as if to say "continue."

Coulton took over, slowly sliding down the zipper, drawing out his striptease. She knew he was being playful, but every action was so sexy, she felt a bead of sweat trickle down the side of her face. When did it get so hot in here?

Once his jeans were unfastened, she expected him to push them down because she was ready to get this show on the road. Instead, he turned away from her, giving her the perfect view of his back, and then, as he slowly slid his jeans down inch by glorious inch, his ass.

God. People should write songs about that ass.

She bet she could bounce a quarter off it.

However, as sexy as it was, it wasn't the part of his physique she was most interested in seeing at the moment.

"Turn around." She'd been going for demand, but her breathless request was too needy to sound like anything more than it was. An outright plea.

Coulton glanced at her over his shoulder, wiggling his eyebrows suggestively.

She laughed. "You're a terrible tease."

He twisted back to face her, his very hard, very erect cock in his fist. "Is this what you wanted to see?"

Her gaze drifted down and held. "Hell yeah."

He stroked his dick, letting her look her fill. "What about *your* show?"

She considered giving him a taste of his own medicine, but her libido had shifted into overdrive. Ainsley attempted to strip off her jeans and panties so quickly, she stumbled and almost fell.

Coulton reached out to steady her. "Take it easy, wildcat. We've got all night."

"I don't want all night," she said, her hands gripping his muscular forearms. "I want it hard and fast and rough and dirty. I want you to drive into me from behind, and if you could sprinkle in some spanking, that would be good too."

Coulton had been all suave charm up until that point, clearly intent on taking his time and savoring the act.

Her request changed everything.

With a firm hand on her upper arm, he twisted her toward the bed before pushing her forward over the mattress.

His bed was ridiculously large and tall, a necessity for someone as big as him. Of course, that meant she felt like a mouse, only taking up the tiniest bit of space on the oversized mattress. In this position, bent over the edge, she hung there, her feet at least two inches off the floor. She loved the helpless feeling it evoked, loved the idea of being totally at the mercy of her Gentle Giant.

Coulton bent over her, his breath hot on the side of her face. "Be careful what you ask for," he warned. "Because I told you, I want to give you everything, spoil you." His hand slipped between their bodies, gripping her ass and squeezing, proving he was completely on board with giving her every aspect of her request.

Thank God.

Ainsley glanced at him over her shoulder. "Spoil me," she begged.

Coulton pushed himself upright, his hand landing on her bare ass before she even registered the movement. He didn't hold back as he peppered her ass, varying each of his swats, some hard, some soft, some right on the meaty part of her rear end, some hitting the top of her thighs.

When he thrust her thighs apart with his knee, she groaned as the next spank landed right between her legs.

"Oh my God," she gasped, the shock, the pain, and the pleasure of it rolling through her body like a tsunami.

"You like that?" he grunted.

She nodded, the side of her face resting on his soft mattress.

Coulton repeated the smack, and her toes curled. Then he did it one final time, his palm resting over the part he'd just spanked, his fingers brushing her clit.

"Is all this wetness for me, dirty girl?" His deep voice was laced with approval.

"Yes," she hissed. She hadn't underplayed her need for fast and… Right. Fucking. Now. She was seconds away from spontaneously combusting.

Coulton was mercifully finished playing. He drove two of his thick fingers inside her, pounding them in and out until she saw stars. It was amazing how quickly he managed to bring her to the brink of her orgasms.

Not even she could work that kind of magic, and she was intimately acquainted with her equipment and desires.

Her fingers clenched against the duvet as she sought

purchase. With her feet dangling, unable to hold her steady, she felt a bit like a rag doll in a hurricane.

"Come on, wildcat. You're right there. I can feel it. Your pussy is clenching tight enough to break my fingers. Come for me. Come for me, and then I'm going to give you exactly what you asked for."

Ainsley responded as much to his words as his actions, something Coulton had figured out early on and used to his advantage.

She came. Hard. Her body jerked like she'd stepped on a live wire, Coulton drawing out the impact as he finger-fucked her through her orgasm, shoving her headfirst into a second.

Ainsley cried out his name, cursed then whimpered, begging for a reprieve.

"I warned you," he said, pulling his fingers out even as she quivered.

She missed the fullness of them the second they were gone, but he didn't make her suffer for long. The head of his cock brushed against her pussy, and she gasped when he shoved inside in one fast, fluid motion.

"Are you ready for this?" he asked as he withdrew, until only the tip remained.

She wasn't entirely sure she was, but she also wasn't about to stop him now. "Do it."

Coulton gave her a wicked chuckle, a kiss on the back of her shoulder, and then it was on.

Ainsley couldn't do anything more than hang on for dear life as he pounded into her with the force of a freight train. Doggie style was hands down her favorite position, because it ensured Coulton hit her G-spot on every return.

His hands gripped her hips, holding her in place, and she relished the thought of seeing his fingerprint bruises there for the next few days, a sexy reminder of tonight.

Not that she was likely to forget.

"God!" she screamed on one particularly deep stroke. Her back arched as her orgasm struck without warning.

Her climax triggered a chain reaction as Coulton growled. "Fuck, wildcat. So fucking good."

She felt the first hot splash of come paint her inner walls as his hands landed on the mattress next to her, his hips jerking until he'd given her every single drop.

"Jesus," he said breathlessly. "Every time," he gasped. "Every fucking time is better than the last."

Amen to that, she wanted to say, but unlike him, she couldn't draw enough air into her lungs to speak.

They held there, connected for a minute or two, both fighting to recover.

When Coulton found the strength to shift away, they groaned as her pussy clenched, trying to hold on to him.

She grimaced when his hands softly slid over her ass cheeks, reminding her of his none-too-gentle spanking. She wasn't sure what it said about her that she loved the tenderness, the soreness, the heat still there.

"Crawl into the bed," Coulton directed, even though Ainsley made no move to obey. He'd fucked her into this inert state, and nothing was going to move her.

Or so she thought.

Coulton lifted her, carefully sliding her beneath the covers, on what had come to be "her side of the bed."

Tucking her in next to him, his chest as her pillow, they lay there, both sticky with sweat, wrung out, exhausted.

"We should shower," he said, the heaviness of his tone betraying how close he was to falling asleep.

"Mmm," she hummed, though not in agreement. That one-syllable response was all she was capable of.

She wasn't sure how long they dozed before she roused, blinking to clear her vision in the dark room.

"Coulton?" she asked, when she realized he wasn't in bed with her anymore.

"I'm here," he said from the direction of the bathroom.

She turned that way, smiling at the flickering light of the candles he'd lit.

"Changed my mind on the shower," he said. "Thought it would be more fun if we took one of those rich-people baths."

Ainsley laughed as she crawled out of bed, crossing the room to him. "How bougie of us."

He took her hand in his as he led her to the bathtub, which he'd surrounded with candles and filled with bubbles.

"Super bougie," she added, as she slipped into the steaming water, groaning in bliss as it soothed her sore muscles.

"Jerome and Tank both thought I was wasting my superpower when it came to women." Coulton joined her, sinking down behind her before pulling her between his outstretched thighs.

"Superpower?" she asked as she reclined, her back against his chest.

"Professional hockey player," he explained. "Who knew my real power was my bathtub?"

Ainsley laughed. "Oh, a bathtub is the greatest of all superpowers," she joked.

Coulton wrapped his arms around her, pressing his cheek to the top of her head. "Best day of my life was the day I walked into Mick's Tavern."

"Mine too. Took one look at you, Thor," she said, using the nickname she'd given him, "and I was hooked. Addicted."

Coulton cupped her cheek, turning her face so that he could give her a kiss. "It was the same with me. I can't resist you, Ainsley Hall."

Be sure to check out the entire Stingrays Hockey series!

Restraint

Resist

Rematch

And meet some former Stingrays players in these books!

ABOUT THE AUTHOR

Virginia native Mari Carr is a New York Times and USA TODAY bestseller of contemporary romance novels. With over three million copies of her books sold, Mari was the winner of the Romance Writers of America's Passionate Plume award for her novella, Erotic Research. She has over a hundred published works, including her popular Wild Irish and Italian Stallions books, along with the Trinity Masters series she writes with Lila Dubois.

Follow Mari:
www.maricarr.com
mari@maricarr.com

Join her newsletter so you don't miss new releases and for exclusive subscriber-only content.

www.ingramcontent.com/pod-product-compliance
Ingram Content Group UK Ltd.
Pitfield, Milton Keynes, MK11 3LW, UK
UKHW041840190726
13854UKWH00002B/641

9 781962 026673